The
Ferry Girls

Rosie Archer was born in Gosport, Hampshire, where she still lives. She has had a variety of jobs including waitress, fruit picker, barmaid, shop assistant and market trader selling second-hand books. Rosie is the author of several Second World War sagas set on the south coast, as well as a series of gangster sagas under the name June Hampson.

Also by Rosie Archer

The Munitions Girls
The Canary Girls
The Factory Girls
The Gunpowder and Glory Girls
The Girls from the Local

ROSIE ARCHER

The Ferry Girls

Quercus

First published in Great Britain in 2017 by Quercus
This paperback edition published in 2017 by

Quercus Editions Ltd
Carmelite House
50 Victoria Embankment
London EC4Y 0DZ

An Hachette UK company

A CIP catalogue record for this book is available
from the British Library

PB ISBN 978 1 78648 331 7
EBOOK ISBN 978 1 78648 332 4

10 9 8 7 6 5 4 3 2

Typeset by CC Book Production
Printed and bound in Great Britain by Clays Ltd, Elcograf S.p.A.

This one is for Charlie Repp, my grandson.
His IT skills helped when I needed them most.

Chapter One

Vee had never stolen a thing in her life, yet here she was, her hands shaking, fumbling with a large brown envelope, terrified that at any moment the lavatory door might open and she would be discovered, about to thieve from her boss.

But what was the alternative? Stealing was a sin, but better than spending a loathsome weekend in bed in a New Forest hotel with Sammy Chesterton. This was her one chance to keep her virginity and morals intact.

She paused. Bing Crosby's voice seeped from the bar into the disinfectant-swilled ladies' room in Southampton's docklands' Black Cat Club. He was insisting there would be 'Pennies From Heaven'. Vee hoped he was right: pennies would be much more satisfying than the nightly rain of Adolf Hitler's bombs.

Holding her breath and listening until she was satisfied there was no one outside, Vee continued her search, fingers rifling through the cardboard and papers, her eyes flying from one false name to another on the identity cards, ration books, birth certificates and passports that her boss had obtained illegally to sell on for payment in cash or, in her penniless state, sex.

And then she saw them! Her own and her mother's Anglicized names!

Twenty-three-year-old Violetta and May Anne Smith of Honeysuckle Holdings, Leap Lane, Netley. Excitement rose as she pulled out the ration books, medical cards and other documents that would make them legal citizens of the land they had been born in, their beloved England.

Vee's eyes filled with tears. 'Oh!' she murmured. 'How wonderful.'

Now she and her mother would no longer be aliens. The false documents would give them their freedom to live, walk around and shop locally, like any other English person, all of which had been denied to Vee, especially since the start of this awful war with Germany.

Of course, owning and using forged papers was a criminal

offence. Hopefully Vee and her mother would never need to produce them, and as long as no one discovered the truth, they could live and contribute to the war effort by growing food on their smallholding just as Vee's grandparents had done.

Vee fingered the papers, which represented freedom. She wondered how she could explain all this to her mother. May would be appalled to think Vee held herself so cheap that she could agree to Sammy's demands. She knew Vee wanted to remain a virgin until she could give herself freely to the man she truly loved. That man was out there somewhere, waiting to love her. But the loss of her virginity was nothing compared to the possible loss of her mother if they were removed to an internment camp for aliens.

Before Vee was born, her English mother had married a German pilot. He'd been the love of her life. Not for one moment had May thought that, due to the Aliens Restriction Act, marrying a German would take away her and her baby's English birthright and make them Germans.

If the law that imposed a husband's nationality on his wife and children was flouted, serious consequences befell the offender, especially when that citizenship was German.

The British people hated the Germans. This war had come so soon after the bloodbath of the Great War, and now the

Luftwaffe was attacking English airfields, sending at least a thousand aircraft every day. Already Hitler had invaded the Channel Islands. Any hint of German blood, and homes were burned. Friendships disintegrated overnight. Shops were boycotted or, worse, looted and torched.

Vee didn't want a fate like that for her mother and herself. For years they had managed to keep secret her father August Schmidt's marriage to her mother.

Both she and her mother had been born in Netley, near Southampton: why should a government Act decree that they were not British?

Living on a smallholding that provided them with food meant they had so far managed without having to present ration books and other essential documentation. Already the two women made do and mended without tendering clothing coupons, but both Vee and her mother knew that, sooner or later, clarification of their status would be required. They were living in fear.

Two weeks ago, the local post office had been set ablaze, and the elderly Martina and Hartmund Braun, who had served the villagers for ten years, had been severely injured by thugs hurling stones. Villagers who had previously been their customers and friends had shouted obscenities at them as they had been taken away in the back of a lorry.

Vee would never forget the terror on the seventy-year-old woman's face.

She stuffed the papers into her handbag. Now she and her mother could present identification without the fear of being different, of being hated.

A door creaked. Someone was coming! Vee fumbled for the cubicle's bolt, forgetting it was broken. With her back against the door she stared at the package. Where could she hide it?

There was no chance now that she'd be able to replace it beside the till behind the bar. She could hear footsteps and someone singing along with the wireless. Now Frank Sinatra was crooning 'All Or Nothing At All'.

Thinking swiftly, she climbed up on the wooden toilet seat and hauled at the metal cover over the cistern. At first it refused to budge. A spider lurking among the grime swung out but disappeared beneath the metal lid as it lifted. Vee shoved the envelope into the dry space between the cistern and the wall, pushed the lid back into place and stepped down. Whoever was outside the lavatory door was still singing.

Vee ripped a few sheets of shiny San Izal toilet paper from the roll and wiped her hands, then dropped the paper into the lavatory pan. Smoothing her hands down her black skirt, she took a deep breath, picked up her handbag and pulled open the cubicle's door.

Vee saw surprise on Greta's face. The singing had stopped. 'I thought I was alone in here,' the blonde-haired girl said. 'You don't make much noise, do you? I never heard the flush.' She let her hand fall from the cubicle's door.

Vee tried a smile, but it didn't come across the way she wanted. The girl was wearing her usual strong freesia perfume.

Greta frowned. 'You all right? You look a bit peculiar . . .'

Vee sent up a silent prayer of thanks. The girl's words had given her an idea.

'Actually, no, I don't feel too good at all. I think I'll go home. There's no way I could be nice to the punters tonight.'

'The boss won't like it.' Greta took a step away from her.

Vee thought of Sammy Chesterton, the tall, dark-haired gangster, who had taken a fancy to her because, he said, she reminded him of a girl he had once loved and lost. Always dressed in smart suits and with a camel coat slung round his shoulders, he looked exactly what he purported to be, a businessman with sway in politics. He strayed on the wrong side of the law but, with his connections in the police force, had managed to keep his good reputation unsullied and his bad one feared.

'I think Sammy would rather I wasn't here than being sick all over the place,' Vee said.

Greta shrugged. The girls weren't great friends but working together had made them allies.

Oh dear! Not only was Vee now a thief, but she hadn't hesitated to lie. She sighed as she waited for Greta to offer to tell the boss that one of his hostesses wouldn't be putting in an appearance. Greta would normally take any chance to cosy up to Sammy – it was well known that she had designs on him.

'I could let him know . . .'

'Would you?' Vee thrust her arms round a surprised Greta in a hug, then pulled quickly away. She was supposed to be poorly, wasn't she? Not bursting with energy. 'I think it's something I ate,' she said. 'Thank you, you're a good pal.' She held the cubicle door open so Greta could go in, and breathed a sigh of relief when the door had closed.

From inside Greta shouted, 'It'd better be something you ate! I don't want to catch it!'

Vee walked back into the smoke-stale bar.

Small wrought-iron tables and chairs with plush velvet seats faced the stage area where a microphone was set up on the parquet flooring. Red velvet curtains at the sides hid the small dressing rooms and were a backdrop for the striptease shows. The bar area at the side of the huge room had mirrored shelves containing bottles of brightly coloured liquids that purported to be exotic drinks. Vee had never heard a single person ask for one. The clientele, mostly merchant sailors and servicemen, preferred beer or the standard spirits.

A wrinkled, stooped man was sweeping the stage, where pale confetti blew about like tiny butterflies. Mindy's strip act included a snowfall of artificial snow. The punters loved it but it was messy and Donald hated clearing it up. He moaned continually. He'd been with Sammy for years, so it was rumoured, and was one of the few people the boss trusted implicitly.

'All right?' Vee smiled at him.

Donald hadn't been in the bar earlier when the young man had entered the club and handed her the large brown envelope for him to deliver to Sammy. She'd stood it next to the till so he'd see it when he came on duty.

'Me dad was hoping to get paid on delivery,' the thin youth said hesitantly.

'Well, there's only me here and no one's said anything.'

He'd looked at her, then at the package. 'I'll call back later.'

Vee hadn't found out until quite recently that Sammy had many strings to his bow and supplying forged documents was one of them. The idea had fermented in her head until she'd finally plucked up courage to ask him for help. She never would have done if she hadn't overheard him collecting the last of the payments from the new Austrian doorman for his birth certificate. The amount of money Sammy had asked for had been much more than Vee could ever hope to give him.

Later, he'd suggested a few days away in the New Forest in lieu of payment and Vee had agreed. She wanted her mother to feel safe and be able to go on selling her produce. Vee had heard that on the Isle of Man women and men were interned in camps. She couldn't erase from her mind the sight of Martina and Hartmund Braun being loaded on to a lorry.When the forger's lad had left the building, Vee's heart had been pounding and she couldn't resist peeping inside the package.

Then she had snatched it up and taken it to the lavatory. As she did so, she wondered how soon it would be before it was missed. Of course the club would be searched. What if the package was discovered? Sammy would know immediately that her and her mother's papers had gone. Only she could be the culprit and he wouldn't like being made a fool of. His peers would laugh at him. He would have to think up a suitable punishment for her. She shivered. Her voice cracked as she spoke again to Donald:

9

'I'm in no fit state for either bar work or welcoming punters . . .'

He leant on his broom. 'You do look a bit peaky, girl.' He smiled at her. She hated lying to Donald, who had always been kind to her. He took out a grubby handkerchief and mopped his forehead. 'Leave it with me, love. I'll get your coat.'

She nodded and he lifted the flap in the bar top and shuffled out the back to return moments later with her coat. Vee shrugged herself into it and made for the door, fearing at any moment that she would be called back. One thing seemed to be leading to another: now she had lied to Donald.

Out in the August evening air she nodded to the doorman, then began walking across the park towards the bus station.

Huge cranes towered over the docks, like praying mantis, and she could smell the oily water where the container ships were berthed. Servicemen passed her on their way to the dark streets where the bars and strip clubs waited to entice them in. Sometimes they took no notice of a lone girl walking quickly. At others they called out to her. She ignored them and the smell of alcohol that often followed them.

But the sun was still shining and the flowerbeds along the pathways bloomed with mauve Michaelmas daisies and vibrant red geraniums. They would not be around for long, as people were being asked to dig for victory and all available land was being used to grow vegetables.

Vee, her mother and their few helpers worked backbreaking hours growing vegetables and fruit on their smallholding, so she appreciated the brightness of the flowers. She took a deep breath of the geraniums' scent before she crossed the road and went into the bus station where, once more, the smell of oil and petrol reigned, and rubbish littered the ground.

Sitting on the top deck of the bus, seeing the shops interspersed with the gaps caused by Hitler's relentless bombings along the south coast made her feel sad. So many lost lives and homes demolished. She knew how lucky she was to live where there were no docks or factories for the German bombers to destroy.

The bus wound its way to the leafier countryside outside the city, but Vee couldn't stop thinking of the crime she'd committed. She had stolen from Sammy Chesterton, one of the most feared men in Southampton. And what would he do to her when he came after her, when he found her? Vee had worked at the club for about six months. Before that she'd worked in a bomb factory and enjoyed the camaraderie but had left when one of the men wouldn't stop pestering her, touching her at every available moment as she worked on the line. She was scared walking home – he had begun to follow her and would hang around outside the cottage. She couldn't see him but when she drew the curtains she could feel his presence outside. Vee didn't dare involve the police in case they delved into her history and found out that her name was actually Schmidt. Nor did she want to worry her mother. Walking past the Black Cat Club one day on a shopping expedition, she had noticed the sign requesting a barmaid-hostess and had left the munitions yard. She hadn't seen the man since.

She caught sight of herself reflected in the window of the bus.

Her fair hair was tied back, showing off her deep blue eyes. She knew she owed her looks to her mother but she'd inherited the impulsiveness of her father. There wasn't anyone special in her life at present. She'd been writing to a local lad serving in France in the British Expeditionary Force, but his letters had stopped coming. Then had come the evacuation of Dunkirk . . . Looking back, Vee remembered his letters had been peppered with the name 'Colette', and decided that Colette was probably more than just a friend. She would rather believe he had fallen in love with another girl than perished.

Not having a boyfriend had meant working at the club

with its odd hours wasn't a problem. She knew very well that some men wouldn't have liked her choice of work or the fact that she was driven home, with some of the other girls, in the early hours by one of the male bar staff. At her interview with Sammy she'd been adamant that she wouldn't dance, wouldn't undress and wouldn't go to bed with the punters.

Sometimes she worked behind the bar, serving watered-down overpriced drinks to the men who came into the Black Cat looking for girls. Sometimes she sold cigarettes and cigars to the men sitting at tables watching girls strip. Sometimes, as the cloakroom girl, she took hats and coats from the customers and was often tipped for this service. Vee now realized her reticence had probably drawn Sammy to her.

Her mother hated her working at the club, but never asked too many questions. May knew that living in virtual isolation and working on the land made for a healthy life, but that it wasn't what her daughter needed for fulfilment. Vee needed the companionship of other girls. Working nights meant she could help on the smallholding during the day. She needed to live her life, and her mother trusted her to continue in the honest way she'd been brought up. She had now broken that trust.

The bus lurched on, and Vee stared out of the window,

but saw nothing of the countryside's majesty. All she could think of was that she had stolen from Sammy Chesterton. She had welshed on a deal with him and he was not likely to forget it. He would want reparation.

Icy fingers of fear crept over her, not simply for herself but for her mother, who had done nothing to deserve Sammy Chesterton's wrath but would now be in the firing line.

Chapter Two

Jem was chopping wood. The sound of his axe cutting logs to stack against the side of the house for the coming winter rang comfortingly through the trees as Vee walked down the lane from where the bus had dropped her. She opened the wide front gate and pulled it back far enough to step onto the path leading to the front door. The smell of late roses filled the air, but already the blooms had the brown-tipped petals that heralded autumn. She felt sad to know that their colour, perfume and beauty would soon be gone.

'Hello.' Jem waved in greeting, a grin splitting his face. Vee waved back and pushed open the front door, which was never locked. She threw her coat and handbag over the newel post at the bottom of the wide stairs and called to her mother.

May appeared at the top of the stairs, her arms full of

clean bedding. A pregnant grey cat watching Vee from the second stair came down to meet her.

'You're home early . . .' May paused, doubtless noticing Vee's worried expression. She left the pressed sheets on the landing table and continued down the stairs. 'It's not Jem and that blessed newly sharpened axe, is it?'

Vee put her arms around her mother. 'No, he's fine. I need to talk to you.' She could smell the aroma of baking emanating from her mother's skin and wrap-around pinafore. 'Sit down, Mum, while I make a cup of tea.' She bent and patted the cat, which butted her head against her legs. 'Not had your kittens yet?' The animal purred. May sat down at the scrubbed wooden table, a frown creasing her forehead.

Vee shook the kettle, decided there was enough water in it and put it on the stove.

'I think Jem should hear what I have to say.' Going to the door she called his name loudly. 'Otherwise you'll have to explain to him later.' There were no secrets between them.

Vee couldn't remember a time when Jem hadn't walked up daily from the village, where he rented a small terraced house near the church. He employed casual labourers for May when the crops were at their heaviest and needed harvesting. He took it upon himself to look after her cottage, and many times May had offered him a room at Honeysuckle

Holdings, but Jem had always refused, aware of the tittle-tattle his living there with the two women would cause.

He'd begun working for Honeysuckle Holdings about the time that May's mother had died of influenza in the pandemic just after the Great War. To Vee, Jem was like the father she had never known – August Schmidt had been killed shortly before the Great War ended.

As he wiped his boots on the doormat, Vee saw Jem frown as he looked first at May, then back at the axe he'd set down against the kitchen's skirting board. He pulled the door closed behind him. He was tall, with broad shoulders, dressed in corduroy trousers and a cotton shirt. He stopped near May and looked questioningly into her eyes.

'Sit down, Jem,' said Vee. 'I've got something to say that will ultimately concern you – and you, Mum.' Going over to the Aga she picked up the brown earthenware pot and made the tea, careful not to spill any precious leaves. Leaving it to settle, she went to the bottom of the stairs and picked up her handbag. Without another word, she took out the documents and laid them on the table in front of her mother.

May's eyes widened. For a while she sat quite still. Then she picked up the brown ration book bearing the name 'May Smith' and stared at it.

Her voice was soft, almost tearful, as she asked, 'Where did you get this? How?'

Jem had risen protectively and now he stood behind May and whistled through his teeth as his hand reached for an identity card, which he scrutinized.

'These are forged, right?' Vee nodded. 'Must have cost you a pretty penny.' He let out a deep sigh.

'I've done something stupid, and I'm going to have to pay for it.'

At first, May didn't seem to be listening because she said brightly, 'We can be like everyone else now.' Then silence filled the kitchen, until she cried out, 'However did you get hold of them?'

Before Vee could answer, Jem asked, 'Are you sure there's no one who knows you married Gus Schmidt?'

May shook her head. 'No one. The few that were in on the secret are gone now, even my friend Annie who was so kind to me, when . . . when . . .' her voice trailed off into a whisper '. . . Gus and I wed in secret at the register office in Southampton. After Vee arrived, I called myself Smith and, as far as anyone hereabouts knows, I'm Mrs Smith. Schmidt is on my marriage certificate so I've been scared to apply for any papers that might show my husband's surname. And now I'm more petrified after reading in the newspapers of the abuse hurled at anyone with a German-sounding name . . .'

Tears filled May's eyes and she put a hand over her mouth.

Vee spoke: 'I thought when I asked my boss for help I was doing the right thing for you and me, Mum. He does this a lot, providing fake identity papers, passports . . .'

'As well as now having a hold over you.' Jem ran a calloused hand through his grey-blond hair. 'Oh, love, whatever have you done?'

Vee took a deep breath. She'd never meant to cause unhappiness. 'I thought I was getting the best of the bargain when he said, at first, he'd take the money from my wages weekly . . .'

'You'll be paying through the nose for these for the rest of your life.' Jem's words were harsh.

'No, no, I won't. He said afterwards he didn't want any money . . .'

'What does he want?' Jem asked. When she didn't answer straight away, Vee saw sadness in his face. 'Don't tell me, you . . .'

'That's just it.' Vee looked first at her mother then back at Jem. 'I knew I couldn't go through with it.' She wiped her hand across her wet eyes and told them how she had taken the package from the lad at the club and, instead of leaving it behind the till for collection had opened it, stolen their papers, then lodged the envelope in the lavatory cistern. The kitchen became silent again, apart from the ticking of the ancient cuckoo clock above the mantelpiece.

Eventually she said, 'There are many women who'd jump at the chance. Not me. I didn't want to spend two nights in a hotel in the New Forest and have him pawing me.'

'Oh, Vee!' Her mother let the ration book she had been clutching fall to the table.

'He said he didn't want my money, but I honestly believed he'd let me pay him in cash, like the other customers he gets false passports and documents for . . .' She was gabbling on.

Jem's face was like marble as he left May's side and stepped towards Vee, enfolding her in his brawny arms. For such a big man, his voice was now surprisingly gentle. 'He's the one in the wrong, not you, love.'

As he spoke, Vee thought of the many other times he had soothed her as any father would his child. Now, clutched to his chest, she took in his calming smell: the earthiness that came from hard work, and peppermints.

May said softly, 'You'll have to go away.'

Vee broke free from Jem. 'Go where?'

Jem said, 'Your mother's right. You can't stay here – he'll come after you.'

'I can't leave you!' Vee was horrified.

'I don't think you have a choice, Vee,' said Jem. 'Sammy Chesterton's well known for his public acts of kindness when he wants something, but that man's reputation goes before him.' He was now staring at her mother and she could see they were both of one mind.

'But where will I go?'

Jem shook his head. 'Get on a bus or a train before Sammy Chesterton comes looking. This will be his first port of call.'

'I can't leave you to face my problem . . .'

'Vee, you have to go. I'm here with your mother. Even if we had money to offer Sammy Chesterton, out of principle he wouldn't take it, not now. You mustn't worry about us. You have to go, quickly and alone. We can't leave. This is one of the busiest times of the year, coming up to harvest.'

Her mother was nodding. 'You know it's the right thing to do. Unless . . .' She grew thoughtful and turned to Jem. 'What if Vee goes back to Southampton today, sees Sammy Chesterton and appeals to his better nature?'

Jem let out a guffaw of dry laughter. 'What better nature, May? Everyone believes Chesterton was responsible for the man who was hacked to pieces and left in a dustbin a few months back. The gossip was the bloke had been stealing black-market goods from him. My love, that man wants to be thought of as a good businessman, a philanthropist, but the truth is very different. Like the huge party he put on at his club last Easter for the kids of the people who'd been made homeless in the bombing. Then he offered some of his rat-infested properties as emergency housing at extortionate rents, knowing it'll be years before the local council can get around to rebuilding and renovating the places that are still standing. Even if you offered yourself on a plate now, he'd refuse because he'll want you shamed publicly.'

'Don't talk like that.' May sighed and turned to Vee. 'I'll miss you . . . You've not left me before.'

Vee said, 'I'll go tomorrow.' The cat wound herself round her legs as if in sympathy.

'No,' May said. 'You must leave immediately. Jem's right. Sammy Chesterton could come next week or he could arrive tonight. You can't take chances.'

Jem agreed. 'We'll concoct some story, but if he finds you here there's no telling what he might do.' She should go. It would be safer for all of them. Jem wasn't saying they wouldn't stand by any decision she made, but he also knew she would never forgive herself if Sammy Chesterton decided to take out his anger on her mother or the smallholding.

'Just promise me you'll keep in touch,' May said.

Vee nodded miserably. She lifted the knitted cosy on the

teapot and felt its heat. As though reading her mind, her mother said, 'Let's drink this blessed tea before it stews itself to death, then I'll help you pack a few things.'

Jem added, 'She's right, love. Do as your mother says. I'm here to look after her, but I'm no match for Sammy Chesterton.' He patted his pocket, took out his wallet and emptied it on to the table. 'Take what I've got.' Vee dissolved into tears.

Chapter Three

May sat on the old armchair by the fire, her legs tucked beneath her. Her beloved girl had gone. Vee, despite appearing self-possessed, had inherited her own youthful waywardness, which didn't bode well when paired with her father's headstrong determination. She wouldn't cry, she told herself. After all, she'd encouraged Vee to leave, and such was the bond between them that her daughter would let her know where she was. The main thing was that, for now, Vee was out of the clutches of Sammy Chesterton.

The flames flickered and burnt red, yellow. The sweet smell from the apple logs was comforting. May's eyes closed and she thought back to June 1917, when more than a hundred people had been killed and at least four hundred injured during the first daylight German bombing raid over London. She remembered the outrage when a school was hit, killing ten children. In those days there had been no early warning system. The government had been loath to admit in 1914 that war was imminent, in the belief that the news would cause pandemonium among the people. Eventually policemen had cycled about the streets wearing notices of impending attacks.

Later on in 1917, August Schmidt was transferred to the Royal Victoria Hospital at Netley and entered May's life, changing her for ever. After he had been discharged, they had lain on the rag rug in front of this same fire making love, and now she could almost feel his strong arms around her.

His words came back to her as though she, not he, had survived hell, and gave her the comfort she needed . . .

The room was white. There was no pain. A sort of calm seeped through his body. From the bed Gus could see a trim young woman in an ankle-length grey dress with a stiff white apron and neat white square covering her blonde hair as she went about her duties in the ward.

He couldn't move his head, but his eyes took in the cage over his lower left leg. He tried to move the toes on that foot but failed. He tried again. Nothing.

In the dark of the night the pain woke him.

He realized he had been holding his breath and exhaled,

then drew in the antiseptic cleanliness of what he supposed was a hospital ward. In an English hospital. This he could tell by the printed signs hanging from the walls. Silently, he thanked his school near Cologne for teaching him English, though at the time he had thought he would never get to grips with the idiosyncrasies of *gh*, *th*, *ph*.

There was a rasping noise. A crackling sound that didn't seem right, coming from his chest. Relax and breathe, he told himself, but breathing hurt. How had he come to be here? All he could remember was pain and a vague recollection of being bumped along on wheels. He closed his eyes – and saw shells bursting like fireworks. He became agitated. Relax and breathe, he told himself. Relax and breathe. He slept.

Later when he woke he thought she was singing, the blonde girl in the grey ankle-length dress. Then he realized the words had no tune, but were more like lines from a play.

'Don't talk about anything you hear in hospital. Duty before pleasure. Stand when seniors enter, obedience to all seniors. You are but one of many.'

The young woman carefully replaced the cage over his leg and smoothed the thin white blanket tidily across the top of it. She then bent down and emerged upright, holding soiled dressings, thickly clotted with dark red matter. She put them into a bag hanging from her wrist. Her fair hair, which was poking out from the white headdress, was very shiny, cut short. Her face was scrubbed, her eyes blue as a summer sky. To Gus she looked like an angel.

'Don't talk about . . .'

She was repeating the words. 'Is that something you have to remember?' His voice sounded like gravel washed up from the shore. It was a long while since he had spoken to anyone and the sound was foreign to his ears.

He must have startled her because she looked at him, eyes wide.

'It's the VAD's oath,' she said softly. 'And you should sleep.'

He didn't understand.

'VAD?'

'I'm a voluntary nurse. I clear up after the doctors and qualified nurses. We have to remember our place in the order of things in this hospital.'

He tried to smile at her, but his face felt stiff, unyielding.

'Careful,' she added quickly. 'Your scar is healing over nicely. Don't break the stitches.'

What scar? He was conscious of his leg, because now there was a dull ache in it all the time. He also knew he had some internal damage because the pain in his chest was similar to sharp spikes being drawn through his flesh. He tried to lift his arm and managed to run his finger down the side of his cheek where he discovered the beginnings of a beard and tenderness from a raised ridge.

'Leave it alone,' she said.

He let his hand drop. Speaking to her, thinking and moving had worn him out. He closed his eyes and slept.

When he woke again the angel was leaning over him.

Panic set in. Her nearness made him remember how close the enemy aircraft had come to his plane. He had been on reconnaissance. The look of recognition, of kill or be killed, he had seen in the bi-plane's pilot's gaze. The wild noises of the wind and the rat-a-tat-tat of bullets. He remembered machine-gun fire hitting him, the piercing pain. His instrument board had been torn to pieces by a shell. He was going down over Mazingarbe, in France, with the battlefront of Vermelles two kilometres away.

His lower leg was shattered by a bullet. When he touched it, his hand had come away covered with blood. He remembered the descent, more wind, the sound of rushing air and blood dripping from his face, warm and wet.

Half the propeller was gone and his plane was spinning like a child's toy. He had no parachute. There was no room in the tiny cockpit to manoeuvre wearing the bulky object; it was preferable to have a lighter, faster plane. Besides, how could he have deployed it from the burning aircraft that was tumbling towards the earth?

He had watched a Fokker pilot without a parachute, arms and legs flailing like a windmill, hurtling to certain death. Perhaps he had thought choosing to jump was braver than waiting to go down with his machine. Gus was sickened as the man hit the ground. He swore he could hear the thud.

Loos was below.

Memories of that enemy plane, when with the cold wind across his face he had got out his revolver and fired at the enemy pilot. Never would he forget the man's fearful look as their eyes had met.

Despite his leather flying jacket, high leather boots and cap he was so cold.

He didn't bail. Instead, forcing himself to use his fast-failing flying skills he tried to steer the plane.

From the corner of his eye he watched the orange burst of flame, like an exotic sunset, that was his plane, hurtling ever nearer to the French soil. All he could hope for was that he could land before the petrol tank blew.

The ground was coming up fast to meet him. He had no memory of landing.

He had blacked out.

And now he opened his eyes wide. Happiness rushed

through him. He wasn't dead. The vagaries of war had washed him up somewhere in England. His eyes rested on his VAD angel.

'What's your name? Mine is August Schmidt.'

'May,' said his angel, and smiled.

May sighed and gently deposited Cat on the floor. She picked up an apple log from the filled basket, setting it on the fire. Tiny spurts of damp steam puffed out into the room as the log burnt. On the mantelpiece lay the documents that allowed May to stay, to shop, to belong in her own country. The price had been her daughter fleeing from her.

In the mirror she examined her face, her eyes lined at the corners from working outside in the sun. Unlike Vee's, her hair held traces of grey that blended with the blonde. She wasn't beautiful but she'd inspired two men to love her. May said a silent prayer asking God to keep her beloved daughter safe.

The moment May settled back on her chair, Cat jumped determinedly up to settle in the space at her side.

Opening the *Southampton Echo*, May began to read. The RAF had struck back at Germany for the bombs dropped on London. Berlin had taken a hard shelling. She made herself read the distressing news, then turned the page.

The headline spoke of a mystery blaze. A photograph showed a Southampton baker, his hands covering his face. Behind him, in the background, a shop was in flames. The man's anguish was pitiful. Apparently Karl Muller's one crime was to have been born in Germany.

Chapter Four

The train rattled along, the view through the carriage window changing from green fields and farms to the backs of grimy terraced houses with grey washing hanging limply on bowed lines.

Vee wished she hadn't been so hasty, first in asking Sammy Chesterton for help, then in stealing the documentation that had meant so much to her and her mother. How could she have been so stupid?

Neither she nor May was ashamed of her father's nationality – her mother had loved Gus Schmidt with all her heart. But war had changed the way people thought about ordinary German people. It was so unfair. People forgot that love knew no barriers. It was ridiculous for anyone to believe that Vee and May might be traitors simply because her mother had married a man considered an enemy.

Another train passed on the other track, smoke billowing in a cloud alongside, wafting in through the slit of open window. It smelt sharp and acrid. A loud whistle startled her.

'Oh, that made me jump as well!' The elderly woman opposite fanned her wrinkled face with a handkerchief. Vee smiled at her. 'Would you like a sweetie?' The woman proffered a white paper bag of toffees.

'No, thank you.' Vee guessed how precious the sweet ration was to her. She made herself more comfortable, glancing up at her suitcase in the mesh rack above the plush seats.

'At least it was only a train and not another of that dreadful Hitler's bombs. Going to Portsmouth, dear?' The bag of sweeties went back into the woman's capacious handbag. A waft of lavender travelled towards Vee. The sailor sitting next to the old woman grinned at her. Vee thought he looked very young to be fighting for his country. He fingered his round hat with the white band. The train was packed, people squashed together like sardines in tins.

Servicemen squatted on kitbags out in the corridor. Smoke swirled in the air from cigarettes and the floor was awash with dog-ends.

'I . . . I . . . Yes,' Vee finally answered. So that was the train's destination, was it?

Upon reaching the station at Southampton, she had climbed inside the carriage of the first train that had pulled in. She hadn't bought a ticket, for she knew the conductor would supply her with one on whichever train she chose to board. She had no idea where she should go, for there were no relatives she could stay with, and even if there had been she could never have involved them with her problems.

Eventually the carriage door opened and the portly inspector entered.

'Tickets, please.' These were tendered and then he stood looking expectantly at Vee.

'I need to buy one, please.' Her mouth was dry.

'Where to, love?' His dark suit was shiny with constant wear.

Vee must have looked confused. 'Portsmouth?' she said.

He clicked a ticket from the machine hanging at his corpulent waist and handed it to her. 'Single?'

She nodded and paid him. He left the compartment, and Vee gave the woman opposite yet another smile, then closed her eyes. She'd never been to Portsmouth before.

'. . . end of the line.'

Vee awoke to an empty compartment. The disembodied

male voice from the loudspeaker repeated, 'Portsmouth Harbour Station, end of the line.'

Sleepily, Vee gathered her handbag and small case, then stepped out into the corridor. Stationary trains and carriages were all around her. The air smelt of oil and the sea, salty, moist and muddy.

At the office close to the exit she handed the man her ticket and, without a word to or from him, began walking down the steps.

Ships and boats were all around her! The railway station was built on a pier-like structure that streamed out from a main road backed by hotels and shops and ended on iron stilts that jutted into the water, with a sturdy jetty that rose and fell with the tide. Small boats were tied to bollards on the jetty, as was a larger ferry with lifebelts attached all around. She could make out figures on the boat and cyclists pedalling towards it, trying to avoid the foot passengers.

Vee looked at her watch, a birthday present from her mother. It was ten thirty, almost dark, and she had to find lodgings for the night. She hoped they wouldn't be too expensive for she had to make her money last. Tomorrow she must find work and somewhere permanent to stay.

Ahead of her the tide was out and more boats lay on

an expanse of mud, some tied to buoys, some leaning drunkenly in brackish water that looked as dark as the sky.

'Hurry, or we'll miss the last ferry!'

Vee was caught up in a crowd of young people rushing past and found herself following them to a small kiosk.

'One, please.' She opened her purse and bought a return ticket just like the girl in front of her, then hurried with the noisy bunch down the rickety bridge towards the pontoon where the ferry waited, now crammed with people. At one end bicycles were piled together in such a way that she was sure they could never be untangled. There wasn't room to sit so, like some of the other passengers, she stood against the warmth of the large funnel and yawned. She didn't remember ever feeling so tired.

'Are we keeping you up?'

The man stood about six feet tall in his turned-down wellington boots. He wore a dark jumper and laughed, showing even white teeth. Beneath his cap she could see dark curls. She felt the warmth of a blush and was thankful the darkness hid it. Ignoring him, she turned away to stare at a notice tied to a metal pole emerging from a slatted wooden bench where a drunken man lolled – she could smell the beer fumes. She could just make out the words, 'Staff Wanted'.

The drunk rolled, allowing Vee to read more of the notice: 'See the Skipper.'

The comforting heat from the funnel made her yawn again. She wondered what the work would entail and where the skipper might be. She could discern no other information on the notice, which was now hidden by the drunk's bulk. There was no way Vee was going to disturb him. Perhaps she could ask one of the men casting the thick mooring ropes at either end of the craft from the bollards.

Mesmerized, she watched as the boat left the landing stage, churning the seawater into white-topped waves as it arced towards another pontoon, which she could just make out in the distance.

If only it wasn't so dark. What lighting there was consisted mainly of green and red dots on the water among larger moored vessels. The sky suddenly allowed a silvery light to pick out the huge boats she recognized as tankers and dredgers. There also seemed to be some naval boats moored on the Portsmouth side that the small ferry was now leaving behind.

If necessary, she could always come back tomorrow to ask about the job. The main priority was a bed for the night. With a bit of luck she'd arrive on the other side of this stretch of water in time to ask at a café or a public house where she might find accommodation – if they hadn't all closed for the night.

It would be awful if the siren blared, announcing that bombs were imminent, when she had nowhere to go. She shivered, and decided to keep her eyes open for the nearest public air-raid shelter.

She wondered what kind of work would be needed on a ferry. Cleaning? Yes, that was probably it. Vee didn't care what job she took: she needed money for lodgings and food. She watched the port opposite growing bigger and bigger. Soon the ferry would land and she would have arrived at her destination, wherever that might be. She wondered where she would be if she hadn't been swept up with the happy band of travellers, whom she could hear still laughing and chatting on the other side of the boat. Would the opposite direction have taken her into the heart of Portsmouth?

Absentmindedly she watched a man in a thick jumper and boots handling a rope near the boat's exit. A thought occurred, and she made her way towards him, pushing through the crush of people.

'Can you tell me where I can find the skipper?'

He looked her up and down and a smile lit his young, ruddy face. His shock of red hair blew in a breeze that seemed to have sprung up from nowhere.

'Where he should be, Miss. Up on the bridge.' He glanced towards some iron steps back near the funnel and Vee followed his gaze to a man high at the front of the boat, his eyes on the water. Vee nodded her thanks and made her way to the metal ladder.

If the water had been rough, she wouldn't have been able to climb the slippery steps, but keeping a wary eye on her cardboard suitcase, left tucked out of the way of people's feet, she was soon inside a small wooden cabin that was completely open to the elements.

The wind, not really discernible below, was biting at her face and causing her hair to whip into her eyes. She tapped the man on the shoulder. His hands were on the wheel.

'Excuse me!'

'My God!' She'd made him jump. 'What the hell are you doing up here?' He stared at her, then his eyes moved quickly back to the water. 'Don't you know this is out of bounds to passengers?'

Her heart dropped. Never had she expected to be shouted at so fiercely, and by the same man who had accused her of being tired in such a jovial manner when he had caught her yawning.

'I'm sorry,' was all she could manage. The wind was trying to take her words away. Vee pulled her hair back from her face. 'The sign says "See the Skipper", and you're the skipper, aren't you?'

'You could have chosen a better place to see me. What do you want?'

His words were gruff, but the twinkle in his eye showed a sense of humour. The wind, becoming more violent, caused the boat to sway, and she fell against him. 'I'm sorry,' she said, scrambling to regain her composure. 'That notice down on the deck says you need staff.'

For a moment he was silent, as though digesting her words, then he began to laugh. If she wasn't so bewildered she would have thought it was a good sound – a real man's laugh, deep and dry.

'You?' He looked at her quizzically and smiled again. But it was a warm smile.

'I can clean a boat, make tea, scrub a deck.' She knew she was babbling but she didn't care. What else would he need a woman for on a boat?'

'You really are desperate for a job, aren't you?' He frowned. 'I thought this was some kind of joke one of my blokes had cooked up.'

Vee was practically shouting to make herself heard above the elements now.

'Look, I need a job and somewhere to stay. I'm a good worker and I'm honest.'

As she uttered the last couple of words she realized she'd just lied to him. She was running away because she hadn't been honest at her last job.

Rain began to fall. Huge wet drops that not only stung her face but were plastering her hair to her head. The man pulled off his cap and stuck it over her hair. He looked down at her – she barely reached his chest. He was staring at her thoughtfully. 'That'll keep your hair dry. It's the best I can do,' he said eventually. 'Now, stand back and let me land this craft.'

Neatly, despite the waves hurling themselves against the pontoon and causing the boat to pitch and toss like a cork, he drew close enough to the wooden jetty for the seaman she had spoken to earlier to throw a rope, encircle a bollard, and haul the vessel against the pontoon. At the other end another man was securing the front.

Only when the boat was steady enough did the young man unclip the chain allowing passengers to safely disembark.

Still standing close to the skipper, Vee watched amazed as the men, once the foot passengers had departed, helped disentangle the bicycles for their rightful owners, who then pushed them up the gangway to disappear into the darkness beyond.

Vee was soaked. She sneezed, then yawned again. The day had been full of surprises, some not so good, and she was hungry, tired and, although she hated to admit it, she was scared. Oh, how she wished she was at home, with her warm cosy bed to climb into.

'Get down in the cabin out of the rain. This is the last ferry for tonight. As soon as I've moored up properly and locked everything away I'll fetch you.'

She looked into his eyes. There were so many questions she wanted to ask but her happiness at hearing him mention a cabin where she would at least be dry overrode everything else. He gave her directions to get to it, then Vee climbed down the ladder, took her suitcase and went down into the bowels of the boat. She sat on a wooden bench in a windowless room that smelt of fags and bodies.

She wondered if Sammy Chesterton had been out to the smallholding. It might be a little too soon as perhaps he hadn't yet discovered that the envelope containing the forged papers was missing.

Before she had left home, Vee had had great difficulty in persuading her mother to hang on to the forged documents. She had put her own into her handbag.

'Even if you never need them, Vee's paid a high price for them and the least you can do is to keep them safe,' advised Jem.

It was warm in the cabin and the floor was littered with rubbish and sweet wrappers. Vee was so tired. How lovely it would be to sit in the armchair in front of the fire with Cat on her lap. Sadness overwhelmed her that she wouldn't see the kittens when they arrived. Already homes had been promised for three and May had decided to keep one. But who knew how many Cat would produce? She was a good mouser and earned her keep. Vee often found her asleep on her bed. She sighed. At present she didn't have a bed.

She smoothed some stray hairs behind one ear and realized she was still wearing the skipper's peaked cap. She took it off, ran her fingers through her hair, put the cap on the bench beside her and closed her eyes. The man with the twinkling eyes would come and find her, if only to claim his cap.

Chapter Five

'Wake up, sleepy-head.'

Vee opened her eyes. For a moment she was unsure of her surroundings and wondered if she was still dreaming. A dark-haired man was shaking her shoulder gently. When he said, 'I think you could do with a cup of tea. Am I right?' she remembered where she was.

She tried a smile. 'My throat feels parched.' The wooden seat seemed welded to her bottom.

'Come on,' he said. 'I'll take you home. We can discuss work there.' He picked up his cap and jammed it on his head.

'I'm not going home with you! I don't know you.' It was as if a light bulb had switched on in her brain. First Sammy Chesterton had wanted to get her into bed and now this stranger wanted to take her to his home. 'What do you think I am?'

'You asked me for a job. Either you want one or you don't. I haven't got time to mess around. There are rooms for workers at my house and my wife will sort one out for you. We can discuss work or . . .' He paused. It was then she saw how tired he was. He rubbed a hand across his chin. '. . . get off this boat and let me go home so I can get some shut-eye.'

She stood up. Without another word, he picked up her case and started towards the doorway. Meekly, Vee followed. When she reached the top of the steps she saw that the rain had stopped. The dark seemed impenetrable and she was glad she wasn't alone. He waited, watching her as she carefully went down the steps, then walked off the boat and onto the pontoon. Because of the blackout he carried a small torch but kept his fingers across its beam so the light shone thinly and only where he needed it. She tried to keep up with him, but his long legs increased the distance between them. At last she cried, 'Wait for me!'

The man stopped, turned and laughed when he saw her struggling to catch up with him in her high heels.

'If you're going to work for me you might think about wearing some proper shoes,' he said. 'Else you'll be in boots all the time.'

When Vee reached his side she took a moment to look about her and catch her breath.

'It's not far now,' he said, striding down a concrete path.

Vee had to step aside – a young woman, looming out of the darkness, nearly knocked into her.

'I'm sorry.' The words came automatically, but the girl didn't answer, just hastened on her way, leaving a waft of cheap perfume.

'Don't worry about Ada,' he said. Vee waited for him to add more, but he said nothing and she carried on walking behind him. Cloud had shut out the moonlight and Vee could feel yet more rain in the air. She made out what she thought was a bus station with several double-deckers silent and empty for the night. There was a ticket office and as they drew close she could make out the boat fares. A board announced, 'Gosport Ferry'. So she was in Gosport. She thought back to the train arriving at Portsmouth Harbour Station, then her journey across the short expanse of water. Just then she heard music coming from what looked like a Nissen hut in darkness across a road. Alongside it, tall, imposing houses faced the water.

'There are no lights in my house,' he said. 'That means my wife's not at home. I don't want you worrying about being there alone with me so I'll take you into the café.' He began to cross the road, slower now so that she could keep up with him.

'Here,' he waved an arm, 'is Beach Street. Known for its boat builders. Tomorrow you'll see the skeletons of small craft and hear the men working on them.' He paused. 'Business is slower than before the war,' he added. 'Take a deep breath.'

Vee breathed in. The smell of wood reminded her of pencil sharpenings.

'I hope that doesn't unsettle you,' he said. He pointed upwards at the windows of one of the tall houses. 'That'll be your room. If you can't stand the smell of wood shavings, you're in trouble!'

Vee didn't speak. The thought of a room with a bed, one she could curl up and sleep in, filled her with relief.

At the Nissen hut he pushed open the door and immediately she was enveloped in light and a fug of fried-food smells that reminded her of how hungry she was. The ever-present cigarette smoke tried to escape out into the road, but the long blackout curtain kept most of it inside.

The skipper stood aside so she could enter. The dance music from the wireless and the brightness of the electric light immediately raised her spirits.

Men and women sat around long tables drinking tea and talking. Some were eating, some laughing and most were smoking. A plump woman in bright overalls, bleached blonde hair piled high on her head, secured with glittery pins and covered with a mesh snood, stood behind the counter.

'Hello, Jack. The usual?' She gave him a warm, welcoming grin. Then a smile came Vee's way.

So, Vee thought, she knew his name now. Jack suited him.

There was a glass container on the counter filled with some kind of pudding on a large plate. It looked greasy and was cut into squares.

'Please, Connie, love, two mugs of tea and two bits of your delectable bread pudding.' He turned to Vee and said, 'Park your bottom there.' He pointed to a seat at an empty table. 'Ever had bread pudding before?' He took off his cap and put it on the table, then ran his fingers through his curly hair and smiled down at her.

Vee shook her head. It didn't look very palatable.

'Connie's bread pudding is the best in Gosport,' he added loudly.

Vee could see the woman was pleased as she poured their tea from a large urn into big white mugs. 'Sit down, Jack, I'll bring it over.' Connie flashed him another wide smile and he took the chair opposite Vee.

'Thank you,' she said, falling on the tea as it was placed in front of her. She eyed the square of pudding that accompanied it with apprehension. Connie stood by the table.

'John Cousins was in here looking for you,' she said.

'He'll catch up with me,' the skipper said. Turning to Vee, 'Now you know my name, Jack Edwards, am I allowed to ask yours?'

'Vee, Violetta Smith.' She forked up a small piece of the pudding. 'Violetta after my grandmother,' she added as she popped it into her mouth and chewed. 'It's lovely,' she gasped, amazed as fruit, sugar and spice flooded her taste buds.

'What did I tell you? The best in Gosport.'

Connie laughed. 'As soon as I can find the mixed fruit to make it, it disappears. We can't always get hold of the ingredients now. Bloody war.' She put a hand on Jack's shoulder and he looked up at her in the way of people who have few secrets between them. The way good friends trust each other, thought Vee.

'I got the baby out the back,' she said quietly. 'Rosie's with her.'

Jack's face clouded and he began to rise but Connie pushed him back into the seat. 'She's fine, asleep. Eat and drink up before you go to her.'

'Where's Madelaine?'

'Gone to see her parents,' she said. 'Didn't want to take the little one in case there was an air raid and she was between

49

public shelters. She knows I got the Morrison in the kitchen.' Connie moved away from the table and made her way back behind the counter, where a small queue had formed.

Already the bread pudding was lining Vee's empty stomach and the strong tea was making her feel better. She wondered who Madelaine was. From the way Connie had spoken of her, Vee decided Connie wasn't enamoured of the woman.

Vee's mother also had a Morrison shelter in their kitchen. The box-like metal contraption held a quilt and pillows, and was just big enough for two or three people when the planes came over, dropping their bombs. Like many others, May had put a sheet of wood across the top and used it as an extra table.

Vee finished eating, then drained her tea. She sat back on the chair and thought how much better she felt. But Jack's demeanour had changed. She thought he seemed preoccupied now, and the light had left him. Whose baby was it? Why was the child out the back?

'If you don't eat anything else until breakfast tomorrow,' he said, 'you won't hurt with that inside you . . . I sometimes wonder why on earth I don't let Connie have a free hand in this place. I suppose I have so much on my mind, I'm scared of changing things.' He wasn't actually talking to her, Vee realized, more voicing his thoughts. There was no need for her to answer him, but she had deduced that the café belonged to him, or was under his management.

He finished his tea, then took a deep breath. 'I'll tell you briefly what I want from you. If you agree, I'll take you next door to my house where not only my wife, child and I live but also Rosie, Connie, and Regine, who works in the ticket office. It's a big old house but there's an empty room overlooking the harbour and the floating bridge . . .'

What on earth was a floating bridge?

Jack answered her unasked question.

'The steam-powered floating bridge takes people and transport across to the point at Portsmouth, and has done since 1840. It can accommodate up to fifty vehicles. At present it's very useful for transporting troops, lorries and munitions. The floating bridge, or car ferry, is nothing to do with me.

'Our ferries transport people to Portsea, near the dockyard, for the princely sum of a penny. We start early, end late, run regularly and don't shut down during the raids.' He stared into her eyes. 'Am I right in thinking you've never been to Gosport before?'

'Never,' she said.

'Well, you've got a lot to learn. But there's no finer folk than true Gosport people. Play straight and they'll do anything for you.'

'But what do you want me to do?' Vee asked. She was mesmerized by his mouth. As he talked the corners seemed to dissolve into upward strokes that made her think he could laugh quite easily if he wasn't being so serious.

'I'm coming to that. The company has lost a few men who decided to join up, even though ferrying is a reserved occupation.'

'What does that mean?'

'It means working on the ferries is a necessary job during this war, so the workers are exempt from joining the forces.' For a moment sadness clouded his face. 'Unfortunately, I can't fight because my heart beats erratically. It also means I've had that blessed notice pinned up there for long enough to know that no one suitable wants a job working on the boats during the war, until you happened along, of course.

'I've had men on their last legs apply, unable to climb the ladder to the wheelhouse. Spotty young lads ready for their call-up, who are no good to me. By the time they were trained they'd be in the services . . . I'm willing to train you up. It'll be hard work, dirty work, and you'll be out in all weathers. You'll probably get some stick from the older ferry men for being a woman in a man's world, but what do you say?'

Vee opened her mouth but that was as far as she got.

Jack didn't give her time to answer: he went on about

the wages, the hours, the room in his house. She noticed he didn't ask where she'd come from or why she'd left.

'Yes,' Vee said.

He slapped his knee. 'Good. I knew you were right when I saw you weren't in the least seasick. No good to me if you're queasy every time you're on the water.'

Vee thought back to the wind, the rain and the heaving of the craft as they'd sailed from Portsmouth.

'No, I wasn't, was I?' She hadn't thought about it at the time and was pleased she could tolerate bad sea conditions.

Just then the thin wail of a baby crying, drowning the music from the wireless, came from the kitchen. 'That's my daughter,' Jack said. Vee saw the pride in his eyes. 'That's my Margaret – we call her Peg. She's only a few weeks old. Got to think about getting her christened soon, keep putting it off.' Vee noted how his voice was soft and his smile reached right to his eyes when he talked about his little girl. 'I'll just go and get her, then take you home and show you your room. Oh, I forgot to ask, you do have your identity papers and ration book, don't you?'

Vee got up from her chair. 'Oh, yes,' she said. 'I have them.'

He stood up, jammed his hat on his head, called good-night to some of the men and women in the room, then disappeared through a door at the back of the counter to reappear moments later with a carry-cot that held the crying child.

'Her mother's gone visiting. I must get my Peg home and changed.'

Vee looked into the carry-cot at the wailing infant. Connie handed her a bag containing an empty bottle and a rolled-up dirty nappy. Vee noted the smell emanating from the little girl. Connie must have tuned into her thoughts for she added, 'Madelaine didn't leave enough stuff for me to make her a feed or to change her again, though I'd have used a dishcloth if Jack hadn't arrived when he did.'

Connie talked of him with warmth, and it was obvious that she was fond of him. Vee wanted to say the baby was lovely, but she thought the screwed-up face and open crying mouth belied that. Yet her motherly instincts rose to the fore.

'Hello, little one,' she murmured. She touched the tiny clenched hand, and immediately the little girl opened her fingers and clutched Vee's finger in a powerful grip. Vee immediately thought of Cat's babies, who would look nothing like pretty little fluffy kittens when they arrived. Living on a smallholding had taught her that newborn animals soon changed and became beautiful. She hoped it would be so with this infant who was surely too small to be without her mother.

Outside the rain was lashing down again and Jack kept close to the walls of the buildings to try to protect Peg. Very soon he stopped, put his shoulder to a door and it opened.

'Put the light on as soon as we're inside,' he said, walking ahead of her. After flicking the electric switch, Vee saw they were in a long passage with doors and stairs leading off it. Ahead Jack had entered a large, comfortable living room-cum-kitchen where a fire was burning low in the grate. Vee relished the warmth after the chill of the rain.

He had put the carry-cot on the table. Miraculously the child had ceased crying. He grinned at Vee.

'Your room is at the top of the stairs at the front. If you open any of the other doors by mistake you'll see they're occupied. Rosie is next to you and Regine is opposite . . . Regine. Don't pay too much attention to her – she has a sharp tongue.' He waved towards a door leading from the room. 'Scullery and garden are through there. Now,' he said, 'you work for me and I expect you to be here in this room at five tomorrow morning. The ferry starts at five thirty. Don't make me late by staying in bed.' He paused. 'I'll expect you to muck in and help in the house – we all do our bit. My wife had a hard birth and is a bit fragile, so Rosie, Regine,

Connie and I help as much as we can. Connie feeds us.' Vee nodded. She was now practically asleep on her feet. Only the strangeness of the situation was keeping her awake. Jack must have seen this for he said, 'Go to bed.'

Vee was only too happy to oblige.

Chapter Six

Sammy Chesterton sat in the layby in his Armstrong Siddeley, smoking. He sighed. Even though the aroma and taste of the expensive cigar soothed him, it didn't stop the memories flooding back that caught at his heartstrings and hurt, like a knife twisting in a wound. He brushed ash off his expensive suit.

The cottage looked the same as it always had: Honeysuckle Holdings, set back a little from the lane with the smallholding and its sheds, fields and greenhouses at the rear. A grey cat, heavily pregnant, walked from the side of the house to flop lazily in the patch of sun on the path.

May had been ten years old when he had first walked her home from school, carrying her books for her, as his father had told him he should. His father was old school, believed in treating women like ladies. Certainly his mother had had his dad wrapped around her little finger, but they'd worshipped each other until that bomb had landed on his village house in 1917. It had happened while Sammy had been away . . .

All these years later his heart still hurt thinking about May.

After college he'd travelled the world, working his way to India, Thailand, Greece, Germany and China, but eventually he'd settled back in Southampton, discovering he could make more money in a place he knew if he kept a finger in a lot of pies.

He imported quality goods made by the Chinese and Thais. Local people were paid a pittance and worked long hours, and he sold their goods at profits he'd never thought possible. Then he had bought his first club, and realized it was easier to slip over to the wrong side of the law, bringing in drink from France rather than buying it from wholesalers in England, his clubs the perfect places to sell it at exorbitant prices. Backhanders to coppers in high places kept everyone happy, most of all him.

He'd even thought about going into politics. Again, cash to councillors made it possible for him to get small changes made in some local laws if they didn't suit him. He'd known early on that he'd never get anywhere with a German name.

At school it hadn't mattered so much. After all, 'Herbert

Lang' was as English-sounding as the next boy's name. His birth certificate told a different story.

Sammy Chesterton was the name of a character in a novel he'd read and admired. So Herbert Lang had become Sammy Chesterton. But his ancestry barred him from the success he wanted. Far too many English Members of Parliament were determined to scour the country of anything or anyone remotely German. The British Nationality and Status of Aliens Act of 1918 contained so many anti-German provisions it was laughable. But Sammy never laughed.

He discovered a brilliant forger who liked being paid for what he was best at, so Sammy put business his way . . . a great deal of business over the years, which was mutually profitable. It allowed peaceful people, who lived and, in some cases, had been born in England to become, albeit illegally, English. It was amazing how many people in high places had skeletons in their closets.

Sammy put a great deal of money into the Nationality of Married Women Bill that had gone before the House of Commons, but even though a Joint Select Committee had been appointed, it had fallen by the wayside, despite the support of at least two hundred MPs.

Sammy reasoned that if the women affected could be given back their own birthright, instead of having to accept their husbands' nationality, their children wouldn't suffer indignity. He firmly believed he could have done much more for his beloved England if his own birthright hadn't been taken from him. Sammy had never suspected that the girl who had worked in his club was the daughter of his childhood sweetheart. May must have married a German lad.

Now the heat rose from his neck and added to the sweat dampening his back. How could he have been so insensitive as to proposition young Vee?

She'd said she had no money and asked if she could pay in instalments. He'd told her she could pay her debt in kind. That a weekend in a hotel in the New Forest would pay for her and her mother's new identities. If only he'd looked closer at the information Vee had given him, he'd have realized her address here in Netley was the home May had been brought up in.

He sighed. Why had he never noticed her resemblance to May? But, then, why should he? He'd driven to this address hoping to catch Vee and instead had spotted May collecting logs from a stack outside the house. His heart had flipped.

When he was a kid, her parents had made him welcome. He remembered apple pie with a latticed pastry top and thick dairy cream, the pie tart and the cream sweet. Fresh strawberries picked in the field, with May at his side. She'd had pigtails then. Sammy drew on his cigar. Best Cuban, hand-rolled. He had money, he had clubs, expensive clothes, things, but objects didn't make a person feel wanted.

He was lonely. Very, very lonely.

Sammy threw his cigar stub out of the window and thought back to that morning when his forger, Tom, had come to the club for his money.

'You're a bit quick off the mark, mate. What's this, cash on delivery?'

Tom had given him a look that would have melted ice. 'C'mon, I need money same as everyone else. Was everything all right?'

He had had nothing in his hands.

'Who did you give the package to?' Sammy was well aware that a few of his employees would like to make a bit more money over and above what he was paying them.

'It weren't me, Boss.'

Sammy looked at Donald. If he said he hadn't been given a package, he believed him. 'It's all right, mate,' he said. He didn't want the old feller's dicky heart playing up.

'My boy brought it in a few days ago.'

Sammy lifted the wooden flap and motioned Tom behind the bar. 'There's the telephone. Get in touch with your lad, ask him who was here.'

Five minutes later it was established that Vee had taken the large brown envelope.

'Search this place from top to bottom,' Sammy growled. 'Likely she won't have stolen stuff that wasn't hers.'

He knew now why she'd left early and it wasn't because she was feeling ill. He hadn't really worried about her absence, thinking she was getting over whatever ailed her, but the little bitch had lied to him, stolen the documents she'd wanted, and made a run for it. Sammy thought quickly. Although there were only a few people in the club who knew what had happened, within hours his peers would be laughing that a chit of a girl had got one over on Sammy Chesterton.

The biggest slap in the face was that she had turned down the offer of a weekend in a hotel with him. He wasn't sure what would be hardest to live down. Women usually flocked to his bed. The bitch had made him look a right fool.

He opened the till and counted out notes, adding a few extra from his wallet to Tom's original price.

'Sorry, Tom,' he said. 'I should know better than to doubt you. No hard feelings?'

Tom shuffled from one foot to the other. There was always honour among thieves. 'None at all, mate,' he said.

Sammy knew they were waiting for him to blow his top,

like he had the other morning when he'd caught one of his drivers with his fingers in the till. Sammy would give money freely if it suited him but if anyone took it without asking . . .

'What are you doing, Al?' He had caught the young man with the till drawer open and banknotes clutched in his hand. He'd tried to return them, but Sammy was beside him and had pinned Al's hand to the counter with one of his own. Like a flash Sammy's fingers went to his breast pocket. His flick knife was out and Al's hand, still holding the notes, was skewered to the bar. Above Al's screams of pain, Sammy said, 'Never steal from the hand that feeds you.' Sammy looked at the young man, the blood, his fractured hand, and at Donald, who had come in to see what all the noise was about.

'Get rid of him, Donald,' he'd said.

The young man hadn't been seen at the club since.

Sammy now looked at Greta, the bar staff and Donald. 'Don't just stand there! Carry on looking for the rest of the documents.' He went to his office, slamming the door after him.

A while later a knock on the door and a small voice asked, 'Boss, are you in there?'

When he opened the door, Greta was standing outside in

the silky siren suit she wore for her dance practice. A turban covered her hair and in her hands was a cobwebbed package.

'I remembered the night Vee said she was poorly, she was in the lavatory for ages. I thought she was being sick . . .'

He took the envelope, shook off the detritus and looked inside.

'Well done, love.' He smiled at her. Running his eyes along the cards and birth certificates, he saw it was as he'd guessed: her and her mother's papers had gone. He threw the package onto his desk. He'd recoup the money he'd already paid out for the forged papers from the punters, but in the meantime he'd think up a suitable punishment for Miss Vee Schmidt.

'Do you want me to get you a drink or something, Boss?'

He looked into Greta's face. She was one of his best girls. She had a look of Betty Grable about her, and her legs weren't bad. A waft of perfume reached him and he treated her to another smile. 'I'll take you out for a meal as a thank-you after the club closes,' he said.

He'd thought the look in her eyes showed eagerness, and she readily agreed. It was another of those nights when he had nothing else to do.

'What a bloody mess,' he said now, taking another cigar and cutting it.

The trouble was, he'd allowed Vee to work at the Black

Cat even though she didn't give out to the punters. After all, some girls were a little shy at first. Stripping came easier when the money rolled in from the men in the audience. The patrons liked the feel of nubile skin. Vee seemed to think he could go on paying her when she wasn't pulling her weight. He'd believed it wouldn't be long before he could entice her to be . . . friendly to his customers. True, she'd stolen from him, but underneath she was a nice girl, a little naive perhaps, but then she was May's daughter.

'What a bloody mess,' he said again.

How could he take May's daughter to task for making him look a fool? But if he did nothing about her theft he'd be a laughing stock, wouldn't he?

He threw the part-smoked cigar out of the open window, started the car and slowly drove back to Southampton and the Black Cat Club.

May had spotted the car in the layby. For a moment she thought the driver looked familiar, but then she laughed at herself. Who did she know with a car as expensive as that?

In her arms she carried logs for the living-room fire. It was really rather warm during the day for a fire but Cat liked to snooze in the corner behind the old chair and at night the cottage became quite cold. May had no doubt that the grey cat would produce her kittens in the house. She smiled to herself. Vee would never forgive her if anything happened to Cat. She wondered which tom had fathered the kittens. Cat had had several suitors. An orange thug with a crooked tooth, a black and white stranger that had hung about, then disappeared, and the black mouser from the barn that didn't really belong to her but that May fed anyway.

Cat had appeared one stormy night when May had been, as usual, sitting in the kitchen trying not to feel sorry for herself that Gus was gone for good. The rain had lashed against the windows and she'd heard the faint scratching on the door and the plaintive miaows. That night she'd let Cat into the house and her heart.

Gus had loved cats. The strays that gathered in the grounds and buildings of the Royal Victoria Hospital at Netley were always in for a petting from him when at last he was able to hobble about on crutches. Sometimes he managed to save them scraps from his meals.

Set on the shores of the river Hamble, the hospital had been built in 1856. Its 2,500 patients were partly looked after by Red Cross volunteers as most of the regular nursing staff were working overseas during the Great War.

May couldn't keep August Schmidt out of her mind. The tall, slim man always seemed to be watching her whenever and wherever she was in the ward. Now he was up on crutches, he wore the thick cotton suit of a detainee with large red dots on the back. The clothing made the prisoners think twice about trying to escape when their injuries had healed. May had known only of one who had escaped. He had reached Waterloo station by clinging to the underside of the train from Southampton before he was captured again.

Most of the Germans, once they had recovered, stayed in the hospital's prison or were sent out to work, returning nightly. Of course, the people living around Netley hated the Germans being treated well at the hospital; they imagined the men were better fed than their own lads at the front. Quite possibly they were correct, thought May.

The hospital was self-contained, with the main wards facing the inner courtyard, the nurses' and doctors' quarters in kit-built units at the rear. As well as the prison, it had its own gasworks, bakery, reservoir, asylum, and even a ballroom to keep the workers happy when time and circumstances permitted.

May and the nurses loved the dances. There was music, of course, and the chance to dress up in clothes that were not their uniform. On those evenings May found it easy to pretend the war didn't exist, especially when she was dancing with a young doctor. That bubble usually burst when the next batch of bloodied, stinking men arrived on a ship from Southampton Water, and moored at the hospital's jetty to be brought in.

'What does VAD mean?' Gus had asked her one day, as she cleared away the detritus one of the doctors had left after cleaning his leg.

'Voluntary Aid Detachment,' she'd replied. 'We're a sort of back-up for the regular nurses.'

'Is that why your clothes are different?'

She'd nodded. 'The hospital needs all the help it can get.' She didn't tell him that some of the regular nurses looked down on the VADs. After all, they had trained for much longer than the volunteers. He'd put his hand on her arm. 'I thought I had died and I was sure you were an angel . . .'

Had those words come from anyone else May would have thought they were taking liberties with her. She knew how badly he'd been injured, so he was trying to tell her how grateful he was to be alive. She'd smiled at him and something inside her had told her he would love her like no one else had ever loved her.

Now May sighed as she picked up the *Evening News* from the table and settled in the armchair to read: young men between the ages of eighteen and forty-one were now obliged to register for military service. Previously many men had volunteered to fight. She read down the list of workers who were exempt. Selfishly, she was happy that Jem was considered too old.

War had taken her first love; she didn't want to lose the second.

Chapter Seven

When Vee awoke to the tinny clatter of the alarm clock she looked around the room in which she had tumbled, unwashed, into bed the night before. Her last memory was of the smiling lips of Jack Edwards.

Last night she'd pulled back the bedclothes, which were clean and sweet-smelling, then wound and set the clock. As soon as she'd closed her eyes, she'd been asleep. Now the morning sun burst into her room as she pulled back the blackout curtains and gasped. Across the road a huge metal monstrosity was half in and half out of the water. Already several delivery vans and cars were parked at either side of the central bridge on the boat-like contraption. People were milling about. Vee opened the window and the smell of the sea greeted her with a torrent of noise. So that was the floating bridge. Along its bow a painted sign proclaimed,

'Brickwood's Sunshine Ale Bright To The Last Drop'. Advertising for a brewery no doubt, she thought. She could also make out the boat's name, *Ceto*. Vee wondered what it meant. People were stepping from the sloping hard on Beach Street on to the weirdly shaped chained craft. Despite the bustle outside she felt calm. Surely Sammy Chesterton wouldn't find her here. Vee put her elbows on the window-sill and took a deep breath of the sunny morning. Not far away, beyond the ticket office, she could see the squat ferry she had travelled on last night. Across the harbour at the Portsmouth side there was another boat. The sea between the two points was filled with craft of all sorts and sizes. Even at this early hour people were working, queuing and laughing, and the greeny-grey sea washed against the sea wall, splashing against the concrete as the movement of the larger ships caused the water to swell.

Vee was pleased with her room. It had a double bed, wardrobe, dressing-table, chair and toe-comfy rag rug, and was very clean and comfortable. There was a basin in the corner and immediately she began a strip-wash, hauling on wide-legged grey trousers and a darker grey lightweight woollen sweater from her suitcase.

She'd slept well last night despite an argument that had been going on downstairs. She had heard a woman's

71

high-pitched voice screaming obscenities and a heavier calming tone. Vee hadn't heard what the couple were quarrelling about, and they had stopped when the baby began crying. Now, tidying the room and emptying her suitcase, Vee took her birth certificates and other papers, for now she had two of everything, and hid the originals, which told the truth, in the space behind the bottom drawer of the dressing-table. She felt they would be safely out of sight there. It ran through her mind that she should perhaps destroy them but somehow that seemed disloyal to her father.

Along with her gas mask, her identity papers had to be carried at all times. But since she had no idea of what her work would entail, she decided to keep her papers in her large purse in her pocket and leave her shoulder bag in her room.

She brushed her hair and pulled it into a ponytail, then took a deep breath and went down the wide stairs to the huge kitchen, following the smell of toast.

A pretty woman with a blonde pageboy hairstyle and a sulky mouth was stirring a cup of tea while she sat at the large table. Her silk dressing-gown gaped open, showing a matching nightdress. Smoke curled from the cigarette she had placed on a saucer.

'So you're the new girl?' she said.

Vee nodded. A dark-haired imp of a girl was toasting bread on a long-handled fork while kneeling in front of the range, which was sending out a fierce heat. She turned to Vee. 'How many bits of toast?'

'Two, please,' said Vee. 'You're Rosie?' She hoped she'd got her name right. She vaguely remembered the names Rosie and Connie from the café the previous evening, and she had already met Connie.

The girl nodded. 'And you are?'

'Vee, Vee Smith. I'm—'

'Oh, we know who you are.' The voice came from a dark-haired young woman who had come in from a door leading into what Vee supposed was the scullery and the back garden. 'You're the girl who's going to be a stand-in for the fellas on our ferries.'

'Well, I—'

'All the decent blokes have been called up.' She set on the table the bag of clothes pegs she'd been carrying. 'What's left are either too young or too old. Jack thought because some of our own men have insisted on going to fight he'd do what the farmers have done with the land girls and train women up.'

Before Vee had a chance to reply, she continued, 'As

long as he doesn't put you in the ticket office with me, I don't care what he does.' She began to move away then said, 'Madelaine sometimes gives me a hand when she gets time off from Peg, don't you, Mads? And that's the way I like it.' She turned to the blonde. 'It's a lovely day. Those nappies I boiled should soon be dry.'

She passed Vee in a cloud of perfume and, with a toss of her dark sleek hair, left the kitchen. Vee heard her going upstairs.

'Here you are.' Rosie held out a plate with two slices of bread toasted to perfection. 'Don't take any notice of Regine. She thinks she's above us all. Put some marge on this before it gets cold. There's strawberry jam if you'd rather.'

Vee gave Rosie a smile and thanked her.

The woman with the pageboy hairstyle asked, 'What's Vee short for?' She took a long drag on her cigarette, blew the smoke high in the air, then stubbed it out in the saucer.

'Violetta – it was my grandmother's name.' Vee began to take in the comfort of the large room: several plump armchairs, a huge table, a wireless on the sideboard and a dresser full of blue and white crockery. A copy of *Tide Times* lay on the table.

'I'm Madelaine, Jack's wife and the mother of that eternally crying child.'

'Hello,' said Vee.

Madelaine blinked her almond-shaped eyes, but didn't smile.

Jack had told Vee he was married, but she would never have thought Madelaine could be his wife. They looked totally unsuited. But that was love for you, she thought. Love made for strange partners. Yet if that was so, why did she feel Jack deserved someone different? She thought of his lips, kissable, smiling . . . Suddenly ashamed of herself, she brushed the thoughts away.

Vee saw that Rosie had poured her a cup of tea and smiled her thanks at her.

'Connie also lives here and she's usually first up in the mornings. She opens the café for the early-bird workers,' Rosie told her. 'I should be there as well by now. Jack said for you to wait until he arrives.'

A few moments later Rosie had gone. Madelaine was reading a newspaper, using her long red fingernails to flick through the pages.

Vee thought about her mother and decided she should let her know where she was. May would be worried sick because she knew Vee's money wouldn't last long. On the other hand, thought Vee, if she told her mother where she was, then decided she didn't want to stay and moved on, May would be even more worried. She decided to get in touch with her as soon as she knew she was truly settled.

'Did you know the government has levied a twenty-four per cent tax on luxuries?'

Vee realized Madelaine was talking to her, reading from the newspaper she was holding. She shook the pages. 'I wonder what they consider luxuries. Some of us might consider them essentials.' She neither waited for nor expected a reply. She didn't move when a cry cut through her voice. 'They've also banned the buying and selling of new cars. How ridiculous!'

Just then Vee heard the front door open and heavy footsteps paused in the hallway. Presently Jack entered the kitchen carrying the grizzling baby. Vee noted he was extremely careful that the little one's head didn't wobble, supporting it with his large hand against his thick navy jumper.

'Morning, everyone,' he said cheerfully.

'Oh, Jack, why not let her sleep?' Madelaine sighed and let the newspaper slide to the floor. She made no move to retrieve it.

'Peg had just opened her eyes, hadn't you, my darling?' Jack said. 'She was telling the world she was awake.' He placed the baby in the carry-cot that lay on a chair. Tiny fists began waving and punching at the air. It occurred to

Vee that the argument she had heard last night might have been between Jack and Madelaine. Possibly he was angry that she'd left the child with Connie for so long. Vee, her toast and tea a memory, got up and went to look at the baby.

'She's got such blue eyes,' she said. 'I wonder if they'll change.' On the smallholding the eye colouring of newborn creatures often changed after a few weeks.

'Isn't she beautiful?' Clearly Jack was smitten with his daughter.

Vee touched a tiny hand and Peg immediately gripped her finger. She gazed down at the baby and something fluttered in her heart.

'Yes,' she said.

Regine clattered down the stairs. 'I'm off,' she said, standing in the doorway with her capacious handbag over her arm. 'See you later, Mads, everyone.'

'Bye,' called Vee, noting she was the only one who acknowledged Regine's leaving.

Madelaine said, 'I wish she wouldn't call me by that ridiculous name.'

Jack walked over to Madelaine and spoke quietly to her, so softly that Vee couldn't hear what he said. Then he turned to her and motioned for her to follow him. 'C'mon, Vee. I'll show you around.'

She glanced at the clock on the mantelpiece. It was a quarter past five. Her first day at work was beginning. Jack already had the front door open.

'I'm going to show you the ropes today,' he said, striding across the road, 'if you'll pardon the pun.' She was almost running to keep up with him, glad she'd put on a pair of flat shoes. 'You're not going to do any work and I'm sending you home when I've shown you enough for you to decide whether you can handle it or not. Then you can take a walk about the town, have a think and let me know tonight if you want to stay. I won't have you doing a specific job, just filling in where I need you to be.'

As they passed the ticket office, she saw Regine sitting on a stool behind a window issuing tickets and taking change. Jack said, 'If you decide to stay I'll get you some boots and black oilskins. If you're helping in the ticket office, you can wear your own clothes. If you work in the café you'll get an overall, same as Connie and Rosie.'

Vee could see a girl standing in the doorway of a cigarette kiosk, holding a large bag close to her side. As Vee passed her, she smelt the perfume she had noticed the evening before. The girl was about twenty, her untidy hair scraped back from her thin face with a clip. Vee was surprised when Jack acknowledged her and went over to her, dipping his hand into his trouser pocket and handing her something that made her smile before he caught up with Vee once more. Had she imagined it or had Jack called the girl 'Ada'?

Two men were busy at the open gate where the ferry was moored against the pontoon. One, who had a shock of dark hair, was clipping tickets as the other waited by the gate, ready to let the passengers on to the boat. Both men, catching sight of Jack, waved and he raised his hand in acknowledgement. Suddenly Vee's attention was taken by the boat's name.

'Why is the ferry called *Galatea*?'

Jack said, 'All the ferries are named after Greek sea goddesses. All craft are "she". *Calliste* is ready on the Portsmouth side, waiting for the bell to ring to announce we're ready for the off. They're steam craft.' He pointed towards the funnel. Vee glanced at it, remembering its comforting warmth from the previous night.

'Such a lot of people,' she said. A heaving crowd was waiting for the gates to swing back, allowing them to board the first ferry of the day. Most were men, some holding on to bicycles, and many carried lunch boxes.

'That's Portsmouth dockyard over there,' he pointed across the expanse of sea, 'and we've got the munitions yard this side. There's a steady exchange of workers backwards and forwards. There's so much Hitler would like to flatten on the south coast. One of the reasons we have so many air raids here.' He smiled down at her. Again she saw the gentle curve of his lips and wondered what it would be like to kiss them. Then she looked away, angry with herself. He was a married man, for goodness' sake! He was talking once more. 'There are other crew members. One's the stoker – we call him the driver. Then there's our rope man, my mate, and the skipper, usually me.' He grinned, lightening her heart again.

'Do you have a second crew?'

'Of course. We can't work seventeen hours a day, even though we work long hours.'

'There's a lot for me to learn.' She didn't want to let Jack down, but she needed the job and the room that went with it.

Already she had decided she would save her money until she had the same amount of cash that Sammy Chesterton charged other people for their forged papers. She'd pay him and be out of his debt. Surely he'd agree to take the money if she offered it to him?

'Who cleans the boats?' Vee remembered that when she'd left the ferry the previous night there was rubbish to be cleared and the decks were filthy.

'The early-morning crew does that,' he said. 'And a lad's paid to haul in the coal and water needed before we start up in the mornings.'

The squat ferry was filling with passengers now. When Jack saw that she had stepped safely on board, he led her towards the engine room. She could see a grey-haired man below stoking the fires.

Jack stopped at the door and put out a hand so Vee couldn't enter.

'All right, Jack?' The man didn't look pleased to see her, even though Vee smiled at him brightly.

'It gets pretty hot down here during the summer,' Jack said, 'but Eddie here keeps these engines running as sweet as a nut.'

Vee saw the brass fittings were polished to within an inch of their lives. Everything gleamed in the engine room.

'Does Eddie work all day and into the night?'

Eddie stared at her as though she'd sprouted three heads. 'No, I don't. The night men clean out the fires ready for me in the mornings. Don't need anyone else in here when I'm on duty, except my lad.'

Beads of sweat were running down Vee's neck, and she saw that Eddie wore a kerchief to soak it up. He was glaring at her. It was painfully obvious he wanted her out of his domain.

'We'll leave you to it, Eddie.' Jack was out of the engine room and climbing up the steps to the main deck. He pointed to *Galatea*'s deck entrance and exit areas. 'There are safety chains to stop passengers falling overboard, and the outside of the boat, as you can see, is festooned with life-buoys. Unfortunately people still go into the water regularly.'

He gestured to a boat waiting on the Portsmouth side of the ferry route. 'There have been ferrymen plying their trade across this stretch of water for many years, and competition between the Portsmouth and Gosport companies was always fierce. The rivalry between the ferrymen couldn't go on so they've joined forces. Families have a bloodline of watermen reaching back to when the very first small boats, wherries, were carrying up to six passengers at a time. Each boat has, as I've already told you, a skipper, mate and, below deck, the driver, plus ticket handlers at the gates and in the kiosks. Extra mates handle the ropes.

'In 1888 an arrangement was made whereby a launch from each company would leave Portsmouth and Gosport simultaneously. This stopped a great deal of the bullying and bumping that the rival boats engaged in and the payment taken for tickets is shared by the companies ... But we've not been doing so well this side, lately. Takings are down.'

Vee could see how much his work meant to him and how troubled he was about the shortfall in money.

'What about the car ferry?'

He laughed. 'The floating bridge runs on chains and is steam-powered. You won't be expected to work on her. Nor will you have anything to do with the island boats.'

She must have looked confused for he added, 'The Isle of Wight ferries, which can be boarded at Portsmouth Harbour railway station.' She remembered then that the railway tracks and stations were built on metal stilts and iron girders that jutted out into the sea. The sea must be pretty deep at that end of the station, she thought, if the huge Isle of Wight ferries could moor there.

Jack unclipped the metal barrier and jumped off the boat at the opposite end from which he'd boarded, Vee following. Then he turned and pointed to a young man holding on to a length of thick rope, most of which was wound around a bollard on the jetty and another on the ferry.

'Mac ties up. It's an art throwing the rope towards the bollards and pulling in so the boat is close enough for the passengers to jump safely on and off. We don't want to lose anyone down the side.' Vee looked at the red-haired young man. She liked his freckled face, with its easy smile. He waved at her.

'We're a close-knit family of workers. We pull together. Last night you had a taste of how uncomfortable it can be up in the wheelhouse. There's very little escape from the elements. It was suggested we put up shields across the bridge to prevent shrapnel hitting the skippers during the bombing. Not good for visibility. The boats don't stop running during raids.'

Jack turned to her. 'I'm sending you back now. Make up your mind if you want to stay with us or not. Go into the café and get yourself a cuppa – we all eat in there from time to time. It's Connie's place to see we're fed and watered. If you decide to stay she may want you to help her. The café does a good trade, sometimes too much for Connie and Rosie to handle on their own. I'll see you later.' He put on his cap, which until now he'd been carrying, then foraged in his pocket and brought out a key, which he handed to her. 'For the front door,' he said, 'though it's hardly ever locked.'

Vee took it wordlessly and stood watching as Jack hopped back on to the boat and climbed to the wheelhouse. At the front of the vessel another pile of bicycles was in a huge metal tangle that she was sure would take ages to unravel.

She heard a whistle blast and the engine growled fully into life. She watched as the metal gates clanged shut and the ropes were coiled ready for use on the Portsmouth pontoon. Then, as the squat boat moved out into the channel, she saw

Jack wave to her. At last his figure grew too small for Vee to distinguish so she began walking up the jetty towards the Ferry Gardens and the town of Gosport. Suddenly she felt very alone.

Chapter Eight

'I hate peeling potatoes.'

Rosie slipped them into a large saucepan full of cold water on the stove in the kitchen of the Ferry Café.

'It's better to make chips than have no job at all,' said Connie. 'At least in here we're more or less our own boss.'

'True – and who knows? One day we might even make some more money,' agreed Rosie. 'Did you talk to Madelaine about that sandwich idea?'

'She don't want to know about anything that goes on in this café. She said she'll mention it to Jack but I'm not hopeful. Her head's full of that Hugh.' Connie began slicing the potatoes into chips and dropping them into another pan of cold water. 'I ought to talk to Jack but he looks worn out so I don't fancy bothering him. Up all night again with Peg, he was.' Connie sighed. A hairpin struggled free from her piled-up bleached hair and dropped with a ping into the sink. 'Botheration!' she said, putting down the sharp knife, retrieving the hairpin then skewering it back through her curls. 'Let's have a sit-down, while it's quiet.' She glanced at the old station clock on the wall. 'In a while we'll be run off our feet. Let's make the most of this slow period.'

Rosie wiped her hands on a tea-towel and went out into the café area. The wireless was playing dance music and she plonked herself down at a table and crossed her legs at the ankles. It wasn't long before Connie appeared and set down two cups of tea on the Formica table.

'Thanks, I could do with that.' Rosie watched Connie park her ample behind on a chair. 'What d'you think of Vee?'

Connie stirred her tea. 'Seems a nice girl. Jack's taken to her.'

'That's because she's a worker, I can tell.' She sipped her tea and looked at Old Tom sitting against the Nissen hut's wall. He raised a hand in greeting.

'I'll give him a refill in a bit,' Rosie said. The old man had been bombed out a while back and had lost his wife in the blast. He couldn't seem to get over it and spent a lot of time staring into space.

'You could make him a sandwich to go with it,' Connie said. 'Poor bugger.'

Her kindness was one of the many things Rosie liked about Connie.

Connie had taken her under her wing when she'd come into the café enquiring about the 'Waitress Wanted' postcard she'd spotted in the newsagent's window opposite the ferry. She knew she must have looked a sight with her black eye and her face all puffy from crying, but Connie had merely asked her if she'd worked in a café before and, when she said she had, agreed to her starting the next morning.

Rosie had known Mick would still be sleeping off the skinful of beer he'd had the night before and wouldn't even remember he'd knocked her down the stairs, so it was no problem for her to pack up a few bits and pieces – not that she had much – and move into Jack's house. Connie had shown her to a room that looked like a palace.

That night she'd slept like a child. No more fears that her husband would come home drunk and start in on her again. Best thing she'd ever done was leave Mick. It had taken her long enough to pluck up the courage. Since she'd lost the baby, she'd also lost all her confidence, and it was easier to let Mick knock her about than strike out on her own.

She never used to be so downtrodden, but it was her own fault for putting up with his temper. Mind, if he'd shown his nasty side before she'd walked up the aisle to him, a big good-looking Irishman, she'd never have married him. Perhaps it was a blessing that that punch had made her lose the kiddie. God forgive her for thinking that. She was grateful that Connie asked no questions, just let her find her feet in the café and in the house.

It was as if Jack trusted Connie's judgement in hiring her. Since then Rosie had worked consistently for Jack at the Ferry Café and she'd enjoyed every minute of it.

Did she wonder about Mick? Where he was, what he was doing? Maybe he was living with someone else now. Did she care? No! She was glad she was away from his flying fists.

'D'you ever wish you had another job, Connie?'

Connie's eyes narrowed. 'Not really,' she said. 'But I'd like to put a bit of money behind me. Maybe then I could visit my family. I got a grandson I've only ever seen in a photograph. That's why I'd like it if we got this sandwich idea off the ground.'

Rosie saw the dreamy look in her eyes.

'If we had them in packets all ready for the customers it would save a lot of time and trouble. I get so fed up trying to cook and make up sandwiches at the same time. If we could get known for having tasty fillings it could become a decent little earner. Who knows? We might be able to sell ready-prepared sandwiches to some of the shops – Woolworth's, even.'

'Maybe Jack could take on another girl—'

'No, Rosie. It's our idea. I just want him to give the go-ahead. I'd work every night if I had to. We could come up with some interesting fillings! I know there's a war on and there's shortages but . . .'

Connie's voice tailed off. Rosie knew how fond she was of Jack – he was like a son to her.

Connie had a grown-up daughter but she was in Australia. The girl had married young and Connie thought she'd never see her again. Brisbane was a long way from Gosport and Connie needed money to get there. She had photos of her grandson but it wasn't the same as holding a little body in her arms, was it?

Maybe Connie's daughter would visit on a holiday. Still, when the café was busy there wasn't the time to think of what might have been or could be. Now Rosie and Connie went dancing with the servicemen in the Connaught Hall and to the pictures together on their time off – a couple of women from the other ferry crew took over the café duties.

Her thoughts scattered as the door opened and a couple of bus conductresses came in. More and more women were taking over men's jobs while the lads were away fighting.

'Egg and chips twice, please,' said the shorter of the two.

'Only powdered egg,' said Connie, rising from her chair.

'Omelette and chips twice, then.' The girl smiled, taking off her Southdown jacket.

Rosie gathered up her and Connie's cups and got to her feet just as the door opened again and three soldiers entered.

'Roses Of Picardy' came softly from the wireless, accompanying May as she attempted to complete her accounts. She was humming along to the emotional First World War song. After adding up the same column of figures four times and getting a different total each time, she abandoned her morning project.

The music made her think of Gus, and of her time at the hospital and how it hadn't always been doom and gloom.

One evening, she and her friend Annie had been told to help decorate the big hall. They were going to have a dance! Once, dances had been held regularly but now that so many men came back from the battlefields with such horrific wounds they had been abandoned. Ceaseless bombardments in Flanders at the third battle of Ypres and the never-ending rain made it difficult for the men to decide what they feared most, the mud or the German machine-gunners.

'Dying men can't dance,' Annie had said, when Matron

had sent the news around that the hall was to be hung with garlands and bunting, and a band was to be provided, along with a buffet.

'We can't dance without proper music,' Annie complained. 'Matron's idea of a band is bleedin' violins and harps.'

'There are several patients who can play instruments and would be willing in spite of their injuries to join in the fun.'

'All right, May,' said Annie, almost smiling. 'I suppose we can push in the beds of those who want to come from other wards. And it will help with morale.'

Annie Bell was also a local girl, born in Southampton. She'd joined the VADs hoping to see something of the world, but Netley was as far as she'd got. May and Annie shared a hut that had a pot-bellied stove, two single beds with lumpy mattresses, oil lamps, wooden floors with a couple of rag rugs, and a small wardrobe each for their things. A spotted mirror had been nailed to the wooden wall. There was no sanitation or water in the hut, apart from the jugs and bowls for washing that had to be filled and emptied daily, along with their chamber pots. The contents were thrown on to the garden rubbish heap, then the pots swilled out at a nearby outside tap. There was a washing block a short distance away that also contained the lavatories. Meals were taken in the main building.

At first May had found it a miserable existence and wished she could live at home on the smallholding. It seemed so silly to her that her family lived a short walk away from the hospital but she had to live in. Annie's normally chirpy disposition helped ease her longing for her parents.

On precious days off they had hitched lifts to Kingston Market in Southampton and spent their wages on colourful scraps of material that Annie fashioned into curtains and cushion covers, sewn on a Singer machine borrowed from one of the other nurses.

'After working from six this morning I don't really feel like dancing,' Annie moaned. She was pulling a screen in front of a stack of wooden limbs in boxes ready for amputees.

'You will when the time comes.' May was looking forward to it.

'Did they find that patient?'

'Not another escapee, Annie?'

There was a long stretch of grassland and trees between the hospital and the jetty, where the boats docked on Southampton Water to transfer the wounded into the ambulances waiting to carry them to the hospital. Most patients were more than happy to be ferried to the doctors and nurses, or were unaware of what was happening, but occasionally a bright spark would make a run for it, either to abscond from the services or perhaps, if a foreigner knew he would be imprisoned after his recovery, to escape.

Netley, a wooded area whose residents didn't hide their dislike of the enemy at the hospital, made a poor hiding place: the few patients or prisoners who took their chances were soon returned to the fold more than happy to be fed and have their injuries attended to. Later, their distinctive spotted clothing announced to all who they were.

May had laughed at Annie as they sprinkled chalk on the floor in readiness for the dancing, careful not to get any on the musical instruments that had been brought in for the evening's entertainment. VADs weren't always allowed to dance but this was a special occasion, Matron had decreed.

Neither was it deemed appropriate for the nurses, VADs and other staff to wear civilian clothing, so the most they could do to titivate themselves was to put on clean cuffs and headdresses. A few brave nurses wore garden flowers in their hair.

Outsiders had been invited, but since many of the patients came from outside the area or, indeed, the country, there were few civilians.

Finally, after washing away the dirt of the day, May and Annie sauntered over to the ballroom, eager to have drinks poured for them by two porter friends, who were in charge of the bar, which was two tables pushed together. Mismatched glasses stood on them, with a very large container of a greenish punch that looked and tasted as though it had been concocted in the chemistry department.

'I'd like it if you'd dance with me?'

May looked up at the tall, slim man. His fair hair fell across his forehead and he smiled at her. She consented, and the young doctor claimed her again for 'A Bird in a Gilded Cage', but this time he seemed tense and held her too tightly. His face against her cheek was too intimate, and he murmured words she was unable to hear properly. She felt that if she could, she wouldn't like them.

May was glad when he led her back to the chairs Annie had found. But almost before she had time to sit down, the young doctor claimed her again.

May didn't like being grabbed and marched towards the floor. Without a word, he had encircled her waist with his arm and pulled her close. His face was scraping her cheek as he moved sinuously in time to the music the band was playing 'They Didn't Believe Me'. In that moment May knew that that song would always remind her of this man and that she would hate it for ever.

She waited until the music stopped, then pushed her partner away. 'I think that's enough for tonight,' she whispered. Without waiting for him to lead her back to her chair, she made her way through the rest of the dancers and was finally able to flop down beside Annie.

'He's like an octopus,' she muttered, 'and he's none too sweet-smelling.'

'If he's been on duty a long time, what do you expect?'

Annie handed her a glass of water that she drank gratefully. A mixture of cigarette smoke and hot bodies made it warm in the ballroom.

'I think he fancies you,' Annie said, nudging her arm after the doctor had reappeared at the buffet table. May shook her head. Her eyes followed him as he poked around the plates, now depleted of sandwiches and cake – indeed, it looked as though a swarm of locusts had flown in and devoured the lot. Since the majority of men in the hall were unable to walk, one didn't have to be a genius to guess that the staff had eaten most of it.

'There's something creepy about him,' May said, and shivered.

'I'd fancy him.' Annie pouted. May could smell the heavy scent Annie had poured over herself, although wearing perfume was against the rules.

'You'd fancy anything!' May laughed. 'Have you worked with him?'

Annie shook her head. 'No.'

Such was the turnover of staff and patients that it wasn't surprising. It had seemed to May that as soon as she became used to certain doctors' habits in the operating theatre they disappeared, moving abroad to work among the wounded or to London and private practice.

'There is one man in here who really fancies you,' Annie confided.

May stared past her friend towards the German flyer. Her heart began to race. He was standing now, able to use a crutch. The artificial foot he had been fitted with emphasized his height. She hadn't known how tall he was, never having seen him standing before. The scarring to his face was healing well. All evening she had taken sly glances at him, only to find him staring at her.

'I'm going to ask him to dance.'

'Are you sure that's wise?' Annie grabbed at her. 'You've just refused that young doctor! Won't it look a bit obvious if you walk over and ask the enemy to take a turn around the floor?'

May ignored her friend's words. The dance was to promote better feeling between the English patients and the enemy, and she saw no difference in dancing with a German or one of the hospital's staff.

'Dance with me?' May asked. 'Leave your crutch. You can use me as a support.' She felt as though she could drown in his dark eyes.

She waited while he propped the crutch against the wall, then leant on her, his feet together. 'You might regret this,' he whispered.

'Phooey!' The word came out with more determination than she actually felt. May sensed he was leaning heavily on the arm that went around her body. The band started to play 'Roses Of Picardy'. It was natural for him to lead and he did, despite her worry that he might stumble.

May felt her blood warm in her veins. No man's touch had ever made her feel so alive. Suddenly she was glad she and Annie had sprinkled chalk on the makeshift dance floor, though he needed no props to help him with the steps except her. She guessed he must have been practising walking all day yesterday when he had first been fitted with his artificial limb.

May had asked him to dance out of the desire to be close to him – or as close as she could be in a room full of people. She couldn't say why she was drawn to him but she was, as a moth is drawn to a flame.

Across the floor Annie was dancing with a porter. The look Annie gave her told her she should be careful. She could almost hear tongues wagging over her obvious enjoyment at being in the arms of a man who had tried to kill her countrymen.

'I think we should make this our first and last dance.' His breath was warm on her face.

She nodded. 'It doesn't seem right to save your life, then cut you dead, though.'

'We shouldn't be dancing together,' he repeated. 'This get-together is a sham, and everyone knows it, yet we all conspire to pretend friendship.' Much as May loved his clipped accent, she didn't like what he was saying.

'The Hippocratic Oath means doctors try to save lives regardless of creed, colour or nationality.' Her words came out in a rush.

'But this dance is a farce,' he said. 'Don't tell me you can't feel something special between us. I'm sure others can sense it. And they don't like it. They can't bear to see you and me so close together and enjoying ourselves.'

She knew he was speaking the truth. Previous dances that evening had mostly involved everyone. 'The Gay Gordons' had prompted much laughter among staff and patients.

May felt his grip tighten as his step faltered. Then he regained his momentum. A wave of sadness engulfed her. She could tell by the way his body moved with the music that he must have been popular on the dance floor with women in his home town. Hatred flared in her for the evening's organizers. It wasn't a morale booster at all. It was an outward show to the rest of the hospital that both sides could get on together. But that was a lie.

As her eyes left his face she became aware that other dancers had left the floor to stand and watch them. For a second she thought he hadn't noticed the sudden exodus.

They were the only couple dancing.

'Are you all right with this?' His words were soft.

Was she? May had never felt like this about anyone before. Was she falling in love? Was this what love meant, showing others that neither of them cared what they thought?

'Yes,' she breathed.

So he held her tightly and she refused to be intimidated. And they moved together to the sad little song, about a lifelong love surviving beyond death. Then, when the dance ended, he took her arm and led her back to where he had been standing. May knew now that without a crutch he was unable to walk, let alone dance: it was too soon after the amputation. As a nurse she should have known it. He had danced because she had held him. He had endured pain to be close to her. So, with her arm tightly around his waist, she managed to turn a chair round so he could sit down. Afterwards she picked up his crutch from the floor where it had fallen.

He smiled at her, then bent forward and kissed her cheek.

She went back to her seat next to Annie, leaving Gus in his ridiculous blue hospital uniform of scratchy material with the markings on the jacket at the back that reminded her of a scoreboard. As if eventually leaving the hospital for the prison wasn't enough, he had to look like a clown while he was at the hospital.

The band were playing again and May looked at the German – Gus, his name was. Now she saw blood seeping through the thick trouser material. His exertions on the dance floor had reopened his wound. She didn't go to him. To do so would have taken away the last shred of his pride. May knew then three things. One was that he loved her, the other was that she loved him, and the third was that life would not be easy for either of them.

The music on the wireless had faded and the news caught her attention. Four hundred deaths in London alone. The city was taking the brunt of the Blitz. So much destruction and sadness, May thought. One hundred and eighty-five enemy planes shot down in a single day. How foolish she was to have thought the Great War would never be repeated.

May looked at the columns of figures and began to add them up. Daily life went on. She might hear from Vee tomorrow. It would be enough to know that her daughter had work and a place to sleep. She hoped with all her heart that, one day, her daughter would fall for a man and know the true meaning of love, as she, May, had with Vee's father.

Chapter Nine

Jack stood with his hands on the wheel, watching the Portsmouth landing stage grow larger the closer his boat sailed. He waved to the skipper of the boat passing him, on its way to take his place at Gosport. The ferries passed each other continually. On average they ran every fifteen minutes, but they'd do faster turnarounds if it was necessary.

The morning sun was on his face, the rain of yesterday forgotten. He liked Vee. She had said she was ready and willing to try her hand at any job and he believed her. He hoped she'd stay on. He'd tried to frighten the life out of her by taking her below deck to show her how hard Eddie worked, but she didn't seem put off, not even by the heat down there. He didn't tell her Eddie's boy usually worked with him. The lad was back on Monday after a few days off. Vee would never need to work in the engine room. Eddie would shoot her sooner than let her into his domain, which had been in his family for generations.

Jack was still angry that Peg had been left at the café while Madelaine had visited her parents. She should have been back sooner. She shouldn't have let the kiddie scream. Peg had missed her mother and needed changing and feeding. Connie and Rosie had enough to do in that busy place without looking after his baby as well.

The argument instigated by Madelaine shortly after her return in the early hours had been one of the most violent they'd had. She'd asked him for yet more money towards a new outfit for the christening; the sum he had already given her apparently wasn't enough. It had ended with Madelaine turning her back on him, but not before she'd screamed to the whole of Gosport that he was a 'tight-fisted bastard'.

He didn't know how he had kept his temper. Of course he'd wanted to hit her, to shut her mouth against the vile invective that spewed out, but he'd never hit a woman in his life and didn't intend to start with Madelaine. She was volatile, highly strung. If he'd had money to throw away he'd have given it gladly: she filled his eyes with sunshine when he saw her beautifully dressed, but she'd have looked good in a paper bag. The dockyard was ahead with Nelson's flagship, *Victory*, moored nearby. She was a fine sight. The panorama of the ships, the sea and Portsdown Hill in the background always made him gasp with its beauty, as did Madelaine. Never in his wildest imaginings had he thought he would be the one she would settle for.

He'd known her since his schooldays, but they were far apart in backgrounds. Her parents lived in Alverstoke in a large house set back from the sea in Ashburton Road. Like most of the other Gosport lads, with their grimy hands and scruffy clothes, he'd worshipped her from afar. In her teens she had played tennis at the club in Anglesey Road and he often caught a glimpse of her in her whites as he cycled by. Or she'd be sitting beside some flash Harry in the front of a car. Jack had had his fair share of girls as he grew older, when his shoulders had broadened and his lanky frame had filled out. Some of the girls would ride the ferries just to chat to him, as they did now with Mac and Paul, the two good-looking mates. Paul, on the tickets, almost had to fight them off.

At the dances held at the Connaught Hall he'd catch sight of Madelaine and her friend of the moment. She never seemed to have a best friend, but there was always a crowd about her and she'd be glowing with health and vitality, dancing her heart out, blonde ponytail bobbing.

Later she favoured a dark-haired man as a partner, and

then there had been a subtle change in her looks. She lightened her already blonde hair and changed its style to a long pageboy, going from pretty girl to beautiful woman practically overnight.

Then he'd had to pluck up courage to ask her to dance with him and sometimes he didn't manage it. When he got home he cursed himself for being such a weakling.

The same year he helped his parents buy the house where he now lived on Beach Street, he had made it to skipper. His dad, and his dad before him, had been on the boats and Jack never doubted he'd do anything different. The sea was in his blood. After the night when his parents had died visiting a London friend during an air raid, his job was the only thing that had kept him sane.

Now he had a beautiful daughter and a gorgeous wife. Everything in his garden should have been lovely, but it wasn't. Since Peg had come on the scene Madelaine had changed.

Their love affair, if he could call it that, had started one night at the Lee Tower ballroom. Amazingly she'd come over and asked him to dance while the band was playing 'The Breeze And I'.

Girls didn't usually do that: it was considered too forward. Nice girls waited, sitting around the ballrooms, until the lads asked them to dance. Sometimes they danced with each other.

Of course, earlier he'd spotted her dancing with the tall chappie, one of the chinless wonders who were always hanging around her. And why not? With that gorgeous blonde hair, deep blue eyes and a figure to rival Veronica Lake's, all the men watched her. But this time she'd made a beeline for him.

'She's coming over,' his friend said. John Cousins was forever trying to get him out and about to take his mind off his parents' deaths.

'I bet it's you she talks to,' Jack said. But it wasn't.

He was like an idiot when he held her, not knowing how to touch the object of his fantasies, let alone dance with her. He mumbled answers to her questions, trod on her toes and apologized so many times he truly believed she must think him an absolute idiot.

'I need some air,' she'd said.

Before the dance had finished he'd found himself walking along the beach at Lee-on-the-Solent hardly able to believe his luck that at last Madelaine was actually with him.

The night was hot and sticky and she sat on the sand, pulling him down with her. And then she was kissing him. He remembered the sea below them, rushing and drawing back, and he'd thought he'd died and gone to Heaven. He couldn't talk to her – he wanted to, but the words wouldn't form themselves in his mouth. He let his instincts take over.

Her body was tanned from the summer sun; in the moonlight he could see the white lines on her shoulders where her swimsuit had covered her.

Her kisses were gentle at first, then firm enough to bruise his lips. He could smell alcohol on her breath. Then he had felt her fingers at his belt buckle. Her touch made him grow hard, more so because he couldn't believe this was really happening.

His conscience was telling him it wasn't right, but his heart and body were saying he wanted her more than anything else in the whole world. Her breasts were freed from her bra by his fumbling, and her jasmine perfume filled his nostrils.

Faintly, in the background, the music was spilling from the open windows of the ballroom and it seemed to be urging him on to take what she was offering.

She guided him into her and her soft wetness swallowed him whole. He pushed her back on the sand and moved inside her with ease. She rose up to meet him and, with his kisses wild upon her face, he remembered only the sense of infinite motion that followed, until the stars above blurred and fell to earth, and he was falling with them.

Afterwards, she lay in his arms, not speaking. He was delirious with happiness. Then, as his senses returned to him, he said, 'I shouldn't have done that, I'm sorry.' He felt like crying but couldn't understand why. After all, he'd achieved his secret desire, hadn't he?

'Didn't you want me?' Her voice was brittle.

'You know I did,' he replied. He began to cover her nakedness and she finished the task herself. 'You must know I worship you,' he said.

They were both silent until she said, 'Let's get back inside,' and he stood up, held out a hand and pulled her to her feet. Standing beside him in her stockinged feet, she barely came to his shoulder. A great feeling of protectiveness towards her stole over him.

But even then there was a coldness about her, as if she was locked in a cage of ice that he couldn't melt.

As they walked back, he looked at the clock on the front of the tower. He was amazed that in such a short time his whole life seemed to have changed.

In the foyer, she turned to him. 'I'm going to the cloak-room. It's best we don't go in together. I don't want people to look at us and know we got carried away.'

'Of course,' he mumbled. He was well aware that her reputation was at stake. But as he walked away he thought how proud he would have been to take her back to the table he shared with John and his friends and announce to them that they were now a couple.

Briefly he wondered why she didn't feel the same. He thought she probably needed time to tell her friends, to do it in her own way. The Alverstoke set were quite different with their snobbish ways.

He guessed she might not be as happy as he was about what had just taken place between them. He shrugged. He hadn't forced her – in fact, Madelaine had instigated the whole thing. Women weren't like men when they fell in love. In love? Yes, without a doubt he was in love with her. Hadn't he always been in love with Madelaine Carter? And for her to allow him to make love to her showed she reciprocated that feeling . . . didn't it?

'What's the matter, Jack? You look like you lost a quid and found a tanner.' John eyed him thoughtfully. 'Don't think I didn't notice you come back just before Madelaine.'

John was his best friend, had been for years, but sometimes Jack envied him his job as a plain-clothes copper and his wife, Emily, who adored him. It was as if Jack was on the outside looking in. 'So Emily's with her mother?'

'Changing the subject? I'll play along. Her mother isn't well.'

Jack took a mouthful of his flat beer, not really listening to John, while his eyes roved the ballroom. When he saw Madelaine sitting with the tall man, with Brylcreemed hair and a slim moustache, who usually accompanied their little group, he waited for her to glance in his direction. A smile, a look, any acknowledgement would have done. Eventually, he gave up.

To Eric, his other friend, he said, 'I'm going up for another pint before the beer runs out. I know it's a shame to waste this as it's in such short supply, but it's gone flat and lost its guts for standing so long.' It wasn't that he wanted more beer – but he couldn't just sit there after what had happened between him and Madelaine. Making love to her had meant everything to him. He couldn't understand her coldness towards him.

'If you don't want it, give us it here. I don't mind flat beer.' Eric didn't wait for his reply but picked up Jack's glass and glugged back most of what was left in one go. 'Thought you was never coming back after you'd had a dance with that blonde.'

Jack rose from the stool and, still mystified by Madelaine's behaviour, said, 'I'm beginning to wish I never had.' He left the hall and went out to the Gents – he'd get his beer on the way back. Or maybe not. The evening had lost its charm for him and he thought he'd leave.

When he came out she was waiting in the foyer for him.

She was agitated. 'Look, it's difficult. Please say you'll see me again?' He could see it mattered to her by the tense look in her beautiful eyes.

'Madelaine!'

Before he had time to do more than nod, the chinless wonder was calling her name from the ballroom's doorway.

He managed to gather his wits and say, 'You know where you can find me.' Didn't everyone know Jack worked the boats?

And she did find him, on a Sunday two months later when he had the day off and was lounging at home reading the *News of the World*. No one could have been more surprised than he was when, on answering the door, he came face to face with her.

Madelaine wore a blue dress that perfectly matched the colour of her eyes, and while he stood gaping, she said, 'Aren't you going to ask me in?'

The house was a mess and he felt ashamed of the beer bottles left on the table from last night, the overflowing ashtrays and the smell of stale food. Last night he and a couple of mates had lazed around listening to the wireless and putting the world to rights after Pompey had won the football match at Fratton Park.

He was about to apologize for the mess, when he realized he didn't have to be sorry for anything. Madelaine had come to him: she could take him as she found him, a hardworking bloke relaxing in his own home on a Sunday morning. During the past few weeks he'd almost persuaded himself that their coupling hadn't happened.

He was hurt that she'd allowed him to make love to her, then ignored him. That she had shared such an experience with him must mean she had feelings for him, he thought, but since then she'd acted as though he didn't exist. Of course, it was unthinkable for him to visit her parents' house to seek her out. He was a bloke and blokes like him didn't run after posh women like her.

It was all very confusing, yet there she was, standing at his front door and looking beautiful enough to take his breath away. He stepped back, and as she entered she raised herself on tiptoe to give him the briefest kiss on his cheek.

He decided a walk might make it easier for both of them to talk. After all, there must be a reason she had come calling. Two of his lodgers, Regine and Connie, were in their rooms enjoying a lazy Sunday and he didn't particularly want them coming downstairs to find Madelaine in the kitchen.

He saw her eyes take in her surroundings. He was proud

of his home, its size, its proximity to the town centre – and it was worth serious money. He grabbed his jacket.

'We'll go down Beach Street. It's a nice day.'

In Walpole Park they watched the swans on the pond. She still hadn't explained why she'd sought him out and their dialogue was stilted. Unable to stand it any longer he said, 'Look, what happened at Lee-on-the-Solent that night, I can't get my head round—'

Madelaine burst into tears. 'Neither can I. I'd been watching you in the dance hall. I wanted you to make love to me. I'd had quite a bit to drink, and now . . .'

She put a hand to her forehead and turned away from him.

Jack didn't like to see her or any woman cry, so he put his arm around her.

She took a deep breath and turned back, looking into his eyes. 'I'm expecting. My monthly friend hasn't turned up.'

It took him a few moments to grasp what she'd said.

'You mean . . . But it was only the first time . . .'

'It only takes once.' Her words came out jumbled, with more tears.

'Oh, my God,' Jack said. 'This can't be happening.' But he knew with an awful certainty that it was.

Now she clung to him, sobbing. 'I don't know what to

do. I can't tell my mother – she'd kill me. It's all my fault. I was watching you long before I asked you to dance with me. I've waited and waited for you to ask me out, but you never have. I'd had a couple of glasses of port that night and it gave me the courage I needed. I'm so sorry. I just did what I wanted without thinking about the consequences. Now I don't know what to do.' The clouds had hidden the sun, the warmth suddenly going from the morning.

He held her. His mind felt like a hive of bees, buzzing every which way. And then a great calm came over him as he asked, 'Why haven't you come to see me before now? After all, something very special happened between us the night of the dance.'

She stopped crying and blew her nose in the handkerchief he gave her. 'I was ashamed. The more I thought about it the more I realized how it must have seemed to you. Nice girls don't do that sort of thing. And now, and now . . .'

The tears began again.

How could he be angry with her?

'I need to think.' Jack pulled her down onto the grass. He looked into her beautiful face.

'Are you sure you're not just late?' He knew little about women's things but he was aware that their internal clocks sometimes lost or gained time.

'Jack, I know.'

The sun came out, the clouds disappeared and, as the beams began to chase away the chill, he said, 'We could get married.'

Jack now drew the boat up close to the Portsea pontoon and Mac began tying up. He looked at Ada's bag, safe in his wheelhouse. Mac had found it this morning. As skipper, Jack knew he should never have allowed Ada to sleep on the boat, but what else could he do? He couldn't deny her shelter. He'd thought to give her a job in the café but he couldn't afford to let his heart rule his head. His café customers would soon dwindle. There might even be further repercussions.

He sighed. Here he was, doing the job he'd always loved. He had a little girl who had entered the world before she should have done, but was as strong as any baby and was the apple of his eye. He had a decent home and a beautiful wife he'd been married to for less than a year.

Why wasn't he happy?

Chapter Ten

'Buy these two marrers!'

The man held two large juicy vegetable marrows, one in each hand. 'If you don't want to eat 'em both today, save one for tomarrow!'

Vee smiled at his cheeky banter. What she had seen of Gosport town, she liked. Stallholders had set up their wares beneath canvas awnings along the high street in front of the many shops. Already people were looking for market bargains and her senses were assailed by sights, sounds and smells that made her glad to be alive on such a sunny day.

She found the library housed in another Nissen hut – a bomb had flattened the original building – and came away happily from the friendly librarian with a card to be signed by a householder before she could borrow books. She felt sure either Madelaine or Jack would guarantee she was now a local resident.

There was a swimming pool and bath house, a museum, a town hall, two cinemas and a boating lake, plus several cafés and public houses. She felt sure there was much more Gosport had to offer but she'd leave further exploration for another day.

She pulled open the door of a telephone kiosk and emptied her purse for change. All the while she was trembling. Suppose Sammy had already been to the smallholding – suppose he had hurt her mother because Vee had stolen the documents. Her heart was beating fast as she inserted the money and pressed the button. Previously she'd decided she wouldn't phone her mother until she was sure she intended to stay at Gosport. Now she'd made up her mind. Within moments both Vee and her mother were crying, but their tears were happy ones.

'Don't tell me where you are, just if you're all right,' May said.

'I'm not too far away and I'm safe,' Vee reassured her. 'Has Sammy been to the house?' Her heart lifted when her mother said he hadn't and that she wasn't to worry about anything.

'Cat's had three kittens,' May said. 'And they're the spit of her. So we'll never know who the father is.' She'd used her new ration book, she added. She'd been wary at first, but after all the trouble Vee had taken to obtain it she'd felt she should. Vee laughed. She'd definitely have to send Sammy the money as soon as she could.

Feeling happier, Vee walked along Beach Street where the noise from the boatyards practically deafened her. Hulks and skeletons of work in progress vied for space in the yards, though she knew it had been even busier in the days before the war when goods had been easier to obtain. Shortages of materials and foodstuffs meant hungry bellies and loss of jobs. Curls of cut planking and wood shavings blew at her feet and the smell of wood made her think that if she closed her eyes and ears to the noise she could believe she was in a forest. Across the water, the huge car ferry was chugging through the waves, laden with passengers and vehicles, and was about to pull in.

The clanking and scraping were deafening as, simultaneously, the two bridge-like structures were lowered on to the gravelled road. She watched as the gates were opened so the vehicles could drive out. The craft was enormous. Dirty, rust-covered metal railings enclosed the top deck where the owners of the vehicles and other passengers could sit on wooden seats as the vessel clunked its way to Portsmouth.

Vee recognized the girl. As the cars rolled off the ferry she stood at the side of the open gates and spoke only to male drivers alone in their cars. Some ignored her, a few listened politely, but from their expressions others were angry to have her approach them.

The girl was thin and her clothing, a black skirt and red blouse, looked as though it needed a wash, as did she.

She had stopped a van and was asking the driver something that Vee couldn't hear. But she saw the awful man hawk a huge gob of spit right in the girl's face. The vehicle passed Vee.

The stink from its exhaust pipes almost choked her as she ran towards the girl, who was still standing there, almost as if she had deserved to be humiliated. Another car passed before Vee reached her and this time she heard laughter.

'You didn't deserve that!' Vee was angry – angry with the girl for not retaliating and with the van owner for his disgusting action. She pulled the girl round to face her. Tears spilled from her eyes. Vee asked, 'Why did he do it?' Silence.

Then, holding her arm, Vee swung her away from the ferry that was still spilling out cars and pulled her across the road to the pavement.

'What did you say to him that made him do that?'

'I asked him if he wanted a good time!' The words were flung at her. Sharp, precise speech from someone who obviously wasn't a Gosport girl. 'Leave me be!'

She made to walk off, wiping her arm across her face, but Vee grabbed her. The strong smell of violet perfume was sickening.

'What do you mean?'

'Do I have to spell it out?'

Vee stared at her. The penny dropped as she remembered how the girls in Sammy's club who were on the game spoke to the men they hoped would give them money to go to bed with them.

'You're a pros—'

'On the game, please,' the girl said, wiping her eyes. 'But not doing too good. There's an annoying woman queering my pitch.'

Vee looked at her. She saw a girl who was down on her luck. 'I didn't realize. I'm sorry. Look, at least let me buy you a cup of tea.'

'And a sandwich?' The girl's dull eyes brightened as Vee mentally added up the money she had left. She nodded. She took the girl's arm again and made to go towards the Ferry Café.

The girl pulled back. 'Not in there. The Dive is better.'

Vee wondered why she didn't want to go into the place where the boatmen congregated but it wasn't her business. She followed the girl across the bus station to the small café on the corner of the marketplace and walked down the steps.

The proprietor nodded a greeting to them. The girl moved through to a table in the bowels of the café, leaving Vee to bring two teas and a sandwich to the table.

'I've got no time for do-gooders. I've not been doing this long. Today was my first go at soliciting. I have nowhere to live, and if it wasn't for your boss letting me creep on to the ferry boat at night after they've shut down, I'd have nowhere to sleep. He lets me stay because I promised him I wouldn't take the punters there, and I keep my promises.'

Then she picked up the sandwich and sank her small white teeth into the tomato and bread as if she hadn't eaten that day. Perhaps she hadn't, thought Vee, who stirred her tea and looked at the girl. Beneath the grime she was quite pretty.

'Let's hope you never sink this low, eh?' the girl snarled, then picked up her cup and drank the contents.

'What's your name?'

'Ada Klein.'

'But that's a . . .'

Ada glared. 'I was born in Sheffield, moved to Kent when I was eight and my mum and dad bought a fish-and-chip shop. They made money, enough to send me to Norland College, where they train nannies. All I ever wanted to do was look after kiddies. Three years' training, and I came here to look after an admiral's children at Alverstoke. The war broke out and I was thrown out of my job.' She took a deep breath. 'Can't have a German looking after a posh Englishman's children, can we?'

'Couldn't you go home?' Vee asked.

'My parents died when the shop was torched one night. We had a flat above it, see? No parents, no home.'

'Surely there's something else you can do.'

'No one will employ me. I'm the enemy. I have no money, so I get by the best I can. At least I can wash in the public lavatories when no one's around, and the other day I found a bottle of scent that someone had left behind. I can't even lie about who I am because the truth is there for anyone to see on all my documents.' Suddenly her voice softened. 'But I've eaten today, thanks to you.'

Vee opened her purse and looked at her remaining money. She took two brown banknotes and slid them across the table. 'A pound. It's not much . . .'

'And I shall take it because it means food to me. But one

day I hope I'll be able to repay you.' Ada stood up and a waft of strong perfume enveloped Vee.

'I really do have qualifications. To attempt what I had to do today I left everything in my bag on the boat. Jack is a good man. He'll look after it for me. I have good references.. One day I'll show you.' And then she was gone, the smell of cheap perfume following her.

Vee sat pondering the cruelties of war until she got up and left. Out in the fresh air, she crossed the road and walked back to her new home. She had liked Ada's honesty. She wanted to talk to her again.

She had no doubt that she would see her again.

At the house, she inserted the key into the lock and heard the baby crying. She went in, and the child's cries drew her towards the pram in the kitchen. Immediately her heart went out to the little scrap who, by the state of her, must have been crying for a while. Her face was red and tears stained her cheeks.

Automatically she picked up Peg, who was wet and smelly. A sudden vision came into her mind of Cat and her three kittens at home, being cared for and fussed over.

'What a to-do then!' Her words were soft, meaningless and meant to soothe the baby, which they did, for Peg snuffled and quietened, staring at Vee with huge eyes. Vee saw a pile of clean nappies on the table. She could change the baby, but it wasn't her place to step in and take over what was essentially Madelaine's job.

Before she had time to decide what to do, the door along the hall opened and someone was striding down the passage from Madelaine and Jack's bedroom.

A tall man with a moustache, his shirt hanging out of his trousers, came in. He coloured when he saw Vee holding Peg. 'What – what are you doing here? No one's due back until this afternoon.'

Vee had no idea who he was but immediately guessed that a half-dressed man coming from Jack's bedroom wasn't quite right.

'I live here,' she said. 'Do you?'

He surprised her then: 'I might as well.' He seemed to have recovered his composure. He looked her up and down. 'And you are?'

'Vee. An extra pair of hands to help wherever it's needed.'

'Well, you've stopped Peg crying. That's very handy.' He ran his fingers through his Brylcreemed hair. Vee decided that the baby was no longer her concern. Her mother had to be within earshot. She began lowering Peg back onto the damp pram bedding. Footsteps behind her suddenly halted. Vee turned to find Madelaine still in the silky dressing-gown of earlier. It looked as if it had been hastily thrown on. Madelaine's eyes met hers.

'I see you two have met.' Jack's wife, in those few words and moments, had tried but failed to persuade Vee that the man's presence was legitimate. 'Hugh, I think you'd better go.'

The baby began to cry again. Madelaine picked her up. There were no soft motherly words as she laid Peg on a chair and began to remove her wet clothes.

'Don't go on my account, Hugh.' Vee walked towards the stairs. She knew her sarcasm wouldn't endear her to her boss's wife but she doubted very much that Madelaine would say anything to Jack. Vee wasn't stupid: she'd come home and walked in on Madelaine and this Hugh who had obviously been in bed together. Perhaps Jack was aware of what was going on. But what kind of man allows his wife to have a lover? The thought entered her mind, then slipped away again. It really wasn't any of her business.

Upstairs in her room Vee sat on the end of her bed. Her heart was racing. Madelaine was seeing that man behind Jack's back. Surely there could be no other reason for him to be coming out of their bedroom half-dressed while Jack was at work.

Her eyes lit on the dressing-table. A corner of her silk

camisole was caught at the side of the bottom drawer. Vee knew immediately that someone had searched through her things. Her fingers felt for and found her original papers. Nothing had been taken, but Vee knew someone had rifled through them. She felt violated. Who would do this? She shivered. She looked at her original birth certificate, at her German name.

From what her mother had told her of her father, he had loved them both. Vee had no reason to feel ashamed of who she was. Were it not for Hitler, she could be as proud of her father's homeland as he had probably been. But that was the problem. She might have a German surname, but she was an Englishwoman. Her first impulse was to repack her few clothes and leave.

And then what? Board another train? Look for another job? The money left in her purse would get her nowhere.

She looked around the comfortable room. Here, she had a bed and a job. Quite what she was to do she wasn't sure, but she could put money by and pay off Sammy Chesterton. That immediately appealed to her.

What of Madelaine and her lover, Hugh? It wasn't any of her business, was it? Except that Jack had shown himself to be a loving father to Peg. He was a good man, of that Vee was sure. And then she realized that if anything happened and Madelaine left Jack, she really would like to be around to help pick up the pieces . . .

It wasn't long before she was pushing open the Nissen hut door of the Ferry Café. The wireless was playing dance music and customers sitting at their tables were digging into plates of food. Rosie was behind the counter, clearly harassed as she wrote down orders and left them on a spike in the hatchway that separated the kitchen from the dining area. Vee saw her wipe her forehead where sweat gathered, as an angry customer complained that his meal had come minus the chips he'd ordered. He was practically shoving the plate beneath Rosie's chin.

'Not only do I have to wait ages but me order's wrong when it turns up.'

Vee saw Rosie's face: she was tired, about to crumble and let fall the tears that Vee could see in her eyes. She remembered Rosie's kindness earlier that morning at breakfast, when she'd made toast for her.

Vee lifted the hatch in the counter and found her way into the kitchen where Connie was turning slices of bacon in a large pan while watching eggs frying and trying to stir a pan of beans all at the same time.

In the chip fryer, the wire basket contained a portion of almost cooked chips that needed lowering into the boiling fat. Vee lowered the basket. The chips sizzled and spat. Vee ran her hands beneath the tap at the sink, grabbed a clean plate from the pile stacked near the hatch and raised the basket, shaking it to get rid of the excess fat. The chips were not quite to her satisfaction, so she lowered it again.

'Thanks,' came the single word from Connie.

A moment or so later, the chips were cooked. Vee was hungry and the sight of them made her mouth water. Picking up the plate she marched out of the kitchen and up to Rosie, who was still apologizing to the man – he wouldn't let her go without a good argument. A small queue had formed.

'Sorry your chips got left off the order. There's a few extra to make up for it.' She gave the man a glorious smile.

'Well,' he said, 'service with a smile.' He turned back to Rosie. 'I'm sorry, love, I've had a bad morning so far.' He picked up the plate and tipped the golden chips over his meal, then gave Rosie a broad wink and went back to his seat at the table, where he began eating noisily.

Rosie stared at Vee, but before she had time to speak an elderly man said, 'Cuppa, please.'

'Egg and chips for one,' another man, in a navy-blue jumper, said, and Vee wrote his order and left it on the spike, which was now empty.

It wasn't until the rush had petered out that Rosie said,

'Thank you. That man was about to make me cry and you saved the day. Usually I can handle the customers but I didn't sleep so well last night and . . . It's obvious you know the café business.'

'I worked in a club and we served meals.'

Vee didn't feel she needed to tell her what else the club had served up.

Connie came to the hatch. 'Thanks, love. I've been telling Jack for ages we need more help but he's got so much on his mind it goes in one ear and out the other. I've been trying to get him to see sense over some changes that would make things easier in here, but will he listen? Will he heck! I was a bit anxious when you tackled our fryer – it can be a bit temperamental, but you showed it who was boss.' She gave Vee a cuddle, enveloping her in the smell of fried food. 'I'll cook you both a meal,' she said, pulling away. She glanced at the wall clock. 'We'll be quiet for a bit now.'

A while later Vee patted her stomach. 'I never realized I was so hungry.' She'd eaten sausage, egg and chips and declared it was the best meal she'd had for a while. Connie, smiling, got up from the table and went behind the counter.

'Well, are you going to stay and work for Jack?' asked Rosie.

Connie brought three teas back, set them on the table, sat

down, took a packet of Woodbines from her pocket and lit up. She blew smoke high into the air and Rosie continued talking.

'We could do with your help here in the café. Though I've got an idea he's going to make you a jill-of-all-trades, train you up in a bit of everything.'

Connie replaced a hairpin that had slipped from her piled-up blonde curls. She was without the net snood she usually wore over her hair. 'If you don't want to stay you must tell him as soon as possible, though. He's a fair bloke to work for and last week he was run off his feet when the other bloke on the ropes had the flu. Oh, he's had plenty of people apply for a job but as soon as they find out they have to graft hard they don't come back the second day. And he won't take on youngsters because they'll get their call-up papers any day. The reliable elderly fellows ain't strong enough. He don't want anyone dying on him, does he?'

Rosie began laughing. 'Cor, you don't talk much, Connie, but when you do, you don't shut up.'

Vee looked at the two women. 'It'll be good to learn how to do different jobs,' she said. 'I might be a woman but I'm fit and strong . . .'

'Just like them land girls,' said Connie. 'Good, that's settled, then. Drink your tea, then go home and make the most of the rest of today. Don't forget to pop your ration book on the mantelpiece. I need it to do a shop for the house.'

Rosie grinned at her.

Vee had so many questions she wanted to ask but, for now, she had a job and a place to stay with people she liked. The sooner she was able to pay off Sammy Chesterton, the better. Being away from Netley had made her see her problems in a different light.

Chapter Eleven

Sammy Chesterton was parked in his usual place on the layby, smoking another cigar and thinking. His car window was wound down and he could hear birdsong. The fresh country air was making him feel better. Word had got out that one of his girls had pulled a fast one over him. He'd been expecting it ever since Vee had disappeared without paying for her new identity.

William Jacobitz, a newsagent from Botley, had spouted that if a girl could get away without paying a debt to Chesterton so could he.

William Jacobitz was finding it extremely difficult to run a business with ten broken fingers.

'You're lucky I'm letting you live. Don't take liberties, mate,' Sammy had told him. So, for now, his reputation was salvaged. But he was racking his brain for a way to catch up with Vee Schmidt, who seemed to have fallen off the face of the earth. He flicked the ash out of the window. What he ought to do was to pay May a visit. But, underneath his sometimes menacing exterior, he was a sentimental bloke and his memories stopped him doing any more than driving to this blessed layby and staring at her house, hoping for a sight of the girl he had once cared for.

He flicked through the *Daily Sketch*. 'Lock 'Em All Up' was today's headline. Of course it referred to the internment camps. The government believed it was easier to herd aliens into camps than allow them to roam at will. But conditions were poor and internees often assaulted. The authorities tried to make sure that those prisoners were fed and housed decently, but it wasn't long before boredom and depression set in.

Sammy thought that if he had his way papers should be provided for any loyal person who needed them, so they could live in peace in England. A simple check would disbar the unwelcome – the rapists, murderers and traffickers. He'd already been doing this for years at a profit. The government was crazy, Sammy thought.

What made ordinary human beings suddenly hate their fellow men simply because their names didn't fit? Why should loyal men lose their jobs because their names weren't

English? Sammy sighed. Perhaps one day a law would be passed to enable a woman to take her husband's name yet keep her own nationality. He himself would be a legal citizen then.

In the meantime he still had a problem to solve. Vee couldn't be allowed to get away with stealing from him. But how could he resolve the matter without hurting May?

He watched as a lorry slowed, then turned into the clearing at the front of May's smallholding. A man appeared from a barn and waved as the driver jumped down from his cab. Sammy heard voices, then May came out and stood on her garden path. Wearing a knee-length skirt and a blouse with her hair tied back, at first glance she looked like Vee. Ah, well, they say the apple doesn't fall far from the tree. He saw boxes of produce and money change hands. With the boxes stacked inside the vehicle, May waved goodbye as, transaction complete, the driver got back into the lorry. The engine started up and he was on his way.

Sammy knew how hard it had been for May and her labourers to work the land, grow and harvest those vegetables, a long, slow process without profits coming in. To the people who bought from her, she was Mrs May Smith. If word got out she'd married a German, her produce would rot in the fields. Her buyers would disappear.

Where was the sense in that, when food was in short supply? No, May deserved her new identity. So did her daughter. Suddenly it had all become so very complicated. He thought about the forthcoming elections. If he could get voted in somehow for Southampton, maybe in time he could get a bill passed so that marriage didn't take away your legal birthright. The fly in the ointment was that changing laws could take years. Probably he was better out of politics. Maybe he could finance another politician, have another shot at getting laws changed to suit his needs. It would certainly give him something else to focus on. Trouble was, he was such a good financier that he had too much time on his hands. If he wasn't at such a loose end, he wouldn't be sitting in this layby, would he?

He was still watching the cottage when May appeared once more. This time she was alone, standing at her front door, her face turned towards his car. For a moment they stared at each other, then May went back inside. Sammy, his heart thumping, started the car and drove off.

It wasn't the first time May had spotted the car in the layby. Who else could it be but Sammy Chesterton? But if that was so, why didn't he come to the house? He reminded her of someone from her past but she couldn't think. . .

May put the kettle on the stove. Jem would leave soon to go home. Of course he'd offered to stay on the premises – she'd had the devil of a time persuading him she could do without the gossip that would cause.

She tipped fresh tea leaves into the pot to mingle with the used ones. Two ounces per week weren't nearly enough, not when you needed tea to keep you going, she thought. May liked being self-sufficient, but there were some items, like tea, that she couldn't grow.

She switched on the wireless just in time to catch the news.

'Ninety-nine German planes were lost while they were bombing Woolwich Arsenal, a power station and the heart of London. Three hundred enemy bombers flanked by fighter planes have decimated the docks, the gasworks and the port. A few hours later there was a repeat attack. Hitler is trying to bring England to her knees.'

Stunned, May made the tea. The south coast was taking the brunt of the beating, which meant Gosport and Portsmouth, with more than their fair share of airfields and armaments yards, were likely to be attacked. May prayed Vee was still safe. She switched off the wireless.

Of course she'd heard the bombing last night as she stood by the window watching the searchlights and explosions fill the sky over Southampton. Out here, in the countryside, she felt relatively safe.

Would the war never end?

May sat down in the comfortable armchair near the fire. A log blazing in the cool evenings made the room homely. A murmur of kitten squeaks cut into her thoughts as Cat left her babies to jump on to her lap.

'Hello, girl,' May said, tickling her beneath her chin, which she knew the animal loved. Cat began to purr. 'Come for a cuddle away from those demanding babies of yours, have you?'

May guessed Cat would soon return to the box behind the sofa. Mothers were all so protective of their babies, she thought, remembering how she herself had felt when Vee was tiny.

Smoothing Cat's soft fur relaxed her. Memories of her work at the hospital came unbidden. Then a memory she didn't particularly want arrived, followed by one she would never forget.

Gus was lying on the floor in the four-bed ward, unconscious and covered in blood. Two of the beds were empty, but one contained an Italian who'd had both legs amputated.

'I was asleep and I heard nothing,' Bruno insisted.

May thought it highly unlikely that he hadn't witnessed the assault on Gus. Annie had rushed into the pharmacy to tell her about it and she had sneaked along to his ward.

The duty doctor said, 'Take Mr Bruno de Pace, bed and all, and put him on Ward Three. Get someone outside this door at all times until I find out what's going on.'

Later, when Gus had come round sufficiently to speak, May was there.

'I was told to stay away from you,' he said to her. 'The young English doctor, home from France and tired of the bloodshed and fighting, advised me to leave you alone. I thought at the time of the dance he might want you for himself. I didn't see why he had the right to advise me of anything and I told him so.'

May sat on the chair at the side of his bed, which she was not allowed to do, poised for flight if a doctor returned. The scar on Gus's face had opened again and fresh dressings obscured part of one eye. The white of the bandage emphasized the dark bruising.

'I was almost asleep when he returned with one of the porters. They stood in this room with the door closed and insulted me in English and in German. The porter had arms like great hams and seemed unable to keep them still while jeering at me and my country. Then the verbal insults weren't enough and they started hitting me as they dragged me from the bed. I tried to prevent them, but they had the upper hand as I was barely able to stand. I couldn't force my legs to move, not without crutches, but I did try to hit back. I felt like a feeble old man.'

May put her hand over his as his fingers clutched at the counterpane. She sensed his anger at being helpless. Gus had no reason to lie about who had hurt him, yet May couldn't understand how a doctor, of all people, would inflict injuries. It didn't make sense.

'But there was something unusual about the young doctor at the dance,' she said. She remembered telling Annie he was creepy. She had had to wait while the regular doctor changed Gus's dressings. She made herself useful by fetching Gus some fresh drinking water, then disposing of the detritus. The room smelt of surgical spirit. Before the doctor left, he had assured Gus that an investigation would take place. 'This is all highly irregular,' he said.

'I do not think they will worry too much about me,' Gus said to May. 'I am the enemy.'

'No, you're wrong. This is a very good hospital. Doctors and nurses do their very best for patients, regardless of where they come from. This was a one-off that will be looked into. It was just a pity it happened to you.'

Gus, upset, was determined to tell May everything he could remember.

'The young doctor swung a right hook that floored me. I could feel blood trickling from my lips. "Fuckin' Jerry," I heard him say, "Stay away from May." While I was on the floor he kicked me in the head. My ear felt as though it was on fire. Again he warned me away from you. Then the kicking began again, this time from the porter.

'"This is for *Lusitania*. My brother was one of the passengers who won't be coming home." He went on kicking me until the doctor pulled him away, finally realizing, I suppose, that he should save lives, not end them. I must have blacked out then. Tell me you didn't go with this young doctor.'

She squeezed his hand. May was aware that the German patients were advised to keep away from the English nurses. Since many of the men were dying when they arrived for treatment, the nurses were naturally compassionate. Sometimes the men formed attachments with them, but when they left the hospital the nurses became wartime memories. May knew all about the resentment among the English for the sinking of the cruiser, though. More than a thousand lives had been lost.

'You weren't personally responsible for the people who drowned on that cruise ship.'

Gus couldn't stop himself. 'I am German. I am the enemy. War is terrible. I can't help how I feel about you, May, but I don't want to cause you trouble . . .' His eyes closed. Gus had fallen asleep.

He remained alone in the small ward, and May found she was making every excuse she could think of to be with him. He told her of his home in Germany, Pulheim. He showed her photographs of his family, who were dead now: the war had killed them too. She told him about her parents, their smallholding.

Every day he grew stronger. The guard at the door was dispensed with. The young doctor seemed to have disappeared. No more was said about the investigation.

Annie said, 'I thought that doctor would be dealt with. This is not a good thing to happen in a hospital. Certainly not in a place like this where everything is so . . . self-contained. Did you have any contact with him after the dance? Has he been bothering you?'

'No,' said May. 'But I don't go out alone at night. Thank God you and I go back to our quarters together.'

She refused to listen for strange night noises. As her one concession to fear, she didn't venture on her own to the washrooms or the lavatories, but instead used the poor facilities in the room.

As Gus grew stronger May took in board games. He couldn't beat her at draughts, so he began to teach her to play chess. They talked of anything and everything. They discussed the war.

'The Americans have entered and are at the French coast,' May told him.

'For more than two years President Woodrow Wilson has been trying to steer a middle course,' Gus answered. 'I fear for my country now.'

'I doubt you'll ever fight again,' said May. 'And your priority is to get well. Well enough to leave the hospital and work. Patients are allowed to work outside the hospital when their health is stable. They're trusted to leave in the mornings and return in the evenings. This is a farming area and many men entered the services, so the prison allows some men to make up the shortfall.'

'I don't think this is possible in Germany. Escape might be on men's minds.'

'The clothing you all have to wear shows you're from the hospital's prison. The hospital can't house men when they're better. Englishmen are sent home or possibly back into the services. Many of your countrymen work in the strawberry fields that this part of Hampshire is famous for.'

'Farmers like this?'

May laughed. 'Since labour is hard to come by, with so many men at the war, the farmers may not be happy to have the enemy working for them, but help is help.'

'I live only for each day so that I can see you.'

His words surprised her, yet she felt as he did. That simple sentence meant everything to her.

Before their conversation she had been reading to him. Supper had come and gone and soon she would help get him ready for sleep. May was still dressed in her hospital clothing but she'd been off duty for some hours, and the regular nurse turned a blind eye to her spending so much time with Gus.

Gus wasn't able to manoeuvre his crutches to use the bath so May fetched water, towels, clean linen and pyjamas.

She began with his arms, soaping from his shoulders to his fingertips. Then his legs, calves first, then thighs. Sometimes they both knew she spent far too long soaping him. She couldn't help herself as she kissed him gently on the lips, loving the feel of his moustache.

He put his arms around her, holding her close.

'You must know how much I want you. Is it all right to tell you?' He let her go and waited for her answer.

May knew that she had fallen in love with him.

She loved the shape of his jaw, his chin, the way his mouth crinkled at the corners, and she ran her hands up his wet body, resting them on his chest. 'It's perfectly all right,' she said.

Before long his arms were around her again and May knew she could wait no longer. If anything was to happen between them it was up to her. The beating he had taken had left Gus unsure. She knew he wasn't worried for himself but was heedful of anything bad happening to her. But May didn't want to wait.

There were few hospital rooms with locks and those were mainly for keeping medicines and important documents safe from prying eyes. Wards were never locked. She left him to put a chair beneath the handle on the door.

May undressed and lay beside him on the small bed while he wiped his body dry. She patted soap from his beautiful face, amazed she'd had the courage to instigate what was about to happen. There was no thought for the consequences: the heat running through her young body needed its outlet. Surely it couldn't be wrong to show the man she loved how much she loved him. 'See what you've done to me?' Her words were soft. 'I've never wanted anyone before you.' She noted how he lay, naked now, his flesh glistening where the towel hadn't dried it. There was a ladder of muscle running from his chest to his waist. His internal injuries had healed, his scars fading more each day. Her fingers moved over his skin. How she had longed to touch him, and now here he was waiting for her touch, her breath, her tongue.

He brushed small kisses on her cheeks, then across her breasts. He reached for her and took her nipple in his mouth. May leant forward to lie on top of him, careful of his amputated limb. She heard herself say all of the things lovers say that sound so silly afterwards, but she couldn't stop herself.

He was slender, taut-limbed, and fine dark hairs glistened on his chest and arms. She knew other things about him: his weight, his height, the touch of his hand, his fingers, the sleepy musky smell of him she'd come to love.

It was unreal and like nothing she could have imagined as he slowly, carefully, drove himself into her. He was practised. He turned her, tumbled her, surprised her with an agility he didn't possess out of bed. It was her first time, and although she had orchestrated the lovemaking, it was every bit as wonderful as she'd hoped it would be.

Afterwards, he said, 'I am your first?'

'Of course,' she said. 'And I must change your sheets or everyone will know you and I have made love.'

She had believed the first time would be painful, but he had loved her, really loved her. Gus had made her a woman. May smiled at him, already gathering her clothes, not speaking but thinking he was her weakness and her strength.

With the chair away from the door she finished his make-shift bath, laughing as he pushed her hand away as she went to wash him. 'No,' he said. 'I want to keep your smell on me, to remember you when you aren't here.'

Chapter Twelve

As May lay in bed, she began to worry about Vee but knew she'd only feel better when she heard from her again and was reassured that she was all right.

Jem had arranged for the pickers to gather the last of the raspberries today – most of the fruit had already gone to local shops. Tomorrow they would start on the runner beans. Freshly picked runners were always tasty. May couldn't remember a time when her life hadn't been governed by the seasons, the vegetables and the fruit on the small-holding. It wasn't a large place, but it was big enough for a good living and she'd spent most of her life working the land . . .

In 1914, after the initial flush of men had volunteered to fight for their country, the government had had to beg others to enlist. May had read the posters requesting women to apply to the nursing profession.

'Have you been told how long it takes to become a fully qualified nurse?' her father asked.

Of course she had. 'I know you don't want me to leave here, Dad, but I feel I must do something for my country.' She'd not left home before.

'Growing food is doing something.'

'I'm going to join the VADs.' He could hardly argue with her. Nevertheless, she had amazed herself by sticking to her convictions.

Sent to London, she felt terribly grown-up sharing a small room and working in a ward at the Charing Cross Hospital with another VAD as her introduction to nursing.

Except that actual nursing didn't come into it: any dirty job automatically went to the VADs. Bedpans to scrub, washing bowls to scour, screens to move, and all the time worrying about being told off because her removable cuffs and white over-sleeves were grubby. She remembered Annie's excitement on being told she was to embark on a hospital ship to help bring home the wounded from France. May was also going on a ship, but only as far as Southampton Water where the Royal Victoria Hospital at Netley needed her assistance. She wasn't even allowed to commute to the hospital daily but was expected to live in. It didn't take May long to find out that the professional nurses weren't happy to work alongside the VADs, so she was relieved when Annie was transferred to the same hospital. The two girls shared one of the huts at the rear of the hospital and May looked forward to the days when she could go home to see her parents. Now, unable to sleep, May went downstairs and lit the gas beneath the kettle.

She sat in her favourite armchair thinking of the time she'd spent at the London hospital. Somehow she'd become the recipient of an 'efficiency' stripe, a scarlet ribbon she was entitled to wear on her sleeve that showed she had reached the high standard required by the London borough during the year she'd spent there.

May often wondered how her life would have been had she not been sent to work on the German ward at the Royal Victoria Hospital.

Stories abounded of how evil Germans were so May was surprised to discover that they were very like their English counterparts, frightened patients who didn't want to die. She was also surprised at the amount of English they spoke.

Three German orderlies helped dress wounds and did everything asked of them by the charge sister, who spoke fluent German, having spent time in Cologne before the war.

Most of the men had horrific wounds and weren't expected

to live long, so Matron had insisted that the window in the ward be left open at the top for their souls to fly to Heaven when they died. May remembered seeing Gus, so still, so broken after he had been unloaded on to the pontoon from the hospital ship, then delivered on a trolley to the ward. She had felt his eyes watching her. Each day she had expected to find his bed empty, his soul claimed by death, but he had survived . . .

She remembered the day in the nurses' canteen when she had heard that an English doctor had been sent to an asylum further down the south coast, and couldn't wait to tell Gus. 'He'd been in France, working constantly with little sleep, watching men die, mostly the British, with shells screaming and bombs dropping. The war had unhinged him. Then his fiancée had ended their engagement, and that tipped him over the edge. His hatred of Germans showed itself when he began operating badly, cutting what wasn't supposed to be cut. His staff, horrified, complained, but with no outward signs of illness, except his erratic work, it was a while before they realized exactly how ill he was. He was sent home to England and was supposed to go to Knowle Hospital but left the ship here at Netley, not as a patient but as a doctor. With little outward sign of instability, he was accepted as the doctor he was.'

'Surely this hospital has records.'

'It's wartime. If a man in a white coat acts like a doctor and speaks like a doctor, who's going to say they don't need his help with a ship full of injured men arriving at the gates?'

Gus sighed.

'You weren't the only patient he assaulted. But it was you dancing with me that upset him. Annie said he carried pictures of a young woman very like myself.'

'But that doesn't explain why that porter—'

'Orderlies, nurses, porters do as they're told. They wouldn't have known he was ill and probably didn't question his strangeness.'

'It might have been better had his past come out before . . .'

'You're lucky to be well. It will be a long while before he recovers from his breakdown. This war has such a lot to answer for.'

'What has happened to the porter?'

'He's been sacked. What he did was unforgivable.'

Gus said, 'Hatred is like a plague of locusts feeding off a field of green shoots.' She watched him. He was obviously thinking about what had happened.

'You might be told officially about all of this,' she said.

'I think not.'

But May knew Gus now understood why the young man

had wanted to hurt him. Perhaps he could forgive. The young doctor had lost everything – his happiness, his job, his mind.

May was woken by a gentle knock on the back door. Before she had time to answer it, Jem came through to the kitchen.

'I knew you were still up,' he said. 'I saw the lights. I had to walk down to make sure you were all right.'

'And why shouldn't I be? I was all right when you left, wasn't I?'

Jem had always had a key to come and go at will. She felt the teapot and decided to make fresh for him. She smiled as she stepped past him.

He put a hand on her arm. The other held a rolled newspaper.

'I had to come down. The car that's been in the layby belongs to Sammy Chesterton. I had a good look at the driver this afternoon and remembered there was an article in the *Echo* about him providing money for a kids' party after their school had been bombed. Luckily, there was no one in the place but while alternative school buildings were being found – he just happened to donate them – the newspaper took pictures.'

He showed May the article.

'We knew he'd come looking for her, Jem.' May tried to sound calm but her heart was pounding. Of course Jem was right. The man in the newspaper pictures and the man in the car were the same person. 'What worries me is that on paper he sounds a nice chap.'

Jem said, 'No man ever made money without standing on a few toes on the way up.'

May stared at him. Jem was always there when she needed him, always had been. There were times when she wished she'd agreed to marry him. She couldn't imagine her life without his solid figure in it. Long ago she'd told herself and him that marrying to change her name wasn't fair on him.

'I wish I could remember where I met him before.'

Jem tucked strands of her hair back behind her ear. 'I couldn't bear it if anything happened to you, May.' He looked at the tea she'd poured for him. 'I'll drink this, then walk back,' he said.

May wondered why she didn't take him up on his many offers to move in with her. After all, he spent most of his time on the smallholding, and Vee looked on him as a father. She knew he cared for them both deeply.

Being outside in all weathers had given her a healthy, if unfashionable, glow, and hard work had roughened her hands but it had kept her supple, too. For a woman in her early fifties May attracted more than her fair share of second glances from the men she met at the markets. Now she smiled at him. 'You won't be leaving this house without a kiss and cuddle, Jem Worthington.'

He put his arms around her and love for him warmed her heart.

'Of course,' he said. 'That's another thing I came back for.'

Vee stepped on board *Eurybia*.

'Goddess of the seas, this ferry,' said Jack, standing on the deck beside her. Vee yawned, tried to hide it, and Jack laughed. 'Yesterday's boat is in for a refit and a quick paint job.' He looked at his watch. 'I'm sorry that you'll do most of your training early in the mornings but with so many passengers crossing to Portsmouth daily, it's the best time for me to bring you up to scratch with what's needed.' He gave her a wide smile. 'I'm glad you've decided to stay around and help.'

'You said the ferries carry on running even through raids?'

'Yes,' he answered. 'Of course.'

That morning, Vee and Jack had left the house together. She'd slept well and eaten a hearty breakfast cooked by Connie. She had even persuaded Jack to sign her library card and looked forward to borrowing books. When he had discovered she liked reading, Jack had shown her a small room in his house near the main bedroom that was lined with books. Some were very old, but there was also a shelf of modern authors, mainly thriller writers.

'You're welcome to take anything you like,' he said. 'Madelaine's not a bookworm like me.' Every day she learnt something new about her employer, Vee thought.

She'd told him she would stay, even though she realized how hard she would have to work. Helping in the Ferry Café had made up her mind for her. She'd liked the camaraderie between Rosie and Connie. If she could work permanently in the café it would be lovely, but Jack had said he wanted someone who could be familiar with most of the work on the ferries, not simply a waitress.

It was a clear, sunny morning and Gosport seemed to be sleeping. Jack stood next to a puddle of rope on the deck near the exit gates of the sturdy launch.

'See how it's coiled? Most important to leave the excess rope like that. Easy to see and hard to fall over. Don't need mishaps on the boat. I'm going to show you the lighter-man's hitch, which is Mac's preferred tying-up procedure. This morning you can do a few trips under his watchful eye and tie up the ferry as he likes it done.' He was looking at her as though defying her to disagree. She nodded. He lifted the rope and unwound it until only the loop was around the bollard on the jetty. He handed her the rope.

'I never expected it to be so heavy,' Vee said. She hoped it might begin to feel lighter as she got used to it.

'It's a dry day. Imagine it wet and heavier.' He smiled. If he went on looking at her like that, Vee thought, she could do anything he asked of her. His next words jolted her out of her sudden daydream. 'This is a bight.'

He wrapped the rope twice around the bollard while the boat barely moved, so still was the water. Then he passed the rope under the end, making a loop. 'A bight,' he said again. Then she watched, fascinated, as he passed the end of the bight through the loop, opened it up and brought the entire knot around to encircle the bollard.

'Sometimes known as the backhanded knot. You're going to practise it with Mac this morning until he knows you can tie and untie this vessel.'

'While there's people about?' Inside she was panicking. Suppose she got it wrong? Suppose people started laughing at her? She looked at the rope holding the boat close to the jetty. Jack had made it all look so easy.

'Mac'll be there to guide you.'

She watched his back as he walked away and began

climbing the stairway to the wheelhouse. 'When he's had enough of you I'll expect you up here beside me so I can explain a few things,' he shouted down at her.

Vee watched the people queuing for tickets at the kiosk. While Jack had been showing her how to tie knots, Gosport had woken up.

The boat had been cleaned before she and Jack had stepped aboard. She looked down at her navy blue dungarees, handed to her that morning. They fitted her quite well, considering they were a men's size medium! She wiggled her toes in the new rubber-soled shoes. They looked heavier than they were and were actually quite comfortable, even though they had newspaper pushed tightly into them to make them fit better. And now passengers were on the boat, chattering, laughing, leaning bicycles against the rails. Vee began to panic. She looked down at the rope and hated it.

Then, striding towards the ferry, there was Mac, his red hair bright in the sunshine. She raised a hand in greeting and was relieved when he waved back.

Chapter Thirteen

At six o'clock Vee climbed down the ladder from the wheel-house, leaving Jack and Albert Haytor, his mate, discussing the finer points of her docking and steering of *Eurybia* across the stretch of water from Gosport to Portsmouth.

'How d'you feel?' Mac was lighting a roll-up, drawing on it deeply. She, Mac and Jack were going home and the second crew were taking over.

'Oh, it feels funny standing on firm ground,' she said. Vee didn't think she'd ever been so tired in her whole life. Neither had her hands ever been so sore and calloused.

She was on the pontoon and it was certainly firmer than the bucking, swaying sea she'd been on since that morning.

At one o'clock Jack had taken her to the café for a bite to eat, handing over *Eurybia* to Albert Haytor. Vee had taken the chance to hurry to the library and hand in her request form. The librarian had allowed her to choose two books. She was looking forward to starting Raymond Chandler's *The Big Sleep*. The librarian had also suggested Christopher Morley's *Kitty Foyle*, and Vee could think of nothing more pleasurable than a bath and bed with two books to choose between.

'You'll soon get used to the feel of the sea beneath you. I reckon you did well today.'

Vee didn't agree. She'd been terrified of docking the craft, but she'd listened carefully to all Jack's instructions and he'd never left her side while she was in the wheelhouse.

Standing beside him with his hands on the large wooden wheel she'd listened carefully as he'd said, 'You need to be part manager, part navigator. Here's how you start up. There isn't time for me to take out a boat without passengers so I'm showing you as we go.'

As soon as the boat was untied, he turned the wheel and moved away from the jetty. 'Good eyesight, quick thinking. You can't afford to make mistakes with passengers' lives in your hands. You'll need to understand the sea traffic in the waters here.' He waved expansively, encompassing the boats and ships moored nearby. 'Before you start a shift it's essential you look the boat over to check everything is as it should be. Check the equipment, check the crew are happy.' Then he explained the function of every lever, every handle, every button. She was sure she'd never remember it all.

She watched his strong, tanned hands turn the wheel and the boat passed an Isle of Wight ferry with ease, then turned and made for the distant shore. 'Take the wheel,' he said. To do this Vee had to stand in front of him and put her hands where his were. She could feel his body behind her, which was unsettling in a good way, almost as if he was sending strength into her by his very closeness. 'See the tanker moored ahead?' She nodded, her eyes judging the distance. Surely he would suggest turning the wheel so they could give it a wide berth. 'It's not like a car where you can press the brake and expect to stop. You need to assess the distance so you can clear any obstacles well before you reach them.' He turned the wheel again and the boat swung out into clear, traffic-free sea. 'There's a great deal of movement in these waters. Small craft can pop up from nowhere. You're doing fine.'

A surge of excitement rose within her.

'You need a licence for this. As I'm in charge, you're covered by mine, and it wouldn't be a good idea to put in for a licence until you're absolutely familiar with the boat and the route.' She sighed. 'Don't worry, it'll all work out in the end,' he said. 'No need to rush things. Bit like driving a car. Can you drive?'

'We have a van at home that I use,' she answered.

'That's good.' He sounded as if he genuinely meant it.

She didn't want to start talking about herself in case she let out more information than she should, so she said quickly, 'Everything on this boat seems different from a car.'

He put his hand to her waist and squeezed gently. 'Well, it would be, wouldn't it? This is a boat!' She laughed and his hand dropped away.

Vee could see the Gosport pontoon looming. If she didn't give out too much information about herself, she thought, when Sammy Chesterton came after her, it would be difficult for him to trace her.

'Slow down,' he said.

It seemed to her that nothing happened when she moved the small black handle. The engine pulsated; she pressed down harder.

'Slow down!' He knocked her hands from the wheel and stepped in front of her just as the boat clipped the jetty, then swung out widely. The boat, now in reverse, was pushing against the rubber buoys hanging from the pontoon. The seawater, churned up by the engines, was splashing high into the air and drenching some of the passengers near that side.

Vee was petrified. If he hadn't been so quick-witted, the boat would have rammed right into the jetty.

'I'm so sorry.' She felt like crying but knew that would be self-indulgent.

'I'm sorry,' she said once more.

A voice called out, 'You want to take more water with it, mate!' Everyone was remarkably jolly about the knock.

'Sorry, folks!' shouted Jack, and cheers erupted.

Vee said, 'I'm—'

'If you say "sorry" once more I shall chuck you in. On my first steering lesson I overshot the jetty and landed in the mud. We've all got to start somewhere and there's no harm done.' The corners of his mouth curved up in a smile and she longed to touch it with her fingers or, better still, her lips. Instantly, she was ashamed of herself. Jack was a married man with a family! 'I can guarantee you'll never go fast when you should go slow ever again,' he said kindly. 'I expect you could do with a cuppa now. There's a flask in that cubby-hole beside you. We'll carry on with this later.'

She had left the wheelhouse and spent almost all the rest of her time with Mac and the ropes. But later Jack had called her to him and, determined she wouldn't make the same mistake again, she went on with her tuition.

'I got a lot of funny looks from the passengers,' she remarked.

'It's not usual to see a pretty girl taking on jobs done by men. But because of this war it doesn't matter who tackles a difficult job, only that it gets done.' Jack smiled at her.

Mac was tall and slim with strong shoulders, and she'd noticed the girls giving him the eye all day. Some had boarded the boat and made their way to the rear so they could stand and talk to him while he coiled the ropes and made sure the chains were fastened securely to stop accidents happening. People got too enthusiastic, pushing against the gates in their haste to be among the first off the boat, and were sometimes careless.

She'd been worried Mac might not take to her, but Jack had assured him she wasn't taking over his job, just needed to be able to do it if necessary.

Walking towards the bus station, Mac fell into step beside her. 'Did Jack tell you about the christening?'

'Didn't shut up about it,' she said. 'I feel honoured to be invited on Sunday.'

'Connie's buying a silver bracelet for Peg. We're all putting in money so it'll be a joint gift. D'you want to be included?'

'Oh, yes.' She was glad he'd asked her.

Vee was happy that Jack had invited her to attend St John's

Church on Sunday morning. She'd seen little of Madelaine, and when she had, the woman had looked at her as if a bad smell had arisen beneath her nose. She knew Madelaine felt awkward with her because she had interrupted her when she was with Hugh.

Vee still had some money left, although not much, but Jack had explained she would be paid weekly. She felt it prudent to keep some money back to telephone her mother. She'd discovered there was a phone at the house, but with it being in the hall, she didn't feel as if she could talk to May in case her side of the conversation was overheard. In any case, she would still have wanted to pay Jack for the call.

Anyway, it wasn't her share of the money for the christening gift she was worried about but what to wear. When she'd left the smallholding, her suitcase had contained only the bare essentials, mostly trousers and skirts with sweaters to match. It had seemed pointless filling the case with the silky and glittery clothes that were suitable for the club but useless for everyday wear.

'Vee!' Up ahead she saw Rosie waiting by the ticket office. Vee waved and Rosie began walking towards her through the crowds wandering in the Ferry Gardens.

'See you tomorrow?' Mac said.

Vee had no idea whether or not she'd see him the next day,

but she smiled into his cheerful freckled face and nodded. From their chats during the day she'd learnt that he lived with his mum in Queen's Road and had been on the ferries since leaving school. His dad had been a stoker, and when he had died a few years ago, Mac had taken over his dad's work with Eddie. Eventually Jack had offered him the job 'up top', which he much preferred. He'd already confessed to her that he liked the attention from the girls but rarely took up their offers. He had a regular girlfriend, Vera, and was saving up to get married.

'She'd have my guts for garters if I so much as glanced at another girl,' he said proudly.

Mac walked towards Mumby Road and was soon swallowed by the crowd.

'I saw you get off the boat so thought I'd wait,' said Rosie. 'How did it go today?'

'I don't know.'

Rosie slipped her arm through Vee's.

'I made a few stupid mistakes with the rope, and my aim for the bollards wasn't so good,' Vee confessed, 'but in the end I got the hang of it.' She rubbed her arms. 'I feel worn out.' If she went to bed at that very moment she'd sleep for ever, she thought.

'Did you get to steer the boat?'

Suddenly Vee was reminded of Jack's closeness, the smell of Imperial Leather soap from his morning wash and his natural male muskiness. His kindness and patience with her had paid off and things had begun to make sense. 'Yes, but I don't know that I'd be any good in an emergency,' she said. 'Or that I'd be asked to skipper the boat regularly. There are other skippers with far more experience who wouldn't be happy to find out I was doing their job. But I understand that Jack needs someone who could take over anywhere if need be. So if he thinks I can be that person, I'm happy to take on the work.'

'It's wartime. Us women are taking on all sorts of jobs now.' Rosie threw back her head and laughed. 'I hope he finally lets you work in the café with us. We could do with the extra help.'

Vee nodded. 'It's nice you came to meet me . . .'

Rosie clapped a hand to her head. 'I forgot. I came to ask you if you wanted to come to the pictures with us some time. Me and Connie.'

Vee's tiredness lifted. She almost felt she could cry with happiness at being asked to join them. Rosie must have taken the pause in her answering to mean she didn't want to go.

'It's George Formby this week. He's not much to look at, but he certainly makes us laugh. *Come On George*, the picture's called.'

Vee threw her arms around Rosie. 'Oh, I'd love to come,' she said, almost knocking Rosie off her feet. In her head she was adding up whether there would be enough money left after she'd put some towards Peg's christening present. If she was careful, there would be.

Together they walked towards the house. Vee knew it didn't matter what she wore to the pictures because it was dark in the cinema. But Sunday was a different matter and it was important to her that Jack saw she'd made an effort. Madelaine always looked so smart – even in her nightwear she was glamorous.

'What are you wearing on Sunday?' The words popped out of her mouth.

'I bought some lace in the market and sewed it on the cuffs of my navy blue dress. I made a matching collar too. It's a nice dress but had got a bit tired. How about you?' asked Rosie.

'That's just it. I only have a few clothes with me . . . '

Rosie stopped walking, turned and looked Vee up and down thoughtfully.

'Have a lend of my strawberry pink dress with the box pleats.' A frown appeared in her forehead. 'You're taller than me, but we're about the same size.'

'I didn't ask you that question because I expected you to lend me something.'

Rosie squeezed her arm. 'I'm offering because you can't go in slacks or a skirt. Perhaps you don't like pink.'

Her face had fallen and Vee felt sure she'd hurt the girl's feelings. 'Oh, I do!'

'That's all right, then.' Rosie grinned at her and Vee knew she was forgiven. She was becoming accepted by the girls who ran the Ferry Café and didn't feel so lonely any more.

Jack was already at the house when the girls arrived. Peg was crying and he was clearly worn out trying to pacify her.

'She doesn't seem to want that, does she?'

The baby was screaming now and Vee's heart went out to the tiny soul.

'Give her here. You get on with making her a bottle, it's possible she's hungry.' Vee took the little one and sat in the armchair. Jack had told her he had changed Peg's nappy, so Vee knew she wasn't crying because she was wet and uncomfortable. 'It must be time for her feed?'

She didn't ask where Madelaine was. At times she seemed to have forgotten she had a baby to look after.

'I'll put the kettle on,' said Rosie.

Vee turned Peg on to her stomach and began rubbing her back with firm circular motions. Presently the little girl gave a couple of deep sobs. Then, breathing evenly, she fell asleep over Vee's knees.

'Where did you learn that trick?' Jack stood with the bottle of milk in his hand, watching her intently.

'I was brought up on a smallholding. We don't have any animals now, but we did when I was growing up and my mum used to cuddle and soothe the small animals when they'd been scared by a fox. She said she used to do it to me – guaranteed to shut me up!'

'It works,' he said, smiling at her. 'Thank you. You say you don't have animals now?'

'No, just a few acres to farm. Tomatoes, beans, strawberries, that kind of thing. My mum has a few helpers. When I was younger I couldn't wait to leave, but now I'm beginning to think it wasn't such a hard life after all.' Vee realized she was talking too much. The trouble was that Jack was easy to talk to and listened to her. 'Anyway, where's your wife? She can't be far away – I'm sure she wouldn't leave this little scrap for long.'

A shadow fell across Jack's face. 'No. She can't be far away.'

Just then Rosie clattered over with the tea tray and the steaming teapot.

'That looks good,' said Vee. Rosie poured the tea, Jack sat on a chair at the table, and Vee sipped from her cup, careful not to drip any on baby Peg, who was still sprawled contentedly across her lap. She could hear Connie singing upstairs in the bathroom and, for a while, she felt every bit as relaxed as the sleeping child.

'I'm going to have a bath,' Rosie said. 'I'm off out later.'

'I think I'd like a soak after you,' Vee said. 'If that's all right?'

'Oh, I'm sorry,' Jack said. 'I didn't know you were going out. Better pass that bundle of joy over to me. You did really well today, Vee. One or two moments when I thought you might not clear traffic in the harbour . . .'

'Rosie's asked me to go to the pictures, but it's not tonight. I think I'd like to go to bed and read. Anyway,' she began to laugh, 'it's a wonder you weren't scared half to death. I saw your knuckles go white as we passed that oil tanker.' Jack coughed and looked down at the floor. Once or twice Vee had terrified herself, misjudging the distances between craft. But when that had happened Jack had quickly taken over the wheel. She'd been glad that he was at her side as she knew he wouldn't let any harm come to the boat, herself or the paying customers.

They heard footsteps click-clacking along the hallway and Madelaine burst into the kitchen.

'This is a cosy little scene.'

Vee guiltily handed the sleeping child to Jack, who was

already on his feet. He slipped past his wife with a grim 'Hello, Madelaine,' and out along the hallway to their room. Vee got up and tried a smile at Madelaine, who was still glaring at her.

'Do you want a cuppa? There's tea in the pot,' Rosie asked Madelaine, but all she received was a stony look.

Vee went upstairs and Rosie followed. On the stairs Vee turned to Rosie and pulled a face. It was quite obvious a storm was brewing between Jack and Madelaine and Vee wanted no part of it.

Ada pulled her coat over herself and closed her eyes. The gentle bobbing of the boat usually lulled her to sleep quickly, despite the lack of pillows and mattress. But tonight the cold was seeping into her bones.

She was hungry, and that was also keeping her awake. She still had money left from the notes that girl, Vee, had given her. Who knew when she could persuade the market stall-holders to allow her to help erect their stalls? The cash they gave her wasn't much, but if she was careful she could make her money last.

Ada sighed. Her hair was still wet. In the public toilets near the bus station she'd attempted to wash it after finding a sliver of soap on the porcelain sink. She'd taken off her petticoat and used it as a towel. Now she glanced at the off-white garment hanging to dry over the wooden bench on the other side of the cabin.

She felt as though she was caught in a trap. She was German and therefore the enemy. No one would employ her in a proper job. 'Bloody Germans, they want shooting!' How many times had she heard that said?

It wasn't her fault that Hitler was at war with everyone. He might be ruling Germany, but it didn't mean she or her countrymen agreed with his way of running their country. The man was deranged, everyone knew that. The trouble was that the English thought the ordinary people were like him. German families were going hungry too, and the constant bombing made life difficult for everyone.

She thought about Vee, who had bought her food and a cup of tea in the Dive. She'd had no problems getting a job. Unlike Ada she had her identity papers. Nevertheless, she was a kind person. She must have known some trouble in her life to enable her to empathize with Ada.

Fancy her being taken on as a ferry-girl-of-all-trades by Jack Edwards! He was a good man. If it wasn't for his kindness, Ada would be sleeping out in the open or in some doorway.

She heard the splatter of rain on the cabin's roof and

the wind, which caused the boat to rock more violently against the dock's buoys. What would happen to her when the winter got a proper hold on Gosport? She doubted very much that the war would be over by Christmas.

If only she was still living with her parents in their home above the chip shop. But they were dead and gone. Or even with those darling children in Alverstoke.

It had been such a wrench leaving little Hannah and George. That was the trouble with being a nanny: you got so fond of the kiddies. But of course her employer couldn't keep her on once he knew she was the enemy.

Her qualifications from Norland College were of the highest standard. She should have known her job in Alverstoke was too good to last. Hitler wanted to rule the world and all the hatred of the Great War had been dragged up again.

'I'm sorry, Ada, but I have to let you go.' She'd had no idea it would be so difficult to find another job – any job.

Ada shivered. Torrential rain was now hitting the boat. Her stomach grumbled with hunger, and the stench of the cigarette butts on the floor was making her insides churn.

She wondered what the time was. At four the lad who cleaned the boat would arrive. That was her signal to be on her way. He would be mopping the decks and hauling fuel aboard. She had a lot to be thankful for. Jack was worth a hundred of that stuck-up bitch he'd married. She'd heard the gossip that Madelaine with her cut-glass accent, her cheating, didn't care a fig about that lovely little girl.

A tear, like a chip of ice, fell down her cheek. If she had a nice man like Jack Edwards, she'd never mess him about. Wouldn't it be wonderful if she could meet an older man who would fall in love with her? She'd love him back so much. More tears fell. She had as much chance of that as there was of the war ending before Christmas.

Chapter Fourteen

Rosie shook some lurid mauve bath crystals into the water. They sank like stones, turning the regulation five inches of water to a salty-smelling pink. The crystals had come from the market and were better than nothing – but, oh, how she longed to be able to soak in something expensive, something that smelt like the picture on the bottle. Maybe after the war was over things would return to normal.

Not that she'd ever been able to buy expensive toiletries. There had been no money left for fripperies after Mick had come back from the pub.

Rosie shook her hair free of the muslin snood she wore in the café to stop hairs falling into the food. Long-lashed eyes stared back at her. Lipstick had settled into the creases around her mouth. Tiny lines had formed that showed how hard her life had been before she had come to live in Beach Street. She leant closer to the mirror and rubbed away some of the Miami red colour. Her knuckle on the second finger of her right hand was pronounced and stuck up at an angle. It didn't hurt now, but it had when Mick had thrown the teapot at her and she'd put up her hand to deflect the boiling tea from her face. Instead a shard had cut the tendon to that finger. It had healed, and the scar on her palm was now a thin white line. Luckily, she had full use of her hand.

She smiled, and now her face was transformed. A wide, white-toothed grin showed her that she was still pretty. Her eyes travelled down her naked body, liking its slimness, the length of her legs, the firmness of her breasts. Maybe one day a customer might come into the café and be the answer to her prayers. A good man, who respected women. A man who would love her. In return she would love him and never leave. They would have babies together, a boy, then a girl . . .

'Will you be long?'

Vee's voice cut into Rosie's thoughts.

'No,' she yelled back, and stepped into the salty water.

At least Mick would never hurt her again. Not now, not after Jack had sorted him out. Her mind went back to that day in the café . . .

*

'There's a bloke sitting over near the door who keeps staring at the hatch.'

Connie dumped a large pile of greasy plates on the draining-board and began to separate the cutlery. Then she slipped the plates into the hot water in the sink. Rosie tackled them. It was late afternoon and reasonably quiet in the café.

Rosie didn't speak, so Connie continued, 'He's got dark curly hair and broad shoulders, looks Irish . . .'

'How can anyone look Irish?'

'Deep blue eyes and something about . . .'

Rosie felt the hairs on the back of her neck jump to attention. Her hands came out of the water. 'Did he speak?'

'No, he just keeps staring at the hatch. He's not in uniform. Got a dark jacket on, bit like a navvy.'

Her words had the desired effect and Rosie had moved, wiping her hands on a tea-towel, to the doorway and stood rigidly while attempting to peep round it.

'Bugger!'

'Oi! I don't want that language in my café.'

'But it's Mick. What's he doing here?'

Rosie scuttled back to the sink and plunged her hands once more into the water. 'If I stay in here, maybe he'll go away.'

'You can't stay in here all the time. I need you to do jobs out there!'

Connie had a point there, thought Rosie. She looked at her fearfully. 'But you don't understand . . .'

'I understand that that's your old man but he won't get near you while I'm here. We have to serve the punters, Rosie.'

'You don't know what he's like.'

'He's a bloke.'

Noise from the café took over. Rosie was scraping dried egg off a plate. She was shivering with fear.

'I got to serve,' said Connie, and went through the door.

'Egg and chips three times, three teas, bread and marge.'

Rosie heard the sound of the till's drawer pinging. The scraps of paper containing the orders grew on the spike. She was well aware she should be taking orders, or out in the café collecting dirty plates and cups. It wasn't fair to leave it all to Connie. Rosie moved to the door and took another peep.

Jack had come in now. He was sitting at his usual table. He looked as though all the worries in the world rested on his shoulders. Rosie's heart went out to him. He had a miserable life and a bitch for a wife.

He called to Connie, who was trying to do several jobs at once while pinning up the front of her hair that had come loose from its snood.

'Can you do me a fry-up?' He had dropped a newspaper, folded, on to the table. 'And a cuppa?'

Connie yelled back, 'Yes, but with scrambled egg?'

He grinned. He was easy to please, was Jack. He nodded and poked around in his pocket for his handkerchief. Rosie dared to look out into the café.

Mick was staring at her. A dark curl lay low over his forehead and his eyes, like forest bluebells, seemed to bore into her. Using his hands flat on the table as a support, he attempted to rise. He was unsteady on his feet. Was he ill?

No. He had been drinking. Now he was upright, but swaying. It was a wonder Connie hadn't smelt the booze on him when she'd served him. She was spot on about things like that.

The queue had dwindled and Connie came back. She didn't look happy. Mick was making a beeline for the kitchen. Rosie grabbed the frying pan. Her heart was bumping against her ribs. Then he was filling the doorway.

He looked at her over Connie's head.

'Thought you could sneak out on me, did you?'

Rosie could smell the staleness of him in the small spotless kitchen. His clothes were crumpled, as if he'd slept in them.

'Keep away from me, Mick.' Her voice was a whisper.

'You didn't think I'd find you, did you?' He put a hand on the doorframe to steady himself.

'Get out of my kitchen.' Connie's voice was calm.

With one hand he pushed Connie aside as he stepped towards Rosie.

'If you thought I'd let my wife bugger off, you got another think coming. A marriage licence means I bought you. I own you . . . like a dog.' The last seemed to have been an afterthought. He laughed. 'Get your stuff. You're coming home with me.'

Rosie's eyes filled with tears as she looked at his big clenched fists. She was waiting for the inevitable punch. She gripped the pan more tightly and from somewhere deep inside her a small voice spoke:

'No!' Rosie seemed to grow in stature. The voice spoke again, louder: 'I'm not coming with you, not now, not ever.'

'You fuckin' dare to defy me?' Mick's face was a black mask of anger. He lunged forward. Connie jumped between the pair, deflecting the punch that landed in mid-air, just as the frying-pan caught Mick on the shoulder. The big Irishman staggered back against the sink as a hand curved in a fist landed on his jaw.

'Get the fuck out of my place!'

Jack's voice was loud and cold. Mick put a hand to his face. Jack, in his shirtsleeves, stood in front of him, the muscles in his arms bulging. His eyes were on Mick as he said, 'No one messes with my girls. Get out now while you're still able.'

Mick seemed to shrivel as he slunk past Jack and out through the kitchen door. Rosie fell into Connie's arms. Jack followed Mick out into the café and the customers' heavy silence. Through the hatch Connie and Rosie watched Mick open the door and leave without a backward glance.

Jack practically fell onto his chair. He picked up his newspaper and shook out the *Evening News* to its broadsheet size. People began chatting again.

In the kitchen Connie said to Rosie, 'He won't come back.'

'I hope not,' whispered Rosie. She smiled damply at Connie, then began to put cut potatoes into the hot fat.

Connie left the kitchen and went to Jack. She stood over him at the small table and asked, 'You all right?'

Rosie watched from the hatch while she spread margarine on slices of bread.

She heard Jack say, 'I can't stand men who talk to women with their fists. I've noticed him hanging around and guessed he was looking for Rosie.'

Connie put a hand on his arm. 'She had the guts to tell him she wasn't going back, didn't she?'

He grinned at her, then asked, 'Where's my tea?'

*

It was the car ferry that woke Vee the next morning. The clanking of chains, the whistling of the men cleaning the decks and laughter as people shared early-morning jokes.

Last night's argument had seemed to go on for hours. It wasn't Jack's deep voice that resonated through the dark so much as Madelaine's high-pitched screaming. Vee thought their bedroom must be directly beneath hers. It had finally stopped when she'd heard Jack leave the room with the baby, who had joined in, crying. Vee wondered where the love was in that marriage.

She thought of her mother and Jem, who wasn't exactly her husband but had been around for as long as Vee could remember. She'd thought Jem was her daddy when she was a little girl because he'd always been there for her.

Later she'd learnt that the handsome man with the moustache in the photograph on the living-room mantelpiece was her father, but she had grown up hearing her mother and Jem apologize to each other after mishaps. She'd seen them kiss and make up after silly disagreements. She'd also witnessed Jem's warmth towards her mother and his face lighting up when she entered the room. She'd smiled at the wild flowers he'd set in jam-jars as small gifts for May. She'd often wondered as a little girl why Jem couldn't be her daddy if the real one was dead.

Jem lived in a small house in the village. He spent all his time at the smallholding, but went home each night. Sometimes Vee was scared that he wouldn't be there in the mornings when she woke.

Now that she was older she understood, which wasn't to say she agreed with how her mother lived her life, but it was her choice, wasn't it? And Jem went along with the arrangement, even if he wasn't happy. Sometimes she wondered if her mother's way of looking at love had affected her own past love affairs. There had been Ben, a librarian, who was serious and caring but not adventurous enough for her, then Alan, who had insisted on caring too much. George had been older and quite moneyed. He'd been married before and couldn't understand why Vee said she wouldn't sleep with any man until she knew she loved him.

Perhaps it *was* her mother's fault. Vee wanted desperately to feel what her real parents had had: a love that could surmount anything. And, she thought, in their own way May and Jem had that sort of love.

Jack intrigued her.

She was drawn to him but he couldn't make a move on her, even supposing he wanted to. He was out of bounds. He had a child, an unhappy marriage, yet she'd had those feelings yesterday when they were close together on the boat. And today he'd decided she was ready for another shot behind the wheel of the ferry, with himself close at hand.

'You can't let the mistake you made put you off. Later you'll be proud of the progress you've made.' His words went round and round in her head. He was her boss, so what else could she do but get on with the job he wanted her to do?

Later, her stomach tied in knots, Vee had stood beside him in the wheelhouse and answered his questions on what she had learnt yesterday.

It was exciting to know that one flick of her wrist could turn the vessel any way she liked, but as she'd stood with both hands in the position he had shown her to guide the boat, all she'd wanted to do was to please him.

Today the water was choppy, with a stiff breeze blowing, and she was glad of the navy blue jumper Jack had handed her before they'd left the house.

'That's good. You're thinking ahead,' he said, as she turned the wheel to make space for a small sailing dinghy to pass safely.

The sun was high overhead, the wind cool on her cheeks, but she was well wrapped up against the cold that the approaching winter was bringing to Gosport.

Seagulls swooped and cried, and a large group of children

from a local school was on board. Vee had heard the teachers talking about the proposed visit to the Isle of Wight to look for fossils. The big white ferry left from the landing stage near the harbour railway station. The children were excited, but Vee kept her eyes on Portsmouth and the craft in the water surrounding the ferry.

She didn't hear the splash but she heard Jack shout, 'That little devil's gone over.'

Then the comforting body giving her the courage to steer the craft was gone. She was alone! She saw his peaked hat had been thrown to the deck of the wheelhouse. She picked it up and put it into a cubby-hole.

Voices were raised, and she heard what she thought was the sound of heavy lifebelts hitting the water – they sounded like the belly-flops people did in the swimming pool. Vee thought quickly. She decided against putting the boat into reverse. Surely the sudden churning of the water could pull the child beneath it. She let the vessel cruise ahead and when she thought she was well away from the place when the child had fallen into the water, she turned back, having made sure that there was enough room for the boat to make a wide arc. Her heart was throwing itself against her ribs. She was terrified. But she'd decided to try to move close to whoever had jumped into the freezing sea to rescue the child so that others could pull them out. The yelling and shouting from the passengers was tremendous.

'Get another lifebelt! He's gone under!' The other children, who were obviously very frightened, were screaming. Vee was aware that the boat was listing to one side as most of the passengers peered into the choppy sea.

Still trying to keep the boat stationary, although the current was moving it towards a tanker, Vee glanced at what was going on. She saw Mac at the deck's rail pulling on a rope attached to a lifebelt. A young boy was inside it, wriggling, and Jack held on to him as he swam towards the ferry.

Even though the child was inside the belt, he was small enough to slip out if Jack let go of him.

Jack reached the side of the boat, legs kicking wildly. Vee saw that his feet were bare. When he grabbed another rope, cheers rose as Mac hauled the lifebelt up. It cleared the water as Jack pushed the boy high so that Mac could reach out for him.

The boy flopped on to the deck and Mac began rubbing his legs, then his arms. Jack looked weary as he climbed aboard but he fell to his knees and turned the little boy on to his back.

Then he took a deep breath and blew into the child's mouth while intermittently massaging his chest. Suddenly the lad threw up. Jack sat back on his heels and laughed. The crowd, who had been silent, erupted with claps and cheers.

A couple of blankets arrived and the boy was wrapped up. A man was now shaking Jack's hand, and a young woman was kneeling with the patient, who was coughing and crying at the same time. Vee supposed they were teachers.

Jack stood up and used a blanket to dry himself. A man handed him his own jacket. It was too tight for him but Jack shook his hand gratefully. As Jack, still carrying the blanket, moved through the passengers to handshakes and shouts of 'Well done', Vee shoved the lever to 'Ahead' and the boat ploughed forward.

When Jack, wet-haired, barefoot and red-faced with cold, reached the wheelhouse Vee was heading towards the Portsmouth jetty. She could feel him shivering as he stood behind her. 'You did well,' he said. She didn't turn but was aware of him as a man, and suddenly it mattered very much that he'd said those words to her.

Vee didn't ask if the boy would be all right. The child was young and strong, and she could see him below her, surrounded by his schoolfriends. He seemed fully recovered from his ordeal, enjoying the chatter among his mates. He'd be the centre of attention for a long while, she thought, even on the boat going across to the island. That was if the teachers didn't insist on calling for an ambulance.

Down on the deck, Mac and another ferryman, whose name Vee didn't know, were using mops to swab up the water in case someone slipped.

'I think you've done that before,' Vee said to Jack.

He put his hand on the wheel. It wasn't touching hers but she could feel the heat of him on her skin. She wanted to hold on to that feeling and to him. He'd just saved a boy's life and was now behaving as if nothing had happened! She studied his fingers, splayed yet firm, his grip secure on the wooden wheel. And she wanted to lean back so that she could feel his body firm against hers. But she didn't. Instead she reminded herself that he had a wife. But his breath was warm on her neck as he said, 'A ferry hazard. I hope you can swim. Maybe a lifesaving course would be a good idea. That's if you intend to stay on. What the heck have you done with my cap?'

She pulled it from the cubby-hole, handed it to him, and he jammed it on to his wet hair. She laughed. 'You lost your boots as well,' she said.

'Mac's looking in the cupboard for another pair to fit me,' he said. 'I had to shake them off, else the weight of them would have taken me down to the depths. Still, the boy's all right. That's the main thing.'

Rosie Archer

The pontoon was ahead. Vee manoeuvred the craft so that, unlike yesterday when she'd nearly hit the jetty, she slowed easily, reversing so that the boat glided in. Mac gave her a thumbs-up as his rope slid easily over the jetty's bollard.

Chapter Fifteen

Rosie had been right. George Formby had made Vee laugh until tears filled her eyes. That had been the main feature at the Forum, with the B picture a crime story starring Ida Lupino, whom Vee thought terribly glamorous. Pathé News had shown scenes of bloodshed amid the war-torn fields of France, later softened by a Mickey Mouse cartoon.

When the film rolled round to where they'd come in, they left the picture house and walked back through the town. Connie and Rosie decided to have a drink in the Royal Arms, a pub along Stoke Road. Through the open doors they could see the bar was full of British sailors in their navy bell-bottoms, and the smell of beer and cigarettes wafted out to them, enticing them in.

Vee left them and began the short walk home on her own. Being out on the water all day was tiring, and she'd been responsible for the passengers' lives while Jack was saving the child. She didn't remember being so weary when she'd been working in the fields in the sun on the smallholding.

Coming off the Gosport ferry, Jack had been congratulated many times and someone had even taken a photo of him. Vee hoped it hadn't included her. They'd had to make the return journey to Gosport so the other team of ferrymen could take over, and Vee guessed the phone wires had been red-hot with news of the rescue. Before they reached the ticket office he said to her, 'I can't stand this. I'll see you later.' He'd handed her the blanket and disappeared. Without him she was nobody so, with a wave to Ada, who was standing near the Dive café, she had made her way home alone. She thought Jack was admirable not to want the limelight. Vee didn't need it either, but that was because she didn't want anyone to discover her whereabouts.

Vee jumped when she switched on the light and saw Jack sitting alone in the house.

'Jesus, you made me jump!' She thought how tired he looked. The fire had burnt low and the house was quiet. She could smell drink on him.

'Just thinking,' he said. 'Sorry, I didn't mean to alarm you. Earlier a reporter came to chat about the boy who fell in the water. He said it was newsworthy, and I told him it happened more often than people realized. But it didn't always end so well. The bloke had brought a bottle of Scotch with him.' He ran his hand through his hair.

'Everyone on the boat thought you were brilliant. Do you know what happened to the boy?'

'Apparently the ambulance took him to hospital. He was yelling and crying because he'd been looking forward to the school trip and insisted he didn't want to be left behind. A teacher went with him, promising that if his parents and the hospital said he could, they'd catch up with the others the next day.'

Vee asked if he'd like some tea. He shook his head. 'I'm not drunk, if that's what you're thinking. I've just got a lot on my mind. You didn't see my wife out anywhere, did you?'

'No, but I wasn't looking. Is Peg . . .?'

'The little one's fast asleep.' He gave her a small smile. 'Sorry about the unpleasantness between my wife and myself. I get so angry when I find she's left Peg alone.'

Vee wanted to say that perhaps Madelaine had had some good reason for it, but even animals protected their young. Madelaine seemed totally devoid of maternal instincts.

Jack was talking again.

'Look, Vee, even though it's unlikely you'll need to set foot in there I'd planned on taking you down to the engine room again tomorrow so you can get to know how it all works, but I'm going . . .'

Vee was aware she'd allowed her face to show her lack of enthusiasm.

'No, no! It won't be necessary for you to shovel the coal!'

'Thank goodness for that,' she said.

'I want you to understand how the engines run, though. Eddie wouldn't let you touch a thing down there. Vince, his boy, is usually with him and will be his natural successor, I'm pleased to say. The other crew respect them . . .' Her confusion must have shown on her face. 'Eddie's brother is a stoker. It runs in the family, see? When my crew and I have finished for the day, the other crew take over, as you know, but the stoker is one of Eddie's family.'

'So I won't be going down into the engine room to work?' On the smallholding she had had to get on with loads of filthy and heavy jobs, but that didn't mean she liked doing them.

He shook his head. 'I'm putting you in the ticket kiosk with Regine. The Portsmouth side have been complaining that ticket sales are down.'

So far Regine was the only person in the house who seemed unfriendly towards her. Or was Vee being silly and imagining things?

'I don't want you to spy,' he continued. 'Just watch her.'

Did he mean for her to check Regine was taking the right amount of money for the tickets?

'You'll be watching what goes on, from the sale of a ticket in the kiosk to its clip before the passenger boards the boat, then the handing back on the return. We don't date tickets. Portsmouth agrees that people who cross on the ferry usually come back. The passenger hangs on to the ticket for the return journey. It is then clipped and collected for disposal. If the ticket has been clipped more than once, the passenger is trying to pull a fast one. If I ever need you to punch tickets I must know you understand how the procedure works, okay?'

Vee nodded. 'So the person at the gate punching tickets on the Gosport side travels over on the boat and does the same job on the Portsmouth side?'

Jack nodded.

'Is there a ticket office on the Portsmouth side?'

Again he nodded. 'Have you forgotten you must have bought a ticket to come over on my boat?'

She nodded, and he carried on: 'The number of passengers should tally with the ticket sales. But something's not quite right . . .'

So tomorrow she'd be in the ticket office? At least he

didn't intend for her to stoke the boilers and for that she was grateful. She stifled a yawn, closing her eyes.

When she opened them he was looking at her intently.

'Sorry I've kept you up.' He gave her a beautiful smile. 'Goodnight. See you in the morning.'

'Madelaine will come back eventually. She always does, I believe.'

'You're right, but I'll wait up all the same.'

Vee climbed the stairs. In the bathroom she washed, then picked up her toothbrush, ready to clean her teeth, but there was no paste. Her pink tin of Gibbs wasn't where she had left it. She opened the bathroom cabinet and saw that it had been put on the shelf. As she picked it up, thinking someone must have borrowed it, which she didn't mind, she noticed a packet pushed behind a bottle of hydrogen peroxide. Vee took it out and found it contained powder. The writing on the packet said it was bleach. She realized immediately that the peroxide and the powder were what Madelaine used to keep her hair that gorgeous pale yellow blonde. Vee smiled to herself. She wasn't a natural blonde then. She looked at her own fair hair. Perhaps she should make a bit more of herself. She put the bottle and powder back.

She was asleep as soon as her head touched the pillow.

*

The bang woke her .

'Vee! Get down here!'

Her first instinct was to burrow beneath the warm bed-clothes but when Jack's voice came again, sharp and clear, her senses took over. It was an air raid.

Vee slipped from the covers and grabbed her coat, slinging it over her nightgown. Her sleepy brain began to function properly and she grasped her documents and purse, stuffed them into her handbag, then ran for the door as another huge bang shook the house, sending slivers of plaster dropping down into the room like snow.

'Vee!'

This time she shouted back, 'Coming.'

Despite the thick walls of the old house the noise of the many planes droning overhead was clear. Fear gripped her. The night raids had fallen across Southampton, aimed at the docks, the ships. At Netley the bombs that fell were likely discharged to make the aircraft lighter on their way home to Germany. Here, as in Southampton, the targets were the dockyard, the factories, the boat builders, the armaments yards – and at any moment she could be blown to smithereens.

'Grab those flasks!' Jack shouted as, clutching his daughter, he made for the back door. Vee saw he had a bag over his shoulder containing the baby's cotton nappies and clothing.

He stopped near the carrycot and put his precious charge inside, covering her with a blanket.

Vee hesitated. Was she meant to follow him?

'There's a shelter in the garden.'

With both flasks in her arms she managed to open the back door, allowing Jack to pass ahead of her. Vee had had no cause to go into the garden in her short time at the house other than to use the lavatory that was just outside the back door. It wasn't her favourite place, with its newspaper squares on a string and fat black spiders sitting on the walls ready to pounce. She much preferred the bathroom upstairs.

Vee followed him, watchful of where he was treading.

'There are steps down. Be careful.'

The Anderson shelter was practically buried in the soil. Jack elbowed open the door and Vee felt the dampness envelop her. He must have read her thoughts, for he whispered, 'We'll soon get it warm. Sit there for a while.' He passed the child to her waiting arms after she'd put the flasks down. It was pitch black. She held the baby close, smelling her talcum-powder freshness. She'd lowered herself gently to what she thought was a kitchen chair and thought it best to let him do whatever was needed to make them and the shelter secure.

Through the open door, she could see searchlights flashing

and hear the returning ground fire. She smelt smoke, something acrid burning. The noise was horrific. It felt to Vee as if the whole earth was moving each time a crash announced that a target had been hit.

Thoughts of her mother, the smallholding and Cat, furry and warm, surrounded by tiny kittens, filled her head and she wanted to cry. But it was Peg who whimpered and Vee lowered her face to her and whispered, 'It'll be all right, my love, I'm here.'

What with the rescue of the little boy earlier and now this, it had been a hell of a day and night, she thought.

Then the door was closed and absolute darkness reigned. Until she heard the strike of a match, which flared, then an oil lamp flickered. 'There, that's better. I'll light the fire as well . . .'

'Won't the fumes . . .' She trailed off. Now it was brighter inside the shelter, Vee could see what looked like a greenhouse heater.

'No, it's quite safe.'

She saw then that there were bunks one above the other at the end of the metal shelter and seating against the walls. No privacy at all in the very small space, but with the warmth from the stove it was becoming cosy. There was a box against the bottom bunk and Jack must have noticed her staring at it.

'There's clean, dry bedding in there. Can't leave stuff out – it would get damp and go mouldy. I dug this Anderson deep into the soil for safety's sake.' He paused. 'I realized too late that the deeper I dug, the more water could seep in. Did you have a shelter at home?' While waiting for her answer he moved the carrycot onto a bunk.

Vee nodded. 'A Morrison. In the kitchen.' He was now making up the little bed for Peg. She watched his hands, sure and nimble. Neither of them spoke as he took the child from her and put her into the cot, covering her lightly with the blanket.

Jack sighed. 'Now, do you want a cup of tea?'

She must have looked questioning.

'The flasks. One's the baby's milk, the other's tea.'

She smiled at him and nodded.

He busied himself with cups. 'There's one in the café.'

He was still thinking of the shelters.

'A Morrison,' he added.

Vee remembered Connie had said she'd put Peg in the shelter.

'Named after Herbert Morrison.'

He passed her a steaming mug, 'Clever clogs,' he said with a grin.

Just then a huge bang shook the shelter and Vee almost

dropped the mug. The tea splashed over her hand, hot enough to make her gasp but not to harm. He handed her his handkerchief and she mopped her skin. 'I take it you've not been in any heavy raids.'

Vee shook her head. He was looking at her intently.

She knew that at any moment he was going to ask her about herself and she wouldn't be able to lie to him. But it was too soon for her to explain about Sammy Chesterton, the forged papers, her guilt. She was still trying to impress Jack: she needed her work, a place to live, wages. She would tell him, but later, in her own time.

Then Fate smiled kindly on Vee as a voice cried above the noise outside, 'Let me in! It's awful out here.'

Jack moved towards the door and pulled the blackout curtain across so no light would be visible outside. He opened the door and the girl almost fell into the shelter.

Regine regained her dignity as Jack closed it behind her.

'I guessed someone would be in here, and I couldn't bear to stay alone in the house.'

'Are you all right?' Vee asked quietly, then put her finger to her lips and moved her head towards the still sleeping child.

Regine laughed, showing small white teeth.

'Amazing, isn't it, that babies can sleep through almost anything except human voices?' She took off her coat and undid the knot tying her headscarf beneath her chin. 'Where is everyone?'

She put her coat and scarf on the seat beside her and looked at them expectantly. She had brought in with her the stink of cordite and the scent of flowery perfume.

'I was hoping you could tell me that,' Jack said.

Vee sipped her still warm tea.

'If you mean your wife, she's round her mother's house. She said something about trying to persuade her to come to Peg's christening. Any more tea in that flask?'

Jack passed it to her with a white enamel mug. 'Why didn't she tell me?'

'Probably because you'd have expected her to take the baby.'

Jack sighed. 'I simply wish she'd discuss things with me first. Then I could make arrangements.'

Regine, carefully pouring hot tea, said, 'Don't go on at me!' She glared at him, then looked towards the cot on the bottom bunk. 'Baby seems okay to me.'

For a moment there was relative silence apart from the *thwump, thwump* of bombs falling. Vee finished her tea and put down her cup.

'I wonder how long . . .'

'Who knows?' Regine answered her question before Vee

had uttered it. 'We could be out of here in a while or stuck here until morning.'

'Vee's helping you out tomorrow,' Jack said. His voice was cold and sharp.

Regine frowned. 'I don't need any help. There's hardly room for me in that office.' She added, 'Congrats for saving that little boy. Everyone was talking about it. I think a few people actually bought tickets just to gawp at you, not realizing you weren't skippering the boat and had already left. Look, I really don't need any help.'

'That's as may be, but I want Vee to get a grasp of what goes on in every aspect of the business.'

The frown deepened on Regine's face and she ran her slim fingers through her dark hair. 'Fair enough,' she said. She put her empty mug on the floor of the shelter.

Only it wasn't, thought Vee. Not fair enough with Regine at all. She watched as the girl pulled her coat around herself, then closed her eyes. After a while Vee, too, dozed in the warmth of the small room. When she looked at Jack, he was watching her. He smiled, then closed his eyes.

When Vee woke daylight was streaming through her window and the clanking of the car ferry had broken into her dream, like a metal monster on the rampage.

The alarm was just about to scream so she put out her hand to still it. She had a vague memory of climbing the stairs to her bedroom after the all-clear had sounded, with no idea of what time it had been, except it was still dark. She remembered lying in bed listening to the argument floating indistinctly upwards from downstairs.

Madelaine had either returned late, or had been inside the house while they'd hidden in the shelter from the bombing.

It was the start of a new day. One she wasn't looking forward to because she would be spending her time with Regine.

Chapter Sixteen

May felt the sun on her face and cherished its warmth, then bent forward to the straw-covered earth. Her fingers were red with the sweet juice of the strawberries she was picking from their hiding places beneath green leaves. The scent of the fruit mingled with that of the rich earth.

The second picking was almost at an end. She was alone in the field that, weeks ago, had held throngs of people, filling wicker baskets for her to pack into containers and send to market. There was something infinitely peaceful about being alone, at one with the earth and sun.

She glanced towards the wooden shack. On the shelves inside, out of the sun's heat, were the fruits of her labours from early this morning. In June, queues of pickers had been waiting for their baskets to be weighed and added to their totals. It was piecework, so they were paid by the amount of fruit they picked. A summer job, strawberry picking, tried and tested over the years. The same people worked in her strawberry fields as had for her father when she was a girl. Travellers pitched up year after year, their wagons pulled by horses, and gathered in the field set aside for them.

This was the last of the fruit before the strawberry runners were transplanted by the few regular workers she and Jem kept on through the winter. The last strawberries always seemed to May to be the sweetest. In the past Vee had picked with her and it had been peaceful, mother and daughter sharing precious time together. Some of the luscious fruit would go to the village shops first thing in the morning, but mostly it would stay with May to be bottled, made into jam or eaten as it was, fat, red and delicious. Above her a skylark was hovering.

Last night Vee had telephoned.

Her daughter was well, she said, happy, and learning new skills. She wouldn't tell May exactly where she was living. May knew she should feel easier about her welfare. Vee had asked whether Sammy Chesterton had spoken to her, and May had told her truthfully that he hadn't. She hadn't mentioned that he came to the house some days and sat in the layby in his car. Of course she felt uneasy about his presence because he had a bad reputation, but the less Vee had to worry about, the better, she thought. Besides, he did no harm. Merely sat and watched. It was as though he was making his mind up about something.

May told her about the kittens. Three tiny bundles of fur and fluff now eager to explore away from their box and their mother's care. They loved paper bags and bits of string. May told Vee how the most adventurous of the three had had to have a long piece of string carefully pulled from his mouth before it choked him. Cat had her work cut out rounding them up. Vee had laughed, which assured May she really was all right, so she had put the phone down feeling happier than she had in ages.

Gus had loved being out in the strawberry fields.

When he was no longer confined to his bed and able to move about freely with the other prisoners, he was encouraged to work for his keep. The fact that the hospital was deep in the countryside meant farming, although some men were sent to work in the boatyards at the mouth of the Hamble river. The prisoners had become a welcome, if peculiar, sight in their distinctive suits, as they toiled in the fields or on the banks of the river . . .

May's father had taken much persuading before he agreed to take on several men. Eventually he concluded that help from the Germans was far better than no help at all. He was allowed two Germans and one Italian. They arrived by truck at seven o'clock in the mornings and were picked up at six in the evenings.

Manfred was blond, a giant of a man, gentle with animals and softly spoken.

Bruno, the Italian, from a village outside Rome, had expert knowledge of horses, and Gus had somehow wheedled his way in, becoming the third man to work for May's family. Of course, Joe, May's father, knew nothing of the burgeoning love affair between his daughter and Gus.

'They are exemplary workers,' he admitted, but all the same he instructed the rest of his team to stay away from them, unless it was absolutely necessary. Joe had applied for land girls and had been a little put out to discover he had to accept the foreign workers or go without.

Sometimes May thought she had spent more time with Gus when he was near death's door than now when he worked for her father. It had become increasingly difficult to steal time to be with him, so they savoured the sweetness of the precious moments they spent together. She knew she must never allow her parents to find out that she was in love with him.

'If it wasn't for the time I can steal away before curfew at nine, I'd never be able to see you,' he would grumble.

Their favourite place to meet was the hospital's church-yard, where she would fly into his arms. It wasn't always to make love.

The sick and wounded were emerging daily now from the boats that tied up in Southampton Water, the extent of the men's injuries appalling. The train, too, brought in casualties. Her dark memories gave May nightmares and she needed to offload each day's happenings on someone besides Annie. Gus was there for her.

'We took in twenty-nine very severe cases today from the train. Most of the men hadn't a hope of surviving. Some had trench foot so bad we had to cut off their socks and parts of their feet fell off too. Poor men, clotted with blood, frightened, with only dirty bandages holding their bodies together. I unwound a man's filthy bandage on his arm to find the bandage was keeping it on . . .'

Gus would hold her, let her talk, and she knew he was remembering when he had first woken at the hospital and had no idea whether he was alive or dead.

There was no way she could keep such hellish daily events inside her. She had been told to wash the occupant of bed fourteen who complained his arm hurt and pulled back the coverings to discover he had no arm. When she went to feed the man in bed three, most of his face had been shot away.

Talking to Gus kept her sane. A nurse who held everything bottled inside her had run screaming from the operating theatre. May never saw her again. But then the young doctor – she never had discovered his name – who had harmed Gus had been driven mad by the carnage he'd witnessed. 'I am so glad to have you,' Gus would say, after she had talked herself hoarse. And they would make love hurriedly, fearful it might be the last time, for neither knew if the other would still be there the next day. She might be sent to another hospital, he to a prison camp. Now that many thousands of prisoners were being brought to England, camps had been set up for them alongside those for the internees. Hampshire's Gosport and Frimley were the camps nearest to Southampton, but that didn't mean Gus, if he was moved from Netley, would be sent to either. May knew that any day she might discover Gus had been sent away and it was quite possible that she would never see him again.

Gus had told her of his childhood in Pulheim. He had been born in a street not far from the abbey and had gone to a good school where he had been taught English. As a boy, he couldn't wait to join the Jagdstaffel, the air arm of the Imperial German Army. His parents had been killed in a train crash and he had no siblings. He had loved a girl named Hildegarde, who hadn't returned his love, so flying had become his life and he had ended up in reconnaissance.

'I think because of my foot it is unlikely I will fly again. If I ever get home to Germany it will be a desk job.' His one fear was of being parted from May.

May had told him of her upbringing in the country outside Southampton, the village school, the strictness of her father, who nevertheless had allowed her to enter the Summer Princess competition, which she had won.

At carnival time, surrounded by flowers, wearing an ankle-length frilly white dress, with the two runners-up beside her, May had trundled along the streets of Netley on a hay wagon pulled by two Shire horses.

As soon as she left school she had worked on the small-holding until, grudgingly, her father accepted she wanted to nurse. She had expected to travel abroad, but so far it hadn't happened.

May found hatred towards the enemy didn't end at the hospital gates.

One day she had time off and was at home in the large, comfortable kitchen. Through the window she watched the three prisoners sitting on logs eating the breakfast her mother had cooked.

'I don't see why we can't all eat together,' she said. Her

father often suggested they set up the big table outside on a fine day so the English field workers could have a meal with the family.

'I'll not sit at a table with my enemies,' her father snapped. 'They get fed well enough, here and at the Queen Victoria. There are men fighting in trenches to save this country who would gladly eat half of what those men are getting. It doesn't matter where they eat.'

When it was wet the men were fed in the barn.

May wondered why her father didn't think of the prisoners as men who had been pressured by their countries to do as they were told.

Regine unlocked the door to the ticket kiosk and ushered Vee inside.

'I've no idea why he wants you to understand about selling a boat ticket. It's not as if I won't be here to carry on.' She put her handbag on the counter, then filled the cash drawer with the float. It was always taken home at the end of each shift so that those who took over started from scratch.

'The tickets are kept here.' Regine showed her a large roll of yellow tickets that had to be torn off according to the number purchased. 'They're all returns. Portsmouth and Gosport know that if a person travels one way they'll come back.' She pointed to a high stool. 'Sit here, opposite the glass window. Take the money first and give change if necessary, then offer the tickets. Don't give them before you've taken the money in case they run off without paying. I'm going to stand here and watch you give the correct change.'

Regine locked the door behind them.

'Don't make it easy for thieves,' she said.

She had spoken to Vee as if she were a five-year-old. Nevertheless Vee sat on a stool beside her to await their first customer.

It seemed to Vee that the tickets were sold in waves. Noisy people queued and were served. Then there was a lull when she was able to gather her thoughts. Regine must have been reading her mind because she said, 'It's the buses. People get off a bus and come for a ticket. When there aren't any buses due in, it's quieter.'

'How many people cross in a day?'

'About the most is twenty-two thousand on a Saturday when Portsmouth Football Club is playing at home.'

'Gosh!' Vee couldn't help herself.

'Course, it's not like that every day.' Vee saw Regine smile, her teeth showing white in the dully lit room. Even though they were enclosed in the small square building, the heavy smell of seaweed and mud pervaded. 'Some people will come simply to ask questions about times of boats.' Regine put a manicured hand on a large dog-eared book at the side of the counter. 'This contains information about our own ferries. If they want to know about the floating bridge, Isle of Wight ferries or the boat trips around the harbour, send them to the tobacconist across the road, who deals with bookings. We just sell tickets.'

Vee nodded. Of all the jobs she'd attempted so far she thought this was the most boring. Earlier her mind had wandered and one customer had nearly received change for a pound when she'd handed over a ten-shilling note. Luckily Vee had spotted her mistake before she pushed a brown note through the hatch into the woman's eager hands.

'At the end of the shift, the number of tickets sold must tally with the amount of money taken,' Regine snapped.

Since that episode Vee had kept a sharp eye on her change. She had also refused two foreign coins. 'Sometimes it's a genuine mistake, sometimes not,' Regine said.

'Would you like a cup of tea?'

Vee could have killed for one. 'How—'

'We can bring in a flask,' Regine took one from her voluminous handbag, 'which the Ferry Café girls fill at no charge.' She glanced at the clock on the wall. 'Usually by now someone's been over to collect it, so if you're sure you can manage I'll take it across the road.'

'I can manage,' said Vee, actually rather proud that she was about to be trusted to work on her own.

Once Regine wasn't breathing down her neck, Vee found she could smile and chat to the customers while dealing with the tickets and change. She could see why Regine resented her intrusion in the ticket kiosk. Now that she was alone she felt as if she owned the place.

All too soon Vee had to unlock the door and let in Regine, who carried the flask beneath her arm and a plate covered with a tea-towel in her hand.

'Rock cakes. Too bad if you don't like them.' She put the plate down, then the flask, and fumbled beneath the counter for two cups. 'These are clean,' she said. 'You carry on while I sort this out. I tore them off a strip in the café for forgetting about us, but they said they'd been extra busy.'

Vee was beginning to think she'd been mistaken about Regine and that she wasn't as prickly as she'd first thought.

Regine said, 'Get that down you. I'll take over while you have a break.'

Vee moved away from the window and stood up. Her legs felt stiff after sitting down for so long. She saw the rock cakes were cut in half and spread with marge, and eyed them hungrily as she lifted her cup to her lips.

Regine was now on the stool Vee had occupied and was about to serve a man who had asked for two tickets.

Instead of tearing them from the roll they had been using, she turned away, took two loose unmarked tickets from her large handbag and gave them to the man, after taking his money and putting it in a jar near the till drawer.

All the breath seemed to leave Vee's body.

Regine said, 'Of course you won't say a word about me reusing tickets. If you do, imagine how you'll feel when everyone knows you're a fuckin' German.'

Chapter Seventeen

Jack stirred his tea. It was just as he liked it, dark and thick enough to stand a spoon in.

'Anything to eat, Jack?' Connie's cheery face appeared before him.

'Not now, maybe later,' he said. He watched as her tidy, plump figure wound its way through the packed tables towards the kitchen. He realized he hadn't thanked her for her concern. She was a good sort, was Connie. His crew were hand-picked and, in the main, he was happy with them. There were two he wasn't too keen on, but as long as they did their jobs properly that was all that mattered.

Like Paul. He was a ticket clipper. Oh, the bloke was sociable enough but not the type to have a laugh with. Sometimes you needed a laugh, he thought.

He drank some tea. He hoped everything would go

according to plan on Sunday. Christening in the afternoon, then back to the café for tea to celebrate. He smiled to himself. He'd heard some of the girls talking about the clothes they would wear. He was glad they wanted to look their best for his daughter's special day.

'So you're not opening on Sunday?'

Jack looked up and caught the bus driver's eye. He shook his head.

'You must be raking it in to be able to take a day off.'

Jack laughed. He didn't want to get into a heated discussion about why Sunday was to be special for his baby and his workers, despite the ferry takings being down. Until he'd sorted out why the money was trickling away, he'd have to keep his fears to himself. The trouble was, there weren't any discrepancies in the takings, not in the amount of ticket sales for the boat fares. Regine showed him the takings and tickets sold, which tallied. People just weren't travelling as much from the Gosport side. Mel, from Portsmouth, couldn't understand it: there were more passengers coming over to Gosport than ever before.

He shook his head. He was tired.

Madelaine had had a go at him last night because he'd gone to her parents' house to hand them the invitation to St John's Church and the do afterwards.

As soon as he'd knocked on the front door of the detached house in Alverstoke he knew he'd made a mistake.

'Not often we see you here.' Madeleine's father, who was ex-navy, was clearly unsure as to whether he should invite him in! Jack had seen the hesitation in his eyes, and if the rain hadn't decided to fall heavily at that moment, they would have conducted their business on the doorstep.

'We have a visitor, Ellen.'

Clearly Madelaine's mother expected anyone but him, because her smile froze when she saw him.

He gave them the invitation, said a few words and left.

There were no promises to 'see you on Sunday'.

Jack doubted Madeleine's father would attend the christening, although her mother might. All this hatred was because he had made their daughter pregnant. As he was Peg's father, that must be why they weren't interested in the little girl.

Of course, Madelaine had had to be married off, and quickly. An unmarried pregnant daughter would have sent her father's reputation tumbling.

Jack swallowed some more of his tea, then sighed. A moment of madness on the beach and look at him now, unwanted son-in-law and unwanted husband. The reason for their dislike? He wasn't good enough for Madelaine. They had insisted, after the immediate shock, on spending a small fortune on the wedding, and Thorngate Hall had been full of people Jack had never met before and never wanted to see again.

He was amazed that Madelaine had decided she wanted to live with him at his parents' house. Later, he worked out that there was usually a steady stream of babysitters present, so she was able to visit her parents unencumbered. He thought that, like him, they would have relished every moment they could spend with Peg, but apparently not. Perhaps he adored his child too much.

'I've brought you over some more tea. That must be stone cold by now.'

Connie's words made him smile.

'Thanks,' he said. His gaze automatically went towards the door as it opened and his smile widened as he saw Vee enter, bearing a flask, plate and cups.

He waved as she made to join the small queue that had formed at the counter.

'Give us them,' said Connie, going over and taking Vee's crockery. 'Sit down with the boss, cheer him up. I'll bring these back in a minute.'

*

The last thing Vee wanted was to sit down and talk to Jack.

The first night she had spent in Jack's house someone had been through her stuff. Now she knew without a doubt that that someone had been Regine. Funnily enough, she didn't blame the girl for seizing the moment but she hated her own stupidity in not getting rid of the documents. After all, she didn't need her old papers when she had the new forged ones, did she? Why, oh why hadn't she disposed of them?

After Regine's outburst Vee had merely stood staring at her, unable to speak, until at last she could no longer stand the torment. With Regine's cruel laughter burning her ears, she had picked up the empty cups and plates and walked out of the kiosk. She needed to think.

Of course she could say nothing of Regine selling unused tickets. How the unused tickets had come to be in Regine's possession she had no idea, but the girl now had a hold over her. Regine could tell Jack of Vee's parentage. Without a doubt Vee would be sacked and then what would she do? Jack would know she had lied to him by omission, and if there was one person she really wanted to be completely honest with, it was him.

So far the work had been hard but not unpleasant. Vee

had made a couple of friends. And Jack? There was definitely a softer side to him, which he didn't show to everyone, and she wanted to find out more.

Then Vee realized that Regine's threat cut both ways. If Regine told anyone of her Germanic parentage, Vee would point out that the girl was stealing from Jack. Regine's fraud was the reason that Jack's takings were down.

Throughout her life her mother had brought her up not to lie, not to steal, and to be a good person. Why, then, was she ignoring May's training? She felt tears reach her eyes and she had to work hard to blink them away. All these lies were for her own self-preservation. But they weren't making her happy, were they?

'I see Regine has you doing the tea run.'

Vee tried a smile, decided it worked, and sat down on the chair next to Jack. The wireless was playing music from *The Wizard of Oz*. When the film came to the local picture-house she would ask Rosie to go with her.

'Did you sleep well after all the bombing last night?' Without waiting for her to answer, Jack added, 'Gosport copped a few bombs. Not as bad as London – the news reckons four hundred people died last night. Bloody Germans.'

'I hope our boys gave as good as we got,' she said. Surely,

she thought, some German people must think like her and wish Hitler dead.

'Apparently we shot down nearly two hundred planes.'

'Such a waste of human life,' Vee said. He was looking at her strangely, but Connie was at the table again. Her flowery perfume reminded Vee of the scent her mother wore. A wave of homesickness overwhelmed her. 'A good cuppa works wonders, Connie.'

'Have you worked out the best way to sell tickets? Not hard, is it?' As usual, he looked tired, Vee thought. Was it because of the crying baby, or did Peg cry because she was woken by her parents arguing? Or was it the pressure of his work?

'No, it's simple,' she answered. All the while she was wondering how Regine was working the racket. And how she could stop her stealing from one of the best bosses Vee had ever worked for.

'If you've cracked the mystery of selling tickets, you can do something else tomorrow, Miss Smith.'

'I'd like that,' she replied. Though she wished he hadn't reminded her of her name. Smith, Schmidt – why did life have to be so complicated?

Jack put a hand across the table and rested it on her arm. A tingle akin to an electric shock ran through her.

'Regine isn't one of my favourite workers, but she gets the job done.' He looked down at the Formica table.

'She certainly does,' admitted Vee. And to her own advantage, she thought. But she kept her mouth closed.

'Here we are. Something to keep you going until it's time to knock off work.' Connie was hovering.

She slipped two clean mugs and a refilled flask on to the table, followed by two plates of cheese and onion sandwiches.

Vee's mouth watered. She hadn't eaten a decent piece of cheese for ages, certainly not since leaving home. Again she felt the tears rise. How could people be so nice to her when she was such an awful person?

'That's so kind of you, Connie,' she said in a small voice, as the older woman smiled at her, then left to return to the busy counter. On her way she picked up empty cups and plates to deliver to the kitchen.

'Tomorrow you can clip the tickets,' Jack said. 'How do you feel about that?'

'I don't mind what I do as long as I'm useful,' she said.

'If you weren't useful, you wouldn't be working for me.' He looked at his hand, which was still on her arm, and hastily moved it away, as though he had just noticed he was taking a liberty. 'Sorry,' he mumbled.

As the heat left her skin, Vee felt sad. She knew then she

would have to find a way to end Regine's thieving, even if it meant that Jack discovered her papers were forged. He was too nice a man to be taken for a fool. Vee didn't know how she was going to do it, but she would.

She was glad she hadn't lost her temper with Regine when the girl had blatantly admitted she was stealing ticket money. She would go back to her now and see what she could find out, without making her questioning too obvious. 'So,' she said softly, 'tomorrow I'll be outside again?'

Jack nodded. 'I gave you wet-weather gear?'

'You did, and a warm sweater,' Vee said.

She got up to leave the table, managing to carry everything.

She thought of the heavy black jacket and trousers. Until it actually rained, she decided, she would take the waterproofs but not wear the cumbersome things. It would be nice to see Mac again. That reminded her of something else: she hadn't given Connie anything towards the christening present. She put everything back on the table and, wishing Jack wasn't watching her every move, walked over to the counter, called for Connie and gave her the requisite amount for the gift, taking the money from her purse in her back pocket. Then, with the sandwich plates clutched to her once again, she went towards the Nissen hut's door.

'Wish everyone was as honest as you, Vee,' called Connie.

Vee felt even worse.

She was just about to open the door when Jack called, 'Vee, you've forgotten the flask.' He was coming towards her with a smile on his face.

Chapter Eighteen

Vee banged on the door of the kiosk with her elbow and Regine let her in.

'Thought I'd seen the last of you,' the girl sneered.

Vee set down the flask. 'Oh? Why's that, then?'

Regine ignored her to attend to a customer with a ticket from her handbag. Vee noted the girl really was surprised by her return. The glass jar near the till was practically full of pennies. Vee could see why Regine carried a large handbag: it held a multitude of things other women didn't carry with them.

Again the pennies dropped into the jar as the customer took the tickets offered.

Vee poured the tea. Regine was now watching her suspiciously. 'I'm not splitting the proceeds with you,' she snapped.

'Why would I want you to do that?' Vee shoved a sand-wich along the counter towards her. 'Just don't expect me to steal for you.' She began to eat. 'This cheese is delicious,' she said. Regine shot her a curious look as she took a bite.

'Are you going to the christening?' Vee moved Regine's tea towards her.

'I think most people have been invited.'

'What? Even the dark-haired bloke with a moustache who's always hanging around Jack's wife?'

'Hugh's an old friend of Madelaine's.'

'Very friendly, if you ask me.'

'Nobody did. Look, if you knew how difficult it was for that girl to settle in this dump after Alverstoke, you'd have a bit more sympathy for her.'

'That's just it, Regine. I can only judge what I've seen with my own eyes . . . '

'Jack's no angel . . .'

'I've heard the rows.'

'She came from money and has no idea how to look after a kid.'

'That's easy to see. She palms Peg off on anyone who'll have her.' There was silence. It was almost as if Regine was assessing the situation before she spoke again. In near silence she served several customers. Then she sat back on the stool. 'They had to get married, Jack and Madelaine. You know what they say, "Marry in haste, repent at leisure."'

'They must have loved each other or Peg wouldn't be here.'

Regine glared at her, then turned towards the ticket window. It was too late, though: Vee had noticed the hesitation, the drawn breath before Regine took the customer's money. There was more information to be had, but the moment had passed. Vee had got Regine talking but it was as if she had suddenly realized what was happening and the time for sharing had come to an end. More about Jack and Madelaine's marriage was ready to rise to the surface and Vee intended to find out what it was.

It was dusk when the customers thinned. Regine began counting the money in her jar. Then she changed it into more manageable notes and put them into her handbag.

Vee watched in silence as she counted the money in the wooden drawer of the till and marked it down in a cashbook that she put back beneath the counter. She also noted the number of tickets sold from the roll, making sure they matched with the money that was now in a blue bank bag. The roll of unused tickets in the bag, along with the money, was destined for Jack.

'It's six. Time for the next shift.' A knock on the door. Regine snapped, 'Bring our mugs and plates.'

Shoving herself past Vee, she checked it was the usual night girl, let her in and pushed Vee out into the fresh air.

'All right, Sal?' Regine greeted the girl.

'Oi! Are we gonna have to wait all night for our tickets?'

'Just changing staff,' shouted the girl, the door closing on her.

Vee was surprised by how cold it was. A wind had risen off the sea.

'I hate the autumn,' said Regine. 'I suppose tonight we'll be treated to more bombing. See you tomorrow?'

'No,' said Vee. 'Jack wants me somewhere else.'

Regine stopped walking and looked at her. 'Can't say I'm sorry,' she said. Then she grinned. 'Don't forget our little secret.'

Back in her room, Regine again counted the money she'd stolen. Soon she'd have enough to leave Gosport. She was fed up with living in this filthy place where drunks spilt out of the town's many pubs and spewed on the pavements.

She glanced at her bedside clock. Her own mother would now be propping up the bar in the Robin Hood at the end of Mayfield Road. That was where she spent her days and nights, cadging drinks from any feller who'd put his hand in his pocket for her.

She smoothed back her dark silky hair. Regine had thanked her lucky stars when Jack had offered her the job in the ticket office. It meant she never needed to return to the house in Old Road and no longer had to put up with the men who came into her bedroom when her drunken mother was asleep.

Sometimes, if she was lucky, one might stammer an apology that he'd opened the wrong door. Most times they'd hover over her, looking down at her, especially when she had been a child in a scrappy nightdress. Some had sat on the side of her bed wanting to 'talk' to her.

She'd taken to pulling the dressing-table in front of the door. Her mother had told her she was 'imagining things'. But the probing fingers and dirty hands had been real enough.

She'd been fourteen when she'd escaped. Got a job working as a barmaid in the Point of No Return in the high street. Her big breasts and curvy body made it easy to lie about her age, until she could no longer put off her boss, Mervyn: he had asked for her National Insurance card, which of course she couldn't produce as she was below the age of sixteen and thus shouldn't have been working.

She was sacked. She moved out of the pub and into a friend's house and began working in Woolworths, telling the same lie: 'Hasn't my previous employer sent my cards on yet?'

Spending her wages on going to the pictures, Regine fell in love with America.

She'd sit in the dark, smoky atmosphere watching the Hollywood sign, the mountains, the men in their flash suits, the cars. Even the water sprinklers and the brownstone houses of crowded New York fascinated her and she longed to be a part of that fabled land. It cost a lot of money to visit America, but Regine was determined that once she set foot on American soil she would never come back. She'd live in Hollywood, maybe get into pictures. To make her dream a reality she began to save her money.

She had never visited her mother since the day she'd walked out, and if she saw her in Gosport, she crossed the road to avoid her.

When Regine was sixteen and legally able to work, she met Paul who worked on the ferries. He was besotted with her. When Jack gave her the job in the ticket office it didn't take her long to come up with her plan. She managed to keep Paul sweet so he would collect clean tickets for her, which she then sold on. The funds in her post-office savings book were growing nicely. Paul didn't know he would be ditched as soon as she had enough money for her fresh start, and things had gone very nicely for her until Jack had realized they were losing money. It didn't make sense to him that Portsmouth was raking in higher profits than Gosport.

Regine studied her finely arched eyebrows in the dressing-table mirror. She knew she was pretty and she was going to make the most of her looks and figure. She would never end up like her mother, a slut living on men's handouts. She looked at the amount in her savings book. Tomorrow she could add more money to it. Her reflection smiled back at her.

In the bathroom, Vee finished cleaning her teeth and put her toothbrush back into the glass. The air was still hot and steamy. Five inches of water wasn't much to bathe in, but when it was scalding it seemed to wash away the cares of the day. She would finish drying her hair in her bedroom, pin it up, then put on her button-through dress before she went along to the Ferry Café for something to eat.

Maybe she could help out in the kitchen for a while before coming back for an early night. It wasn't part of her job and she certainly wouldn't be paid for her services, but what was the alternative? Go to bed with a book? Listen to the wireless? It really was too chilly to go out for a walk. Besides, the Germans sent bombers over practically nightly, so it wouldn't be long before she ended up in the shelter. Anyway, she rather liked the jolly atmosphere in the café.

Back in her room Vee knelt in front of the gas fire and shook out her hair. She had brought up the *Evening News*, and began to read.

She turned the page and there was a photograph of a fire in the high street. So many fires caused by the bombing. She was about to move on when she saw the name of the fish shop's owner, Karl Baum. The man was pressing two small children to his side. Apparently his wife had gone back into the burning shop to find the family dog. The newspaper said he had begged her not to go, but when his back was turned, unable to stand the little girl's fears for the dog, his wife had disappeared.

And so it goes on, Vee thought. Not a bomb blast, a mysterious fire. Her heart went out to the children. Not only had they lost their mother, but the two little girls were on the receiving end of the country's hatred of anything or anyone German. Again she berated herself for not destroying her original papers.

The brush flew through her now almost dry hair. Vee thought about Regine. If by some remarkable chance Sammy

Chesterton discovered her whereabouts, Regine wouldn't keep the bargain she had made. She would be the first to point the finger at Vee.

She decided she would telephone home before she went along to the café to eat. She needed to make sure her mother was safe. And tomorrow she would keep her eyes open: surely Regine had an accomplice. If she worked every day in the kiosk, how did she get hold of the unclipped tickets?

She nimbly plaited her hair and fastened the end with a piece of wool. Then she picked up the newspaper, intending to return it to the kitchen table for someone else to read. Her eyes lit on a short piece about 2,500 potentially dangerous aliens, interned in Britain, who would be taken to Canada and housed in camps.

So that was where men like Karl Baum would eventually end up, was it? It stood to reason that internment camps in Britain could hold only so many 'dangerous aliens': men like Karl Baum, who had worked in England for many years, raising a family, only to have their businesses burnt down in front of them because their names weren't right. A wave of disgust rose inside her.

One word from Regine about her parentage could mean her mother's smallholding being torched. She had to find out who else was involved in defrauding Jack, before

Regine grew bored with keeping the secret of Vee's false papers. She was about to get up when she decided to read the entire newspaper article about the aliens. It stated that those men had the chance of their status being reclassified as interned refugees, friendly aliens, with a view to being offered Canadian citizenship.

Was there light at the end of the tunnel?

Canada was trying to show the rest of the world that if you had the wrong name you didn't necessarily mean any harm to your chosen country.

How long would it be before England realized that making an Englishwoman take her husband's nationality on marriage was wrong? Vee's mother and father had married, believing that giving their child a name was the right thing to do, to show the world that Vee wasn't a bastard. Now, with a German name, Vee and her mother, like so many others, lived in fear of being classed as aliens.

She sighed. If it hadn't been for the war she wouldn't have needed the ration books and other documents that denied her true parentage. Well, one thing was for sure: she would destroy the original documents – now, tonight. Her ration book in the name of Smith was lined up neatly downstairs on the mantelpiece with all the others, ready for Connie to use when she was shopping.

So, dressed warmly, Vee decided she'd telephone her mother, get rid of the old documents, then eat in the café. She'd have a reasonably early night and her next job tomorrow as a ferry girl.

When she opened the drawer to take out her documents, they were gone.

Chapter Nineteen

Inside the church the air was filled with the smell of flowers that brightened the stark interior. Vee looked at the board on the stone pillar announcing the hymns to be sung and opened her hymnbook at the first. A rumble of thunder broke the relative silence. The weather forecast had promised a wet day.

St John's was Church of England, and although Vee had never been a regular churchgoer, her mother had made sure she adhered to the Commandments. Now, standing in the solemn peace of the beautiful old building, she knew she had broken at least one. Vee was mortified.

'That's Madelaine's mother.' Rosie nodded towards a woman in the front pew, who was alone, wearing a navy outfit and a white hat. Rosie's cheery voice had interrupted Vee's thoughts.

'No father?'

Rosie shook her head. 'She doesn't look like she wants to be here either, does she?'

'Sssh!' Connie looked very pretty in her grey woollen dress. She stood at the end of the aisle, ready to go forward when required: Jack had asked her to be a godmother to Peg. Vee knew she was both excited at being asked and terrified she would do something wrong. The other godmother was a woman Vee hadn't seen before.

'Who's she?' Vee now asked Rosie.

'That's Emily Cousins. Her husband, John, is a detective based at Gosport's South Street police station. John is going to be Peg's godfather. I saw him talking to Jack earlier. They've been mates since school.'

Vee liked the look of John. Tall, fair, and dressed in a dark suit, he had a commanding presence. He'd walked up the aisle and now stood next to Madelaine, who was in a pale blue costume with padded shoulders. She was carrying a navy handbag and it was Jack who held the sleeping child. Vee noticed a silver bangle on the child's chubby wrist.

'Look at Peg! She's wearing the bangle. And I've never seen Jack so smart,' she whispered. The required group was ready for the service to begin and Connie walked forward and joined them.

The vicar, in cassock and surplice, began to speak and the congregation quietened. And so the service began.

Vee was happy with the way her two friends had dressed her. The strawberry-coloured dress had required very little alteration and Connie had lent her a hat that had a pink flower on the band and was practically the same colour as her dress.

Jack looked over at her and smiled. Vee felt the familiar jolt of electricity pass through her as their eyes met. She didn't want to look away, but she did. It was Peg's big day and Jack was so handsome. Vee had a sudden vision of herself standing next to him as he gazed down at her with love in his eyes.

She apologized to God for the thought. Jack was a married man with a child. So many times lately Vee had ignored her mother's warnings about how she should behave that she was certainly not about to throw herself at Jack, no matter how she felt about him.

And how did she feel? She wanted to make him happy. She felt sure he had been miserable for a long time.

'They make a nice couple,' Rosie whispered. 'But look who's at the back of the church. Her fancy man, and he looks angry.'

Sure enough, Hugh was staring at Madelaine as though

he could have killed her. He swayed as he adjusted his hat, and Vee wondered if he had been drinking. She glanced at Madelaine, but her face gave nothing away.

The vicar was saying a prayer and had yet to touch Peg's head with the holy water.

The church was packed. Vee saw many of her fellow workers from the boats standing in the pews. That told of the loyalty Jack instilled in his workforce, she thought. There were many male faces she couldn't put names to and she guessed that even the Portsmouth watermen had come out of respect for him.

Vee followed Jack's gaze, which rested on Hugh. Something inside her told Vee that the man hadn't been invited. Jack's face was as black as the thunder roaring overhead. Thunder that wasn't anything to do with the inclement weather, but was the dull, heavy noise of enemy planes.

The congregation, white-faced and shuffling in their pews, were definitely uneasy.

'I baptize this child Margaret Eleanor—'

'Saunders!' shouted Hugh from the rear of the church, just as the water trickled over the unsuspecting baby's forehead. His voice had drowned Jack's surname. 'She's my child, not yours!'

Gasps rose. Hugh was pushing past the guests, his hat

askew, and Vee saw that he was unsteady on his feet. He stumbled, swore, and she realized he was indeed drunk. As he reached the aisle he fell.

'No, Hugh, not now!' shouted Madelaine. She left Jack and ran towards him. Jack clutched Peg so tightly that either that or the shock of the wetness on her forehead caused her to cry out just as the siren announced a raid.

Even through its wail, Jack's voice could be heard: 'You bastard! I'll kill you!'

'Please leave the church in an orderly manner,' advised the vicar. His voice was brittle yet as calm as possible under the circumstances and his hand went to Jack to still him.

Madelaine was now pushing her way back through the tide of people eager to leave the church for the safety of a shelter. 'You go if you want. My daughter stays with me.' Vee heard the coldness in Jack's voice, which, despite the noise, was loud enough for everyone to hear. From the back of the church Hugh, trying to rise, was knocked off his feet again by the crowd of people heeding the siren's call to get to safety.

'C'mon,' said Rosie, tugging at Vee's arm. 'It's starting again.'

And then the first bomb fell.

Vee fell to her knees, pulling Rosie down with her beneath

the pew. The church shook and slivers of plaster and dust rained down from the exposed beams. Ornaments and sconces fell from the whitewashed walls. Brightly polished brasses tumbled from the long table below the stained-glass window depicting the Crucifixion.

A second crash, this time even closer, caused the roof trusses to move.

'We must get out of here,' yelled Rosie. All around them people were rushing towards the rear of the church, where there was a crush of bodies trying to escape.

Grabbing Rosie's hand, Vee moved along the pew and escaped into the side aisle.

Smoke was making it difficult to see inside the already dim interior, but it wasn't so dark that Vee didn't see Madelaine move back towards Hugh, who was miraculously already at the exit.

It was then Rosie shouted, 'Connie's hurt!'

Jack looked as though he was in difficulties. He was holding the crying child, yet trying to drag Connie away from the pulpit, part of which had split and toppled from its elevated plinth. It now lay across Connie and blood was coming from her shoulder and neck.

'Come with me!' shouted Vee, dodging around the front row of pews. She dropped Rosie's hand to take the baby from Jack. At first he was reluctant to let Peg go, until Vee shouted, 'Help Connie,' and grabbed the child. Then Jack heaved the pulpit off Connie and dragged her clear just as the stained-glass window caved in.

Glass fell like a multi-coloured hailstorm. The strange creaking noises that Vee could hear were of the lead breaking away from the ages-old glass, as fire raged from a burning room behind the altar.

Vee moved as quickly as she could up the side aisle, seeing people lying on the floor with blood oozing from cuts. She wanted to help but her first responsibility was to the now crying baby in her arms.

Rosie was holding Connie's good hand. Connie's other arm hung loosely over Jack's shoulder, bumping against his back. The church was filled with smoke that stung Vee's throat and eyes. She had pulled Peg's long dress up and over her head, partly for protection from the smoking wooden slivers dropping from the rafters and partly to keep the child breathing freely, for acrid smoke now filled the holy building. She reached the open doorway and, gasping, almost fell outside on to the wet pavement and into Emily Cousins's arms.

'Thank God the baby's safe.' The young woman led Vee across the road and into the Queen Charlotte pub.

Vee was suddenly enveloped in the warmth of the bar and was led to a chair. She sank on to it gratefully.

Aircraft screamed overhead. Vee hugged Peg to her breast and was instantly comforted by the feeling of safety that surrounded her.

'So near, yet so far,' said Emily. 'Give Peg to me.'

Reluctantly Vee handed her to Emily and was rewarded with a mug of tea thrust into her hands by John Cousins. 'Thank God so many of the congregation's accounted for.'

'Where's Peg's mother?' For some reason she couldn't utter the woman's name.

Bits of white dust clung to John's Brylcreemed hair and thick eyebrows. He put a hand to her shoulder. 'She got out all right.'

'Put some music on,' came a disembodied voice. A moment later the noise of the enemy aircraft was diluted by big-band sounds.

Vee felt the strength returning to her brain and body. She moved her feet and arms, realizing she was still in one piece and thankful for it. 'Where's Connie?'

Emily said, 'She looked worse than she was. We're lucky that one of the pub's regulars is a doctor, so he's sorting her out now.'

Vee glanced around the bar and saw Mac with a small

plump girl. His intended, she thought. Regine was near the bar with Paul.

'Shouldn't we be in a shelter?'

John waved her question away. 'Andersons and Morrisons are fine, and so are the communal ones if they're near enough, but a lot of people take their chance and stay just where they are. We're better in here than out there. Remember, lightning doesn't strike the same place twice.' He gave a smile that made it easy to see how he had won a pretty wife like Emily. 'Who'd have thought a pub would be safer than a church?'

His answer lightened Vee's heart. She finished her tea. Through the curtained window she could see the church, flames leaping from its rear where the altar was. Rain was pelting across the sky and for once Vee blessed it. She couldn't see Jack and didn't want to ask where he was, even though she longed to know. She peered around the pub again, and then she saw him.

He was sitting near the fire with his head in his hands and appeared to be in a world of his own.

John said, 'If you want to go and talk to him, I'll come along, but I wouldn't advise it. He loves that kiddie. To find out she's not his, on what should have been one of his happiest days, is not good. Not good at all.'

Somehow it didn't seem wrong to be talking to John about Jack and his marriage. John was his friend, after all.

'Did he know about that man and Madelaine?'

'He had his suspicions. Not about his child, though, I'm sure.'

'I can't just sit here while he's in pain.'

'Well, don't worry about Peg. She's in safe hands with my Emily.'

Vee stood up. She wove her way between tables and chairs to stand in front of Jack, who looked up at her. His eyes were red-rimmed.

'I saw you with Peg,' he said. 'I don't know how to thank . . . I couldn't bear it if you've come to gloat . . .' His words tailed off.

'I'm not gloating and neither is anyone else. You should know people aren't good at saying how they feel about things that don't concern them.'

'I'm a laughing stock . . .'

'You're sitting here on your own repelling people, daring them to come and talk. Don't you think you ought to take a deep breath and show these good people what you're made of?'

'What d'you mean?'

'You won't be the first man whose wife has pretended a

kiddie belongs to him when it doesn't. There's going to be a few men coming home from the war to find out their dates of leave don't coincide with a child's conception. Are you going to take it out on Peg?'

'No! Don't be stupid!'

'Steady,' said John. 'Vee's only trying to make you see a bit of sense.'

She put out a hand and laid it on his arm. 'Peg is still the child she was first thing this morning. You're the one loving her, getting up to see to her at night . . .'

His eyes were boring into hers.

For the first time, she noticed his jacket was missing a sleeve and his arm was scratched. There was also a cut on his chin.

'You're right! If that streak of piss thinks he's going to step in and take her he's got another think coming.'

'That's it,' said John. 'Possession is nine-tenths of the law. Peg's here with you, as she should be. Make sure it stays that way.'

Just then Emily came over with Peg in her arms. 'This little tinker has made a right mess of her nappy. Don't suppose there's a bag anywhere with her clean stuff in?'

Just then another bomb fell close by, and the bar shuddered. The noise from outside killed the chatter, and glasses shattered as they slid from the tables.

'That's another too close for comfort.' John, Emily, Jack and Vee crouched on the floor. Jack put out his arms and Emily handed over Peg.

'She stinks.' Vee wrinkled her nose.

Jack looked down at the baby. 'Let's ask the manager's wife if she's got a spare towel to clean you up, shall we?'

Emily smiled at Vee, who grinned back at her. He might not have been the child's biological father, if what Hugh had shouted was correct, but Jack wasn't about to let his daughter go without a struggle.

Emily said, 'I've already asked her to make up a bottle of orange or something and luckily she's got some of her grandson's baby stuff here.'

'Well done,' said John. 'Look, mate,' he turned to Jack, 'Madelaine and her fancy man aren't here in the pub. I've done a head count. Most of the christening guests are accounted for . . . One way and another—'

'Casualties?' Jack broke in. Vee watched as Emily made her way to the bar where the landlady was filling small glasses with whisky tots. She left what she was doing and went out the back through a curtain at the rear of the bar.

'Your Connie's shoulder looks worse than it is.' John gave a knowing smile. 'Poor woman fainted when the doc shoved the dislocation back.' Vee winced. 'Panic causes lots of problems.'

Jack whispered, 'It's over now between me and Madelaine, John.' He gave an enormous sigh. 'I've tried for a long time to get things on an even keel between us, but now I know it would never have worked out. I've had my suspicions for a long time. I think she had that Hugh at my house. I've often smelt hair cream on the pillows . . .'

'Stop it!' John shook a finger at Jack. 'What's the point in torturing yourself?'

Just then Emily returned and Vee saw she had managed to carry four glasses of whisky, a nappy and a baby's bottle of warm milk.

'Well done, lass,' said John, taking the glasses from her and handing them round. 'Let's drink to a new beginning.'

'I'll second that,' said Jack, leaving his empty glass on a table while he fed Peg.

Chapter Twenty

May dropped the corner of the curtain. She had been spying on the car parked in the layby opposite her cottage.

'I'm going out to ask him what he's up to,' she said to Jem. There was determination in her voice.

'Do you really think that's a good idea?' He folded the *Evening News* and put it down on the small table. The saucepans on the stove were bubbling. On the scrubbed dinner table was a freshly baked pie, made with vegetables and no meat, the crust a glorious golden brown.

'I can't go on wondering what he's hoping to achieve by sitting out there, can I?'

'I'm here to look after you,' Jem said gruffly.

'I know that.' May went over to him and put her hand on his shoulder. 'But I have to ask him what he wants.'

She heard Jem sigh. 'You want me to come?'

'Keep an eye on the dinner. I'll be all right.'

Collecting her coat from the hooks near the door, May went out into the sharp air of the early evening. In a little while it would be dark. Since Vee had left, the summer had disappeared. May wondered if her daughter would ever come home again.

As she neared the car he started up the engine. May banged on the window. Up close he was just an ordinary man, good-looking in an over-the-hill way but nevertheless just a man, and May decided she wasn't scared of him, no matter what Jem or the newspapers implied.

'Stop the car,' she demanded. Amazingly, after looking at her closely, he did. 'I'd like you to come inside. It's too cold to talk out here.' Then she turned and walked back across the road, her heart drumming, giving him time to follow.

She heard the sound of the car door opening, then closing, and pretty soon he caught her up. In silence they walked towards the house together. May thought of the man's villainous reputation. Perhaps she was being extremely silly, inviting him into her home. Suppose he turned on her, hurt her? She swept those thoughts away. Jem was in the house, perhaps deflated that she hadn't allowed him to accompany her, but no doubt he was watching every step she was taking.

'Come on in.' She pushed open the oak door and stepped

into the warmth of the kitchen. Sammy Chesterton followed. 'Hang your coat up there.' She waved towards the pegs where she was draping her coat. So far he hadn't spoken a word.

May went over to the stove, checked the vegetables and, after replacing the lids, said, 'We're just about to eat. Would you like to join us?' He looked about the room and nodded at Jem, who returned the greeting but didn't speak.

A soft miaow made her look down. One of the kittens, a kitten no longer, was at her feet. May quickly scooped a potato from the pan on the stove, mashed it with meaty-smelling thick gravy in a saucer and set it down where the cats' water bowl was. The little cat began lapping, quickly joined by her mother. May smiled again.

She turned, saw the surprise on Sammy's face and almost burst out laughing.

'You don't like cats?' She didn't give him time to answer. 'I do know you're keeping an eye on me. If it's in case my daughter comes back . . .'

'I – I—'

'It's all right,' May said. She walked towards the table, moved a place setting further along, then took out cutlery and proceeded to lay a place for him. 'The only way to sort this is to talk things through, and that won't happen with you sitting in the layby, will it?'

Jem rose from the comfortable chair and pulled out a kitchen chair for him. 'Better do as she wants, mate. She can be a Tartar if you cross her.' Jem, May knew, understood that she needed to get to the bottom of things so he was willing to do whatever she wanted to help her.

May moved the pie to the centre of the table.

'No meat, I'm afraid, and I don't want to kill another of my chickens. It's Polly's turn for the pot, but I've had her since a chick and she'll be a bit stringy now. Besides, I'd rather see her scrabbling about in the yard.'

Sammy sank down on to the chair, still with the look of surprise on his face.

May drained the vegetables and Jem set the dishes on the table when she'd filled them.

She knew the smell of the cooked dinner was enticing, especially the gravy that Jem put in the centre of the table. It was in the white gravy boat her mother had used.

The three of them sat, food steaming, and May said, 'I'm not waiting on anyone. Serve yourselves.'

Jem spooned potatoes on to his plate.

Sammy Chesterton looked up as May said, 'I know my daughter stole from you but she's been sending me money. I've been able to make up the shortfall and after dinner I'll give it to you. It's almost the original sum you asked for, before you decided to get her to spend a couple of nights with you in a hotel.'

Jem coughed and Sammy went bright red.

May was suddenly aware he wasn't used to women saying exactly what they thought. She shrugged. She'd been her own boss too long to mince words.

'There's no point in beating about the bush. That's why you've been keeping an eye on my house, isn't it? Take some of the sprouts. They're the first of the season and so sweet.' She pushed the dish towards him. 'For goodness' sake, don't be scared to dig into the pie.' Jem passed it to him.

'Didn't you ever wonder why my Vee kept to the menial jobs instead of dancing about half naked?'

Jem looked at her pleadingly. 'May—'

She interrupted him and went on: 'Vee's not been with a man. Not in the biblical sense. What you wanted of her went against everything she's been brought up to believe is right.'

Sammy said quickly, 'Yet she stole from me. Asking me to provide false documents is a crime.'

She stared at him. 'But don't you agree that what's happening here to people whose only crime is to have the wrong name is worse?' He stared at her. She could see in his eyes that he agreed. 'Eat up,' she said. 'Your food'll get cold.'

Amazingly, Sammy put a forkful into his mouth. May

watched as he closed his eyes and chewed. She guessed he didn't eat too many home-cooked meals. Of course she was aware he sold overpriced meals in his club, but she was willing to bet they weren't cooked half as well as this.

'Look, Bertie . . .'

Jem put down his knife and stared at Sammy, who had gone as white as a sheet.

'Bertie?' He echoed May's voice.

'Jem.' She turned to him. His mouth was hanging open. Quickly she leant across and touched his chin. He closed his mouth but still stared at her. 'This man used to be one of my greatest friends. He was very young at the time and his name, Herbert Lang, means he's also of German lineage. Just like I am now. At school it didn't matter a jot, did it? Or if it did, we weren't aware of it.'

'If I'd known Vee was your daughter I would never have suggested . . .' Sammy was blustering.

'Of course not. And, for the same reason you've put your original name behind you, Vee wanted to protect me.'

She could see Sammy wasn't sure what to say next, so she said kindly, 'Eat up, the pair of you. There's apple crumble for afters.'

To May Sammy seemed relieved that everything was out in the open. Jem nodded at her. His plate was almost empty and he gave a big sigh of contentment. She knew later she'd have to explain how it had suddenly dawned on her why the man sitting in his car in the layby looked familiar. And also that because he knew who she was and obviously still cared about that long-ago friendship, his threats to her daughter had remained just that, threats that hadn't been fulfilled.

Sammy pushed his empty plate away. 'Thank you, May. That was one of the best meals I've had in a while. I don't have to ask how you are after all these years. I can see. I've listened to everything you've said and I agree wholeheartedly, but I've a position to keep up. Vee stole from me. I've been laughed at because I've not done anything about it. Accepting payment in cash is all right but it's not enough. Of course, you can do something to help.' He looked at her expectantly. 'It isn't in my own interests to give out that I'm part German, and there's an awful lot of us about, May. More than you'd think. Germans who love England and have to lie to live here. Suppose I make you pay, because Vee did what she did partly for you? In a small way and only if you agree.'

'I'm not coming away with you for a weekend in the New Forest!' May laughed. 'You were always my friend, not a lad I fancied.'

'That's not what I had in mind.' He grinned at Jem.

'Though you're a fine woman, May.' He made a face at Jem to dissipate the man's sudden jealousy and show he meant no harm. 'Would you give me a box of fresh vegetables every week? I'll collect them. Even pay for them, if you want. The meals in my Southampton club would certainly improve . . .'

'I can do that,' May said. She'd digested his strange request. After all, wasn't it fair she should help her daughter pay for the forged papers? Vee had been thinking not just of herself but of them both. 'You'd have to take pot luck, though. I send to market weekly, but this time of year it's mainly greens. It's too late for salad stuff and fruit.'

'That would be fine. Are you all right with that, Jem?'

Jem nodded. 'It seems little enough . . .'

'When people see how the problem's been resolved they'll either think I'm an idiot or that I'm a good man for forgiving my childhood friend. Either is fine by me.'

'Do people have to know May's business?' Jem asked.

'Things have a nasty habit of coming out. Gossip is, a girl employee stole from me. How, what, isn't public knowledge. Nor need it be. If I personally collect on a Friday afternoon or early evening, can I invite myself to a meal again?'

'It'd be nice to chat over old times,' said May.

'I could bring a bottle of whisky, Jem.'

'That'd be all right, I guess,' Jem said.

May glanced at Jem. She saw that he, too, had realized the man was lonely. For May to invite him for a meal was a small price to pay for Vee stealing from him. 'Good. Glad that's settled. Bertie, you're welcome to my home any time.' May got up and walked over to the stove. She picked up a home-made oven glove. She'd been right all along, she thought. The big man wasn't so big after all, but he was in need of friends. Money doesn't make for happiness and if she could spend a little time every week talking over how their lives had changed since childhood, it might not be such a bad thing. She smiled at Jem but he was grinning at Sammy. They were two men cut from the same cloth, she thought.

She'd certainly have a lot to tell Vee when she next phoned.

'Anyone for apple crumble?' May asked.

Chapter Twenty-one

'I suppose she'll be able to say she was the last child christened in St John's Church before it was bombed.'

An uneasy breakfast was taking place in the kitchen at Jack's house. Both Vee and Emily glared at Rosie.

'Bad taste?'

'Extremely, Rosie,' said Emily. She and John had stayed the night. When Madelaine had failed to come home, Emily hadn't wanted to leave Peg, and John had had a few drinks with Jack, sitting in the darkened kitchen until they'd fallen asleep. Both men had now left for work, slightly the worse for wear.

'Wonder where Madelaine spent the night?' Rosie mused.

Vee had slept fitfully. 'Where d'you think?' she said.

'Who are you talking about?' The click-clack of heels announced Regine, already made up with bright lipstick and her hair just so. She went to the teapot, pulled up the cosy and felt the side. Vee watched her take a cup from the dresser and pour herself some tea.

'Madelaine didn't come home,' Emily said.

'Why would she? It's all out in the open now about her and Hugh, so you don't have to be a genius to know she'd be with him,' Regine said. She examined her red nails.

'Did Jack ever suspect . . .?'

'Shut up, Rosie,' said Emily.

Vee had heard Emily offer to take care of Peg until Jack made other plans, or Peg's mother came home.

Connie, who liked to have the little one in her carrycot in the café with her, had offered but couldn't yet use her arm properly. Her shoulder still hurt after the dislocation. Vee, too, had offered but Jack had told her he still wanted her to shadow Paul with ticket-punching, for today at any rate. 'I didn't hire you as a babyminder!'

Knowing he was under a great deal of strain, she'd held her tongue. She wondered if she should confess to walking in on Madelaine and Hugh that day but decided against it. That would be like throwing fat on the fire.

'According to John, Jack had guessed he wasn't the love of Madelaine's life, but he always hoped the affair would blow itself out,' Emily said, folding Peg's white cotton night-dresses that she'd draped over the fender to air overnight.

Regine said loftily, 'I don't want to speak out of turn but it nearly broke Madelaine's heart when Hugh married.'

Vee and Emily stood transfixed.

Happy she had their attention, Regine carried on: 'Hugh is married with two little girls. His wife has money. He strings Madelaine along with lie after lie. He'd leave his wife when the children were older, so he said. Madelaine married Jack to give a name to Hugh's baby. She thought she could get away with it, still see Hugh.

'Until yesterday, Hugh had never acknowledged the poor little mite in there.'

Rosie tutted.

'The reason it came out yesterday, like it did, was because Madelaine was going to tell Judith – that's Hugh's wife – everything unless he owned up to fathering her baby. She knew there'd be a rumpus but thought she'd get her man. Hugh likes money too much though, and the status it gives him, if you ask me. At times I felt so sorry for Madelaine.'

'Don't see why,' Vee said. 'I don't think she's a nice person. She doesn't care a jot about Peg.' She put down the slice of toast she was eating.

'She couldn't help falling in love with Hugh. She told me she met him at a party when she was very young. He turned her head.' Regine was relishing being the centre of attention.

'So she married Jack, believing him to be the best bet moneywise if she couldn't have Hugh? That's awful.' Vee looked at her plate. She'd lost her appetite.

Regine said, 'She couldn't be an unmarried mother, could she?'

'That's still a dirty trick,' said Vee. 'Jack loves that kiddie.'

'Welcome to the big world, little girl,' said Regine.

Vee glared at her. 'And so he could still have Madelaine, Hugh shouts out to all and sundry, telling Jack that Peg belongs to him?'

'I suppose he was hoping it wouldn't get back to his wife. After all, none of his posh set was at the church.'

'Except Madelaine's mother. I mean, it was a foregone conclusion her father wouldn't attend the christening. He thinks Jack's common. I expect Hugh was surprised to see her mother in the church.'

Vee put her head in her hands. 'Maybe he didn't notice she was there. Poor Jack. What a terrible business.'

'It'll be worse if we don't get to work,' Rosie said. 'And it's raining, so you'll need wet-weather gear.'

Vee groaned.

'I'm going to be here all day with Peg if anyone feels like coming and sharing a cuppa with me—' said Emily.

'So you're not working with me today?' Regine broke in, glaring at Vee. 'You won't need wet-weather gear in the ticket office.'

'No, I'm not.' Vee shook her head.

'See you all later, then.' Regine pulled her mackintosh from the back of the chair and Vee watched her walk down the hallway towards the front door, her high heels clattering on the hard surface.

'I'm off as well,' said Rosie. As she passed Vee, she said, 'If I was you I'd stay away from Regine. She's trouble. Think about it. She's just been saying awful things about Madelaine, yet she's supposed to be her friend.'

'Thanks for the tip,' said Vee.

'I expect you're beginning to feel as though you've landed in a nest of vipers,' said Emily. She looked at her wristwatch. 'You've time for another cup of tea?'

It was quiet in the warm kitchen now that the others had gone and Vee had about fifteen minutes before she needed to get to the ferry for the first boat of the day. She watched Emily top up the pot.

'He thinks a lot of you, you know,' Emily said.

'Who?'

'Jack.'

Vee stared at her. 'Did he say so?' Her heart had begun to thump alarmingly.

'Not to me, but he told John.'

'Oh, well, I like him too, but he's got a lot of problems and I'm not sure I'm strong enough to take them on as well.'

'If you care enough, you can.' Emily stirred the pot, then poured the tea. 'I've known Jack a long time. Madelaine has shaken his faith in women. He feels he can't trust us.'

'We're not all like his wife.' Vee thought about Emily's words. It would be wonderful if Jack did think of her as more than an employee. She could understand that he would need to take his time before he could love again.

'If you want him, Vee, you'll have to show him he can trust you. And it's not going to happen overnight. How about Peg? Are you willing to take her on as well?'

'Peg's a lovely little kid. It's about time she was shown some decent mothering.'

'I'm glad you think like that, because Jack won't give her up. They come as a pair.'

'But at the moment there's three of them. Jack's married to Madelaine. If he left her, I'd go with him like a shot. But he wouldn't do that. It's not in his nature, is it?' She was hoping Emily would say otherwise. When she didn't,

Vee saw that the situation was hopeless. She couldn't get involved in a divorce. The scandal would open up her own life to examination. She hadn't told Jack the truth about her parentage. Besides, how could she bring such shame on her mother?

'Anyway, apart from being friendly, giving me a job when I needed one and a place to stay, he's not shown the slightest interest in me . . .'

'Would you prefer a married man to be all over you? Would you think much of him if he sailed quite happily from his wife to you?'

'Of course not!' She'd heard the old saying that 'if a married man strays from his wife to you, he won't hesitate to stray to someone else'. Jack wasn't like that.

'Well, perhaps I'm speaking out of turn, but I'm telling you what my husband thinks.' She laughed. 'And my John doesn't mince his words. As I've already said, they've known each other for years.'

The clock on the mantelpiece chimed a quarter past the hour and Vee pushed her cup aside. 'I'd better get going,' she said. Outside the rain was hitting the windows with force.

She hauled on the heavy wet-weather trousers over her grey slacks and stuck her arms into the shiny black coat.

'Smells all new and funny,' she said, grabbing the sou'wester and stuffing it into her pocket with her purse.

'If Peg was older you'd probably frighten the life out of her dressed like that,' Emily observed.

At that the baby's cry shattered the relative peace of the early morning.

Vee called, 'Good morning little girl!' into the room where Peg was, opened the front door, grinned over her shoulder at Emily, and then she was gone, running past the car ferry.

She saw Ada walking up from the boats clutching her bag.

Since their first meeting she'd had several cups of tea with the girl, who was older than Vee had first thought. It had been hard persuading her to take gifts of warm clothing, the skirts Vee had no use for now that slacks were her more usual form of workwear. Harder still for her to accept food and sometimes money. She didn't ask Ada how she was surviving, but she was definitely in better shape now than when Vee had first met her.

Vee's forged papers enabled her to work, but Ada wasn't so lucky. She waved and Ada waved back.

Vee ran past the queue of people buying the first ferry tickets of the day and down to the wire mesh gates that separated the boat from the pontoon. She could feel Jack's eyes on her, so she looked up through the rain that was coming down like spears and waved. His face split into a grin and he raised his hand in welcome from the open wheelhouse.

Moving through the sea of people, with their early-morning smells of perfume, soap and sleep, she took her place next to Paul. The purring of the ferry's engine as the boat bobbed against the jetty and the smell from the funnel made the boat a haven for those passengers who could find a place in the downstairs cabin. Those who couldn't would make for the funnel, to stand around its warmth. Though the smell of her new waterproofs wasn't good, at least Vee was dry. Except for her feet. The rain had run down the shiny surface of her coat and trousers to puddle in her shoes.

Paul grinned at her with large white teeth. His hand went to his pocket and he pulled out a pair of clippers.

'You do the people your side and I'll do this. Just one punch. If you make a mistake and clip twice, the ticket will be invalid for the return journey.'

She nodded. The clippers were heavy, a bit unwieldy, but she'd soon get used to them. They were like a pair of scissors that, instead of cutting, made a hole.

The piercing whistle blew from the Portsmouth side, there

was a sudden lull in the noise of chattering people and Mac pulled back the heavy gate. He gave her a huge wink, then went towards the rope, ready to unwind it from the bollard. The people surged forward, tickets in their hands.

Chapter Twenty-two

May poured the strong tea into two cups. She decided to leave Jem out because, with his long legs sprawled in front of him, his hands over his stomach, she thought he'd rather continue sleeping than be woken to drink another cup of tea.

There had been a moment earlier in the evening when she'd thought the two men might come to blows.

'So you think it's all right to force a girl to go to bed with you in payment for something you've done for her?' Jem had asked Sammy.

May wished he'd leave the subject alone, but sometimes he was like a dog with a bone.

'In my line of business the women sometimes see that as the only possible form of payment.'

She had seen Jem bristle with indignation. But her glare

had been enough for him to drop the subject. They were, after all, different men from different backgrounds.

She was happy with the way things had gone tonight. Both men lounging in the armchairs in front of the fire looked contented. She'd fed them well. Damn the war and the lack of food, she'd made a tasty meal they'd all enjoyed – it was certainly true that the way to a man's heart was through his stomach. She'd achieved deliverance for Vee from Sammy Chesterton's wrath by agreeing to provide vegetables for the foreseeable future to be collected each Friday. She smiled to herself. It was a fair bargain. Of course he'd kept the money Vee had sent. He was a businessman, after all. And Friday evenings had become something to look forward to. Especially tonight, when Sammy had arrived with a huge joint of beef!

Actually these evenings were more than a fair trade. It was a ridiculous way to settle things, and if the poor man hadn't had such a crush on her when she was a girl, it would never have worked so well to her advantage. Sammy Chesterton, alias Herbert Lang, might have travelled the world, and now owned clubs that made him money, but he needed a family, and May was quite happy to include him in hers.

Nevertheless she had seen the way he looked at her sometimes. She certainly wasn't in the first flush of youth, but she believed the word that best described her might be 'comely'. She had no intention of his visits ever amounting to anything. If – when – she decided she wanted to settle with a man, he would be Jem. That was how she felt now, and the future could look after itself.

'So you married him?'

May looked at Sammy, for it was he who had spoken, bringing her out of her reverie.

'The German?' he prodded.

'I did,' said May. 'As soon as I announced I was pregnant, Gus, with the aid of my friend Annie, worked out a way we could marry.'

'Surely that presented problems?'

'Actually, it didn't. Finding clothes for Gus did!'

Jem's eyes were closed and she could see his chest rising and falling with the even breaths that signified he was deeply asleep. He'd arrived at five that morning and was cleaning out the chicken run when she'd stepped outside with a mug of tea for him. She smiled fondly.

'You have to explain yourself,' Sammy said..

'When I discovered I was pregnant I had no idea how I'd be able to tell my parents without an almighty row, which would be even worse because Gus worked here.'

May told him how she and Gus had met and fallen in love.

'No doubt your father would have been extremely hurt at what he would have seen as your betrayal.'

'He hadn't wanted me to leave this place, and when I did, I'd got myself pregnant. I felt as though I'd let my dad down, but I just wanted to be with Gus every moment I could, so I didn't think about anything else.'

'Surely he couldn't simply say to the authorities at the hospital that he wanted to marry you and they'd let him.'

May frowned. 'Of course not. I discovered where Southampton register office was and found I needed to present documentation in the form of birth certificates and passports, before they would give me a diary date for three weeks hence. They were wonderfully helpful, maybe because there was a war on. Gus had no papers. Actually, that wasn't true. He had a wallet that had survived his plane crash. But his identification had been taken from him and was now locked in an office at the hospital, where all identity papers that survived their owners' demise or hospital stay were kept.

'Annie had access to this room. She made Gus promise to allow her to return his passport to his wallet if she borrowed it for the registrar.

'In due course, along with my birth certificate, I had a single paper sheet folded in eight with a cardboard cover – Gus's details and his photograph. The passport was charred but legible and amazingly presented no problems at Southampton's register office.

'It was decided Gus would come to the smallholding as usual and we would go on the bus to Southampton. Everything went according to plan, except for the distinctive hospital clothes Gus was forced to wear. He could move about fairly freely as long as he wasn't late for curfew. The prison authorities had begun to trust him. At the small-holding he was under the jurisdiction of my father. As long as Dad thought Gus was working there wasn't a problem.

'I begged a few hours off and met Gus with some of my father's clothing.' May began to laugh. 'My dad's trousers were very short in the leg even though Gus pulled the turn-ups down. But we had to ignore all that. I had on the ankle-length dress I had worn at the village carnival. It was made of white lace, you see, and still fitted me. Annie made me a coronet of flowers and I felt beautiful. At least I wasn't going to become an unmarried mother and heap further shame on my family. We had discussed the future. Gus was determined to marry me and I decided that being wed to a German was infinitely better than becoming an unmarried mother. How naive we were.'

May got up, went to the corner cupboard and took out a shoebox. She flicked through a Bible. Nestling inside was a faded white rose, which, even though it was flattened, was still strangely beautiful.

'I had two white roses,' she said. 'Gus kept one. I don't know what happened to his, though.' She couldn't help herself, and a tear rolled down her cheek.

For a while she stood with the faded flower in her fingers. Then Sammy took it from her, put it back in the Bible and replaced it in the box.

'Surely you couldn't live together, you and Gus.'

May shook her head. She seemed more composed now. 'No. I was surprised that everything in Southampton had gone without a hitch. Lots of young couples were getting married – it was the war, you see. Neither of us needed permission as we were over the age of consent. It was all so easy.'

'I would have thought, being away from Netley, Gus would have made a run for it.'

'You don't know how it was between us. He wanted us to be together. Besides, where would we have gone? Our situation at that time was the best one for us to be in, with him having relative freedom and me as his wife. He hadn't shamed me by giving me a child out of wedlock.

'When we got back here, Gus had to get on with his work. Bruno and Manfred had covered for him while he was away. My friend Annie returned Gus's passport. She'd wanted to come with us but it wasn't possible so we called in two people off the street as witnesses. I managed to replace my dad's clothes and went back to work at Netley Hospital. It became like any other day, except that I had a marriage certificate, proof I was married to the man I loved.'

He nodded.

'It wasn't the wedding my parents wanted for me, I knew that, but I was selfish in those days. I also knew that as soon as the baby began to show the whole story would come out, not to all and sundry but certainly to my parents.'

'But Gus's part in it was deceitful, as was yours . . .' Sammy finished his tea.

The sound of the cup being replaced on the saucer must have woken Jem, for he yawned, stretched, and gave May a sleepy smile. She nodded towards the teapot and he mouthed, 'Yes.'

'We were in love, it was wartime, and if I'd suggested to Gus that we fly to the moon he would have done it to make me happy. He wanted to be my husband for the child's sake. I got my comeuppance later.'

'We've all done things in the past that have hurt other people,' said Sammy. 'Does Vee know all this?'

'You're very inquisitive,' said Jem.

'It's a very unusual story,' said Sammy.

May nodded. 'Quite so. I think because I acted in such an outrageous way I wanted something better for Vee. We don't have secrets, not ones that really matter, and I've tried so hard to bring her up knowing right from wrong. That moment when she stole from you was out of character, but I was the one who persuaded her to run away.' She had taken the lid off the teapot. 'This is stewed. I'll make some more.' Then she bit her lip. 'I was wrong. You have no idea how much I miss her.'

'You can tell her to come home now,' Jem said. He rose from the table, stretched, and took the teapot to the sink to rinse it out. Then he went to the kettle, shook it to make sure it held enough water, and lit the gas.

May felt the tears rise so close to the surface that she fumbled in the pocket of her skirt for a handkerchief, but Sammy beat her to it and handed her a snowy white square.

'I don't know where she is. She telephones . . .'

'We must find her, then.' Sammy patted her arm. 'We must put her mind at rest, and yours.' He looked at Jem for assurance.

May nodded. 'It's not good when you can't be proud of who you are. I loved Gus so much and yet now I'm ashamed . . .'

'Don't forget I, too, have to pretend to be someone I'm not, just like thousands of other people.'

'Will it end?' May asked. She watched Jem busying himself at the stove, then went to the fire and put on another log. The smell of the wood as the flames licked beneath it was comforting. 'I never realized I was taking on Gus's nationality when I married him.'

'Change is inevitable.' Jem's voice was calm and clear. 'There are rumours of the open-door policy that Canada hopes for. If you live in a country for five years you can apply to become a national. I don't know why in our country each person can't be treated as an individual. Do you want to hear of another ridiculous thing that's happening?'

'Ridiculous or funny, please.' She dabbed her eyes. 'I hate talking about my past. Sometimes it makes me so sad . . .' She smiled. 'Go on, tell me.'

'People of German origin, not already interned, are being forbidden to live along our coastline as they might be spies and could possibly use torches to enable the enemy to land on our shores.'

'That's propaganda leading to hysteria,' said Sammy. 'How silly.'

'How about the banning of German composers like

Beethoven and Bach from community music?' offered Jem. 'Apparently we mustn't be influenced by them.'

May started to laugh.

'There's one more,' said Jem.

'Go on,' said Sammy.

'I believe German measles is now called liberty measles!'

Chapter Twenty-three

Vee stood at the front rail of the boat. The back of her neck was wet, her hair hung in rat's tails and her feet were freezing. Across the water the majestic floating bridge puffed and clanged, the waves spilling to either side as it cut through the sea. Passengers stood on its decks near vehicles that shone with the never-ending rain.

'That's a magnificent sight,' Paul said. He lounged against the wooden seat that for once was empty: very few passengers liked to stand on top of the boat in the rain, preferring instead to squeeze up together in the smoky cabin below deck.

'How long have they been running?' Vee asked.

'*Alexandra* replaced *Victoria* around 1864. But don't quote me on that,' he said.

She thought of the noise that sometimes woke her in her

room overlooking the landing stage at Gosport. 'Have you always done this job?' she asked.

'No, but I started quite a while ago. Then I met Regine and we became friends. I was a builder's labourer before that.'

Vee was surprised. 'Are you and she . . . ?'

'I'd like to think so, but she's after bigger fish than me.' He smiled at her. 'But you never know. I might be able to win her.' They'd travelled backwards and forwards across the strip of water between Gosport and Portsmouth all morning. Vee was cold, hungry and fed up with clipping tickets.

The different jobs she'd tackled so far had given her a better understanding of how the ferries ran. It was hard work, but she'd never felt so fit or well.

'When we've done the return journey why don't you go to the café, get yourself warmed up?' Paul said.

A vision of the warm Nissen hut, a cup of tea and possibly a sandwich suddenly seemed very appealing.

'I'm supposed to stay with you until the other lot takes over,' she said. She was fearful of upsetting Jack, who was preoccupied over the weekend's events.

Ahead loomed the Portsmouth landing stage – she could just about see it through the sheet of rain. Automatically her head turned towards the wheelhouse. Jack had left the boat a couple of hours ago. One moment he'd been there and the next he'd been replaced by a man of about fifty with a full beard, who reminded Vee of the sailor on the Player's Navy Cut cigarette packets. 'I'd ask Jack but he's not here, and I don't know him.' She waved towards the man with his hand on the wheel, staring straight ahead towards the jetty.

'That's Si. He won't mind. Another couple of hours and our shift's finished for the day anyway. Wait a bit.' Vee watched as Paul caught Si's attention by doing arm movements that ended with him pointing to her, then miming drinking a cup of tea. Si nodded back furiously. 'There! Told you it'd be fine, didn't I?'

'That's given me something to look forward to,' she said, thinking how nice it would be to be warm and dry again. A seagull landed on the rail. Up close it looked huge and menacing. It turned its head towards her and cawed loudly, making her jump before it flew off to join its mates.

'Every seagull contains the soul of a dead mariner.'

Vee was about to come back to him with a quick retort but realized he was serious. Perhaps that was what he believed and, if so, who was she to say otherwise?

She watched as Mac skilfully threw the rope and pulled the ferry towards the jetty. On the landing stage, despite the rain, people were queuing to board. Colourful umbrellas jostled, lending a little brightness to the dull day. When the boat was secured, and only then, the chains came down so the passengers could leave. They hastened up one side of the gangway towards the railway station and the buses into the heart of Portsmouth.

Eventually the ferry was empty and the gates to board the boat were opened so the flood of wet people could trail in, stepping aboard from the wooden jetty. Vee was standing beside Paul and no passenger was allowed on without a ticket.

'I'll be glad when the shift's over,' said Paul, but his voice was almost drowned in the noise of people eager to get out of the worst of the rain. With their tickets in wet fingers they surged forward, and Vee began the chore of clipping and collecting them.

Her line of passengers dwindled before Paul's, the passengers no doubt thinking that Paul as the regular ferryman would allow them on the boat quicker than the girl who was unsure of herself. Vee was watching him when he took a ticket and, without clipping it, put it into his cavernous pocket. She wiped the rain from her face, left him to deal with the stragglers and stood back on board.

The whole operation of a boat coming in and completing

a turnaround was swift so that one left every fifteen minutes from either landing stage.

'I'll put these boots back,' called Vee, making her way through the disgruntled crowd to the cupboard to replace them and change into her own shoes, which were still soggy from earlier.

Sitting on the bench and pulling off her wet boots, as the boat bucked and slid over the waves, took most of her concentration. It was still windy and the rain was coming down harder.

Nevertheless, the memory of Paul putting the ticket into his pocket played on her mind. The clipped return tickets were passed to Regine at the end of the shift and should in theory add up to the number of tickets sold, but because passengers didn't always return the same day there were minor discrepancies. What nagged at Vee was that Paul had pocketed an unclipped ticket.

A clean unclipped ticket returned to Regine could be used and paid for again. She'd not noticed Paul pocket tickets before . . . Because the tickets handed to him were wet! He only wanted dry clean ones!

Her body felt heavy as she trudged up the Gosport gangway towards the Ferry Gardens. At the kiosk, warm and snug inside, she could see Regine doing her job. And that was when the penny dropped.

Vee remembered Regine handing out tickets from her bag and making no bones about the fact that money from those tickets went into her jar. They had been sold and not punched. Passengers kept their return tickets safe so they were always in pristine condition. How many really noticed that they were supposed to have them clipped? If a ticket was shown and you were waved through in the stream of people, the clean ticket could be presented at the gate for the return journey. If it wasn't clipped it could be reused. A penny a ticket. It didn't sound a great deal of money, but when Portsmouth Football Club played at home and upwards of twenty-two thousand people travelled across the water to watch the match, the pickings would be very good indeed.

Vee's heart lifted: she'd discovered the answer to Jack's problem about the takings being down. Then it dropped. Hadn't Regine said that if Vee breathed a word about it, she would tell Jack that she had forged papers? She would tell anyone who would listen that Vee Smith was Vee Schmidt.

Vee would be back where she started. Running away from her heritage. Oh, she could run – she'd done it once, she could do it again – but leave Jack?

Vee felt as if all the air had been knocked out of her.

Part of her wanted so much to help the man she cared for. But once he found out she hadn't been honest with him, she would be just another person who had lied to him.

The dance music from the wireless enveloped her, along with the fug of cigarette smoke, as soon as she pushed open the café's door.

A few people were sitting at tables and Vee could almost taste the pleasure a cup of tea would bring her.

Rosie saw her first and called her to the counter. 'Look at the state of you! You're wet through and you look frozen!'

Vee gave her a half-hearted smile. 'At least I'll get warm in here. How's Connie?'

Evidently hearing her name, Connie poked her head out from the hatch. Her blonde hair, covered with the snood, made her look quite glamorous. 'I'm fine,' she called. 'Arm aches a bit but I'm one of the lucky ones. Doctor's put it in a sling and I'm to try not to use it.' Her voice dropped to a whisper: 'Go and talk to Jack. I'm worried about him. Got baby-minding problems. Emily's mother's been hurt, fell down some stairs. I don't think Emily's going to want to take the little one along to see her, do you?'

After divesting herself of her waterproofs and hanging them on the wooden pegs near the door, Vee walked across to the table where Jack was sitting, looking disconsolately through what appeared to be invoices.

Connie and Rosie seemed almost like substitute mothers to Peg but it wasn't an ideal situation, especially if Connie had been advised not to use her arm too much. But if Emily had to look after her mother and Madelaine didn't return soon, how would Jack cope?

'How are you?' Her voice was soft but loud enough to rouse him from his miserable reverie.

'I thought you were punching tickets.'

For a moment she'd forgotten she was supposed to be on the boat with Paul.

'They took pity on me because the weather's awful.' She expected him to come back at her with some retort but he didn't.

'How did you like the work?'

'It was one of the most boring jobs I've ever had to do.'

His whole face seemed to light up as he said, 'I guess at least you're honest.'

Just then Rosie arrived with two mugs of tea and Vee pounced on hers. 'I need that to warm me up,' she said, watching as Rosie found a space for the other mug among the papers on the table.

'I'm trying to make sense of the accounts,' he said.

'Thought I'd look at this lot before I go back to the house to take over from Emily. I suppose you've heard about her mother?' He must have guessed Rosie had told her.

'I take it Madelaine's not returned yet?'

He took a swig of tea, then shook his head. When he'd put his mug down he said, 'I'm babyminding this afternoon.'

'I could look after Peg. I'd like to.'

His voice became hard. 'I told you before, I didn't take you on as a babyminder.'

She smiled. 'No, honestly, I'd like—'

'Don't you understand what "No" means?'

His glare made Vee's stomach turn to mush.

'I'm sorry,' she said quietly. She looked down at the table. Jack began sweeping the papers into a pile.

Vee thought of the accounts she and her mother needed to keep up to date for tax purposes and for billing to customers. She was every bit as competent as her mother. Maybe she'd ask Jack if he'd like her to take over some of the office work. Not now, though. She'd already said enough to make him angry.

Then he said, 'I've involved enough people in my marriage . . .'

'It's not your fault.'

'Peg needs her mother.' He folded the papers and dropped

them into a brown carrier bag. Then the chair scraped as he pushed it back, stood up, took his coat from the back of the chair and put it on. Vee watched as he walked to the door, which swung shut behind him.

Rosie returned to the table for the empty crockery. 'I told you he doesn't know what he's doing.' She sighed, twisted a length of her hair behind her ear, then said, 'We've got some vegetable soup that I think would do you good.'

'I'd like that.' A gust of wind hit the side of the hut with force and rain began rattling down again. 'I could help you after I've eaten . . .'

'Go home. If this bad weather continues, the ferry will stop running. Already our customers have been few and far between – we might even close early. Take the chance to catch up on some sleep. Or you could come with us to the Connaught? There's a dance on later.'

'Surely if the ferries run through air raids they won't shut down because of the weather?'

'Oh yes they will. Safety of the passengers is paramount.'

Rosie left her, and returned second later with a steaming bowl.

Vee toyed with her spoon. She might like to go back to the house, maybe have a bath and sleep for a while. Going dancing, she wasn't so sure about.

The vegetable soup made her mouth water. Rosie had put a great doorstep of crusty bread on the side of her plate.

'That looks and smells delicious. Tell me, has Jack's wife ever been gone this long before?'

Rosie shook her head. 'Not to my knowledge, but she might be scared to come back. Who knows what happened after she caught up with that Hugh last Sunday? She dotes on him. Maybe the two of them have gone away together.'

'What – and leave her daughter?'

'She's not the motherly type, is she? She knows Jack won't let anything happen to Peg.' Rosie paused, then said quietly, 'I don't know what that Hugh has, apart from looking like Zachary Scott . . .'

Vee must have looked confused.

'Zachary Scott is going to be a big star. There was a bit about him in *Photoplay.*'

Vee had forgotten how much of a film fan Rosie was but she was reminded when Rosie said, 'The latest issue's on my bed. You can read it if you want.'

Connie shouted for Rosie, and Vee was left to eat her soup.

It was still raining when Vee walked out of the café holding her waterproof coat over her head to keep off the worst of the weather. It was quiet when she entered the house. The fire was burning and Peg's terry-towelling nappies were steaming gently over the fireguard. The kitchen was tidy, no dirty washing-up on the wooden draining-board.

Vee left her wet-weather gear in the shed, propped over an empty box. Relishing the peace and quiet, she went upstairs and ran a bath.

On Rosie's bed was the copy of *Photoplay* with a picture of Joan Crawford on the front and Vee took it to her room. She went to the window and stared across at the space where the car ferry drew in. There was no queue of vehicles waiting to cross the water. The rain was hitting her window so hard she was fearful it might break. But common sense told her the tape stuck on the glass would stop it falling inwards. She looked longingly at her bed and the magazine, then went to have her bath.

Chapter Twenty-four

May felt Jem's hand on her shoulder as she waved goodbye to Sammy, then closed the door on the man who had previously fed fear into her and her daughter.

'Whoever would have thought that sitting down and talking through problems could make them practically disappear?' she said.

He turned her around to face him. 'It's when people can't share their thoughts and talk about them that difficulties arise.'

May didn't move away. 'And you, are you all right with him calling here weekly?'

'You are your own woman. You always have been. But winter isn't the best time of the year to provide vegetables.'

'Sammy won't care about the produce.' She frowned. 'Seems funny thinking of him as Sammy when I knew him as Herbert. Can't you see how lonely he is?' She walked over to the table and collected up the dirty crockery. When she glanced at Jem, she saw he was still standing by the door. She replaced the plates and went back to him.

'Don't tell me that after all this time you're jealous?'

The blush rose up his neck into his face. He turned his head away.

She said, 'After all we've meant to each other, you can't possibly think . . .'

'You're a very desirable woman, May.'

She took his hand and looked at it. At the calluses and the hard skin that had come from working on her smallholding.

'And you are a wonderful man, Jem. I'd never hurt you.'

She thought of the times they had made love. Though never once had Jem stayed overnight for fear of her name being sullied.

'Vee was a baby when I came looking for work. I loved you the moment I saw you. You told me enough times that you'd never marry again, and that Gus was the only man you could ever give your heart to. I never minded being second to a dead man.'

May held on to him and pushed him towards the sofa. She sat down with him. 'You and I don't talk much nowadays, either.'

'I always thought that was because we've said all that had to be said to each other.'

'Well, that's where you're wrong. If it hadn't been for you, Vee and I couldn't have survived after Mum and Dad died of influenza.' Her mind went back to the terrible pandemic that had swept the world at the latter end of the Great War.

She thought back to when, instead of nursing men from the forces, she'd turned the large bedroom into a nursing section where only she was allowed to go. For days she'd bathed and cooled the feverish bodies of both her parents. Even so, when flu was known to be on the smallholding some of the hired staff had refused to work, even while wearing the cotton masks people were advised to wear to ward off the germs.

'I only did what most people would have done.'

'No, you did more. You also cared for Vee.'

She smiled, remembering how he had taken the pram out into the fields and at times had wheeled the child home with him to the village so May could spend more time in the sick room and away from Vee, in case she became infected.

Before Gus died she had stopped nursing at Netley Hospital. Her father had never accepted Gus, not even when he was told Gus was the baby's father, but his feelings had thawed towards his daughter. He had allowed her to come home for the birth. What else could she have done? There was nowhere she could go. Her VAD life was over.

But the price she paid was never to admit to anyone that she'd gone behind her father's back and married a German.

No one could have foreseen what would happen to Gus.

May would sometimes take out her memories and examine them. She hadn't been with Gus when the end came. But she had known the man she loved so well that she could imagine everything.

Gus felt he had a friend in Annie. The notes she carried back and forth between him and May gave him something to live for, as did the coming child. May's father had banned him from the smallholding.

One Saturday night, Annie found him in the small cell-like room he shared with another prisoner.

'May's gone into labour,' she said. 'Tomorrow you'll have a son or daughter.'

He let the news sink in, then asked, 'Why aren't you with her? Surely she needs you.'

'Because I'm like you. This place dictates all my movements. Her mother's there, so don't worry.'

But he did worry. How could he not? All night he tossed

and turned in the bed in the hated room with the locked door, waiting for the new day so he could at least be out in the fresh air working, hoping Annie would come so she could take another letter to May.

'You're being irrational. Childbirth's normal. At least let me get some sleep.' His cellmate, who was older and a father, understood his worries but tossed them aside.

'I should be with her. I want to be with her.'

'Women in childbirth don't need men cluttering up the place,' the man said. 'Try to rest.'

His May was having his child.

Many times he had wished they hadn't been overcome with lust and love. He should have tried to spare her the indignity of becoming pregnant. Because of him she had lost her job and was on bad terms with her family.

After queuing for breakfast, the long line of prisoners in their distinctive suits set about their duties. As he wasn't allowed to go to the smallholding any more, he now worked in the hospital gardens.

But he had to see May. His desire to go to her became unbearable.

'Where are you going?' the armed guard barked. Gus had thrown down the hoe he was using.

He didn't answer. He guessed the guard would think he

was going to relieve himself in the bushes. As long as Gus didn't leave the grounds, he could do as he liked. But he continued walking towards the furthest corner of the park-like area where the gate led on to the road.

'Nothing matters except that I have to be with May.' His words were swept away in the breeze as he walked determinedly along.

Men were watching now.

'Turn around and come back.'

Gus ignored the guard, walking like someone possessed. Nothing mattered except his May.

Gus could feel the cold wind blowing off Southampton Water. It was like a caress.

'Stop!'

Still he walked.

'Come back, you fool!' That was his roommate.

The first shot hit the gate, splintering the wood as Gus put up his hand to draw back the bolt. He flinched.

The sudden pain in his back was excruciating as the second shot hit him and felled him to his knees.

May's features filled his eyes as the darkness descended.

Vee was twenty-four hours old before May was informed that Gus was dead.

*

It was thought the soldiers had brought the flu home from the trenches where disease of all kinds was rife. But it was indiscriminate with its victims. May found out much later that five hundred million people worldwide had been affected by it and fifty million had died.

Life ended in less than a day for her father. He felt shivery in the morning, had a sore throat, and his skin changed colour to a fiery purple. Before midnight he was choking on globules of scarlet jelly-like blood. May had seen it before with the men she nursed. Her mother lasted almost a week.

May remembered screaming at Jem because he wouldn't let her see her baby after her mother had breathed her last. Afterwards she praised him for his unfailing care. Had she been with her child she could so easily have passed on the virus.

'I always felt Vee was like my own daughter,' he said later. 'I didn't want to lose her.'

May kicked off her slippers and leaned against Jem. She could hear his heart beating. She ran her hands over his shirt. 'Your body is still beautiful.'

She wanted to have him always in her life. And now she could. It had taken the loss of Vee to show her how fleeting happiness was. It should be grabbed with both hands.

Jem pushed her down into the softness of the sofa and began brushing her cheeks and neck with kisses.

'I want you,' he said. 'Is it all right?'

'It's more than all right.'

He removed part of her clothing, then drove himself into her, slowly, slowly. May found once more she was saying all the silly things that come to mind when making love. But it seemed right. Everything was so perfect, so amazing, so unreal, and he waited for her.

The next morning she was awake before Jem. It had rained in the night, and she could smell the freshness through the open window. Birds were singing. Cat looked up from her place at the end of the bed and blinked lazily.

May was surprised he was still with her, for she had expected him to disappear in the night. It was so nice waking up beside him. His mouth was slightly open, his lips curved in a smile. She always loved to kiss the corners of his mouth. He had grown stubble during the night. She couldn't help herself – she leant over him and kissed his lips.

His eyes opened and he ran a hand over her nakedness, stopping when he reached her bottom. He gave it a small friendly slap.

'Don't look at me,' May said.

'But I want to look, to touch you. Or have you changed your mind about what we said last night?'

May realized she'd been hiding from happiness all these years, forgetting how it felt to give in.

'I wouldn't agree to marry you before because I wanted to be loyal to Gus, no matter how hard it was, and when you first asked me I thought if I agreed you'd think it was to make my life easier, to have a new name, not because I really loved you. Mind you, I'm not sure you'll be allowed to marry an alien! It's taken me all this time to see what a fool I've been. I've said I'll marry you and I will.'

Chapter Twenty-five

The siren cut into her sleep. Like a person drugged, Vee hauled herself from her bed and threw on her coat. Downstairs she found a hive of activity. Regine was making up flasks, yawning as she did so. Jack, hair tousled, was getting in her way making up bottles of milk for the baby, and Peg was screaming in the downstairs bedroom. Vee looked at the clock: it was two thirty.

'Butter that bread,' demanded Regine, and Vee immediately got on with scraping margarine on to a loaf that had already been cut into slices.

Vee saw a tin of corned beef upended on a saucer. 'This the filling?'

'Don't turn your nose up. There's many won't have even that,' snapped Regine. Vee felt as though she'd been cut down a peg or two.

Already they could hear the sound of planes droning overhead.

'That's the trouble. We never have enough time to get anything done.' Jack put a basket containing Peg's paraphernalia on the table, then found room in it for four bottles. He moved swiftly to the bottom of the stairs and yelled, 'Rosie! Connie!'

He disappeared, coming back moments later to push a wet child into Vee's wide open arms and take over slicing the corned beef.

Vee loved the milky smell of Peg, who was now examining her face, poking tiny hands into her eyes. Vee kissed her tear-wet cheek. 'It's all right,' she said. 'Nasty planes woke us all up.' Then, 'I expect those two went to the Connaught after all. There was a dance there tonight.'

'But it's been pouring with rain practically all day,' Jack said.

'They wouldn't be dancing in the rain, silly,' came Regine's voice. 'And all the more reason to get out for a bit of enjoyment. They've probably stopped over with a friend.'

'So it's just us three for the shelter, then?' Jack said, putting the sandwiches into a bag and settling it in with Peg's stuff. 'This is full now.'

'We ought to make up some food and leave it in the

shelter in case it's needed,' Regine said. Then, 'Where's my handbag?'

'I prefer to eat something fresh, thank you very much,' said Jack. 'And food that the rats haven't had a go at first. All ready?'

'Almost,' said Vee. She passed Regine her big handbag, noting that the girl never went anywhere without it. She had changed Peg's nappy and transferred the wet one to a bucket of water mixed with Milton. Regine grabbed her coat, threw it over her shoulders and made for the back door. Vee was a few paces behind her and saw her take a small torch from the shelf. Jack returned to the front door and turned off the electricity.

The house was plunged into darkness but the stench of cordite had already seeped in from outside and Vee could see quite clearly the back path down to the shelter – the sky was bright with searchlights, and over Portsmouth it was orange, tinged with smoke, which told her that the city, just across the narrow stretch of water, was getting a beating. The returning ground fire was no match for the enemy planes. The noise of the aircraft was interspersed by huge bangs as shells exploded, sending up sparkles of fire.

'Hurry!' shouted Jack from close behind her. She pulled the child closer and followed Regine, head down, watching the path so she wouldn't trip.

'Jesus, it stinks down here.' Regine was at the air-raid shelter, pulling at the latch to open the door.

'The place gets damp. And I wish I could make sure of keeping rats out,' Jack said.

Vee followed the small light that disappeared as Regine shone it inside.

'Careful,' shouted Regine. 'Something's on the floor.'

The scream that followed was unearthly.

Vee saw a small animal scuttle into the darkness. Something smelt bad, like meat gone off, she thought. She clutched Peg even tighter. The door of the shelter banged shut as she and Jack followed Regine inside. The oil lamp was lit.

Flies flew like tiny Spitfires in the confined space. With one hand covering Peg's face for safety, Vee looked down at the body of Madelaine. Regine's screaming was hurting her ears.

'Shut up!' Jack threw down the bag he was carrying and everything spilt across the floor. He shook Regine with both hands as though she was a rag doll. 'Stop screaming!'

Vee tried to move further into the shelter, away from the smell and the flies. The sudden silence hurt as Regine quietened, then fell against the chair and slid to the floor, moaning softly.

'We've got to get help,' Jack said.

Vee, shocked, began to shiver. 'She's dead, isn't she? We can't stay in here with her.'

'Best get back to the house.' He fell to his knees and touched Madelaine's grey face. He stared at her, then seemed to shake himself back to normal. Vee saw Madelaine's hair was matted with dried blood. Her eyes were open as if she was looking for something she couldn't find. 'Yes, get back to the house,' Jack snapped. 'There's many people never leave their own fireside when a raid comes.' Then he rose and said to Vee, 'Are you all right?'

She nodded, then gestured at Regine. 'She's not.' She glanced back to Jack and their eyes met and held.

'I need to telephone for help – the police first.' He gathered up Peg's things, then handed Vee the bag. 'Can you take this as well as Peg?'

Vee nodded.

'We've got to get out of here. Take a chance.' He opened the door so Vee could step into the night. The smell of cordite and burning was a welcome relief after the stench of death. She looked back at the couple still in the shelter.

'C'mon.' Jack put his hands beneath Regine's arms and pulled her upright, while Vee waited on the path, taking deep breaths and willing Regine to gather her wits enough to walk back to the house.

Then she heard the shelter door close and felt Regine slip an arm through hers, the one that was clutching Peg so tightly. 'All right, Regine?' Vee asked.

'Let's get indoors,' the girl said, and they began walking carefully back up the path. 'Those flies . . .' She shuddered, and Vee knew she didn't expect an answer.

Vee took Peg through to the main bedroom and put the baby into her cot against the wall. The noise coming in from outside wasn't so bad, but the searchlights lit the front bedroom, despite the heavy blackout curtains.

'You'll soon be in Dreamland,' she said, and covered the little girl with a knitted blanket. The light came on outside the room – Jack had switched the utilities back on. Her eyes moved around the bedroom. No pictures on the walls, no photos in frames. It was quite Spartan, unfinished, as if no one cared about the decorations. She saw Jack's suit thrown over a chair, the hanger on the floor. Madelaine's silky dressing-gown was hanging from the hook on the back of the door. Impulsively she picked up Jack's suit, shook it out and hung it straight on the hanger before opening the wardrobe.

Madelaine's clothes were in there, alongside Jack's shirts. The wardrobe was full, so it didn't look as though Madelaine had intended to run away. She noticed her hands were shaking. Madelaine was dead. She heard Jack on the telephone. She couldn't catch what he was saying but his voice was brisk and business-like.

She looked again at Peg, whose eyelids were fluttering as children's do when they're being overtaken by sleep, so she felt it was safe to leave her. There was a small table lamp next to the unmade double bed so Vee switched it on, glad it wasn't too bright. She remembered when she was a little girl how she'd hated waking in the dark. She didn't want Peg to become scared of shadows, like she had been.

She pulled the door to and went out into the hall. Jack was staring at the telephone. His shoulders were slumped. He had his back to her. He put his hand to his forehead and sighed. Vee was sure he didn't know she was there. After a little while she saw his shoulders rise, then fall. He was crying, and her heart went out to him.

He didn't turn towards her but said, 'It had got so I hated her. But I never would have wished anything like this to happen.' He wiped his hand across his face. 'The police will be here as soon as possible, but it mightn't be until the raid's over.'

'What do you think happened to her, Jack?'

Vee thought it was possible she had gone down to the shelter, slipped perhaps and hit her head. The body had obviously been in the shelter for a couple of days – the smell and the flies proved that.

'I think someone hurt her.' She saw his throat rise and fall as he swallowed his emotion.

A huge bang made the house shake. Flakes of ceiling plaster drifted down and Vee fell against Jack. She scrambled back, standing upright once more as someone shrieked outside on the street. The bell of a fire engine cut into the sounds of thumps and crashes. Vee heard water splashing.

'Incendiaries,' he explained. 'They scare me when I'm out on the boat.'

He took a deep breath. 'Look, I'm going to ask a big favour. I don't know what's going to happen when the police get here, but there's every possibility I'll be asked to go down to the station in South Street. I'm going to phone the other crew in case I'm not back for my shift. They'll find someone to cover for me. The girls in the house can work as usual, if that's possible. I know they'll not let me down. It's Peg.'

'I begged before to look after her. It'll be no bother—'

'There's something else. I'm going to give you my keys. To the house, the safe . . .'

'Why?' Vee thought he'd trust one of the others more than her.

He sighed. 'Someone's stealing from me. There's

something going on and until I find out who is behind it, everyone's under suspicion, except you.' He took her arm. 'It was going on before you arrived. Find someone to help with Peg so you can carry on working different shifts and keep your eyes open for me.'

'Anyone would think you expected to be gone ages. You'll only be in for questioning and they might not even want you down the police station for that. It's your wife lying out there, remember. You'll be home in a few hours.'

'I have to be realistic, Vee. I'm the obvious suspect. Of course it might have been an accident, and I sincerely hope her death was accidental. But I have to make sure every eventuality is covered and the ferries must keep running. You know all about writing the log and you said you were used to paperwork . . .'

'The others aren't going to like me taking over. And I'm not sure I feel capable.'

'The others, if they want to keep their jobs, will back you up, and maybe I haven't said it but I reckon you're more than capable of standing in for me.'

The kitchen door opened and Regine stood in the doorway. 'I've got to keep myself occupied – I'm going mad. Do you want tea?'

She looked as if she'd been crying.

'That's a good idea,' Jack said, going over to her and putting his hand on her shoulder. 'I know how friendly you and Madelaine were. Did she contact you during the last few days?'

Regine shook her head.

'I believe you,' Jack said.

Regine turned away but he touched her arm and said, 'I did care about her. No matter what she might have confided to you.' She shook him off and walked towards the stove. She picked up the kettle, went to the sink to fill it, then put it on the hob. She lit the gas and orange and blue flames crawled up from the kettle's base. 'Vee's going to be in charge if I'm kept at the police station.'

'Why?' Regine whirled round.

'Something's going on here – oh, I'm not saying you're involved, but I know Vee has nothing to hide.'

'You sure about that?' The words hurtled from her mouth.

'Regine!'

It had the desired effect. Vee meant only to stop her telling Jack she was working on forged papers. If her secret was revealed she'd have no compunction about telling Jack she was sure Regine was stealing from him. But this wasn't the right moment for the ticket fraud to be revealed. Vee needed more proof. Regine and her accomplice could deny everything. How could she prove what she knew to be the truth?

Regine drew a deep breath and Vee sighed with relief. The moment had passed. Jack hadn't realized anything was amiss except cattiness at his decision to put Vee in charge.

Moaning Minnie, the all-clear siren, began her mournful wail as the kettle boiled. Regine glared at Vee, then stalked off to put a small spoonful of tea onto the used leaves.

'So, you're all right with my decision?' Jack said.

Regine said, 'I have to be. Thank God the raid's over. The other two will comply. You're acting as though you expect to be found guilty. The poor cow's body has only just been discovered. What if her death's an accident?'

No one answered her, because a man's voice, accompanied by loud knocking on the front door, shouted, 'Police! Open up!'

Chapter Twenty-six

Vee was upset that her name had appeared not only in the local *Evening News* but also in the *Southampton Echo*. The press had decided a body being discovered in the air-raid shelter of the ferryman who'd saved a little boy's life recently was more than newsworthy.

The papers had praised the ferry's 'other skipper'. Vee suspected the bottle of whisky no doubt given to him by the reporter loosened Jack's tongue. He had no reason to suppose she might not be pleased at receiving approval.

Peg didn't like it that her daddy wasn't around and grizzled constantly that first evening. As he had feared, Jack had been taken in for questioning.

'You'll have to sleep in their room,' Regine said. She gave a wicked smile.

'I don't think so,' said Vee, who could think of nothing

worse than sleeping in a bed where not only the dead woman had slept but also Jack. Since she didn't want to start moving furniture about and she was convinced Jack would shortly return, she made up the carrycot, put Peg into it and took the little girl upstairs with her. Peg seemed to like the sound of the voices and the wireless floating up the stairs and, to Vee's delight, promptly fell asleep.

Madelaine's body had been taken away. Luckily there was a back way into the garden near the shelter so it hadn't come through the house. The police said they would arrange for a post mortem, and Rosie and Connie arrived home in the thick of all the questioning.

One by one the girls were taken into the scullery to speak privately with a policeman.

'I was Madelaine's friend,' began Regine, before anyone asked her a single question. She was bundled into the scullery but her loud voice betrayed her: they all heard her tell of the christening and Jack's outburst.

'She'll have him hanged, drawn and quartered, will that girl,' said Connie, who shed a tear as Jack was taken away.

Eventually the police left and the women sat around discussing the night's happenings. No one shed a tear for Madelaine.

Even though Vee doubted she would sleep, she eventually

went to bed. The baby's snuffling somehow comforted her and she dozed.

She was first up in the morning and had bathed and fed Peg when Connie stumbled downstairs, closely followed by Rosie.

'If you're in charge, there's a couple of changes we'd like to make in the café.'

They made her sit down, then got on with the breakfast chores, all the while telling her of what they'd decided. Vee blessed Rosie and Connie that first morning for their forced cheerfulness because it certainly lightened her mood.

'Don't go expecting me to agree to things you wouldn't ask Jack about,' she said. 'He'll be back shortly, and I'll get it in the neck for agreeing to your demands.'

'We want to start a takeaway service for sandwiches.' Connie grinned at her. 'Customers eat food on the premises and sometimes ask if we can pack up a sandwich for later. We do, but we both think if we advertised, word of mouth, we could do a roaring trade. And having some sandwiches already made up would save us time.'

'Where will the extra food come from? There's a war on, you know, which means the café can only sell what can be bought.'

'We can order differently. Use more salad stuff, ideal

in sandwiches. Corned beef tastes better with lettuce, tomatoes.'

'It's too cold. The season's over for that kind of stuff.'

'Tinned beetroot, shredded cabbage, onions, pickles . . .' Connie had jumped in with stock they already had in abundance.

Vee thought quickly. 'If you're so set on this, why hasn't Jack given it the go-ahead? What's in it for you?'

'A percentage,' Connie said. Vee frowned. 'When we came up with the idea, Jack said to talk it over with Madelaine. But she didn't want to know.'

'Why?'

'She didn't care about making money for Jack, only about meeting up with Hugh.'

Rosie put her hand over her mouth. 'I shouldn't have said that. That's speaking ill of the dead.'

'You should if it's true. I hope when that copper took you into the kitchen to talk to you in private you told him everything you know?' Vee could see from Rosie's face where her loyalty lay. 'Look, if you want to do this, go ahead, but if the profit goes down instead of up, that's it, finished.' Their eyes told her they would make it work. She guessed they'd put their hearts and souls into the idea.

As both of them trudged towards the front passage, she

heard Rosie say softly, 'See? I told you she'd listen and I know we'll make a profit.'

'You'd better,' called Vee. 'I'm going through the books today.'

Connie laughed and blew her a kiss before the door closed behind them.

Vee berated herself. Jack had been out of the house just five minutes and she was changing the way things were done. When he'd told her to look after his business, he probably hadn't expected her to agree to Connie and Rosie's scheme.

'Regine!' Vee shouted up the stairs. 'You'll be late if you don't hurry.'

A short while later the girl came downstairs.

'Jack not back yet?' Dark rings circled her eyes. Vee guessed she'd been crying.

'Not yet,' Vee answered. 'There's tea in the pot and I'll toast you some bread, if you like.'

'I'm not hungry,' Regine said.

If Regine had found it so easy to talk about Jack's shortcomings, would she disclose that Vee had forged papers? Since no one had confronted her yet, Vee was able to breathe as the front door closed on Regine, leaving her and Peg alone in the house.

One of the first things she had to do was make sure Jack's job was covered.

'The ferries must keep running,' Jack had said. A phone call made sure that was so. Si was sincere in his agreement to help Jack all he could until his return.

'When they find someone dead like that, the culprit is nearly always someone who knew the victim well. It's normal to take the husband or boyfriend in for questioning,' he said. 'But I know Jack wouldn't have harmed a hair of her head.'

As Vee poured a last cup of tea for herself, deciding to make a list of what needed to be tackled first, Peg woke up and this time Vee couldn't settle her.

The rain hit the windows with force. One of her priorities had to be finding a good babyminder. Peg's cheeks were pink and she was hot. She'd have to take the child out in the rain – there was no way she could leave her on her own, even if she was completely well.

Peg let out a great howl and Vee picked her up. Her tiny body was rigid. Surely she couldn't be ill.

The announcer on the wireless was discussing the Germans' raid on Coventry last night. So it hadn't only been along the south coast that the bombers had done their worst. She gasped. At least a thousand people had died.

As Vee drank her tea, she wondered how her mother was. She hadn't telephoned her for a while.

Walking up and down the warm kitchen, trying to soothe the fractious child, Vee knew she ought to let May know she was safe and well. She worried constantly that Sammy Chesterton would find her and had now sent her mother almost enough money to cover the normal price he charged for forgeries. She was surprised the time had passed so quickly while she'd been living in Gosport. Each week she bought little, just necessities for herself, but what if the money wasn't enough? What if he had decided interest was due? Soon it would be Christmas.

Thinking of the festive season, she realized this would be the first year she wouldn't be involved in cutting down the mistletoe and bunching it, ready for market. It was one of the jobs she loved helping with.

There was an old apple orchard behind the house where the trees were now too old to bear good fruit but still supported *Viscum album* or mistletoe.

For many years her grandfather had supplied mistletoe for Tenbury's yearly festival, as did some other local small-holdings and farms. As a girl Vee had sat in the barn, making up holly and mistletoe wreaths that Jem sold at market. She missed the smallholding and her mother. Vee shook herself.

This little scrap of a baby in her arms now had no mother, so it was up to her to make sure she didn't suffer because her father wasn't there at present.

Peg refused her bottle and instead grizzled continuously.

Perhaps a visit to the doctor, or at least the duty nurse, was necessary.

When Vee finally had the child ready to leave the house, Peg was sick, and she had to start all over again washing and dressing her. Now convinced Peg was ill, she set off with the pram towards the doctor's surgery.

The streets were full of rubbish, broken slates, bricks and rubble from the previous night's bombing. Vee walked carefully with the pram, fearing she might buckle the wheels as she pushed it over the uneven ground. As she passed Walpole Park she spied Ada sitting hunched in the rain on one of the wooden seats.

Ada rose and came towards her. 'Sorry to hear all about the troubles Jack's having. Oh, don't worry, nobody believes he did it. Have you time for a cup of tea?'

'I can't – I need to get to the surgery. This little madam's been sick – she's ever so hot and I'm worried.'

Ada looked into the pram. 'How long has she had those bright spots on her cheeks?'

'I didn't notice them before this morning but she's done nothing but grizzle and she's hot, sickly . . .'

'Have you tried rubbing her gums with a cold spoon?'

What on earth was Ada on about? It was only these past few days that Connie had suggested Peg could possibly be started on different foods besides milk. She couldn't eat with a spoon!

Ada laughed and fell into step beside her. 'The cold spoon will soothe her hot gums. Or a piece of clean material soaked in cold water – let her chew on it.'

'But she's been sick!'

'She's teething,' said Ada. 'Lean over the pram and see if you can look into her mouth. I daren't touch her – my hands aren't clean enough.'

'Well, it's easy enough with her screaming like this, isn't it?' They both stared into the baby's gaping mouth.

Vee saw two tiny white pinpricks in her bottom jaw and her top gums were red and inflamed. Peg was crying real tears. 'Ada, how clever! And Peg, you're such a brilliant baby! Your daddy will be pleased!'

For a little while Vee had forgotten that Jack was still at the police station. Now it all came back to her. If she went round to South Street, would they let her see him? Everything looked so black at present . . . Perhaps if she could have a chat with him, tell him about Peg and her new teeth, it would cheer him up. She sighed.

Ada said, 'They must realize surely that Jack loved the woman. There was no way he would have harmed her.'

Vee knew Jack wouldn't hit a woman. She didn't know how she knew but she did.

'Ada, I've such a lot to do today, but now you've told me what to do for Peg, I must go home. If you'd like to come with me, I'll make us tea and get you something to eat.'

Ada stared at her. 'I'm not a charity case, Vee.'

Vee was taken aback. 'Have you never thought I might just like chatting to you?'

Ada squeezed her arm. 'Sorry,' she said. 'I get prickly because people look down on me. I feel so ashamed of myself. I think that man spitting at me was the last straw. I haven't been back to that pitch near the car ferry and I haven't sold myself for money. What you gave me eventually ran out, but I manage to earn a few coppers on market days helping pack up the stalls, and if I'm there early in the mornings, *very* early,' she added, 'I help the stallholders set up. A hot cuppa and a sandwich can sort me out for the day. I've been getting by . . . No one's asked my name. I just get called, "Oi, you!"'

Vee put her arm through Ada's. She'd already turned the

pram round. 'I'm really pleased to hear that,' she said. 'You're too honest a person to sell your body.' And then it dawned on her that it was possible her troubles could be over if she asked Ada to look after Peg. Then she could get on with the other things she should be doing for Jack. There was the paperwork, wages . . .

As soon as she got home, Vee put the kettle on. She was disappointed Jack still hadn't got back. Within minutes, Ada had washed her hands and was busy with Peg, somehow stopping the little girl's crying. Vee noticed Ada carried the bag with her in which Jack had said she kept the certificates that showed she was a qualified children's nurse. She decided to take a chance.

'How would you feel about looking after Peg permanently?'

She was astounded by Ada's clipped reply. 'I can't . . . Look at me. I have nothing, not even an English name.'

Vee wasn't going to suggest the obvious, that the girl had something that mattered more: on paper she was extremely qualified to look after Peg. Vee trusted her. She wasn't going to ask to look at her documentation. 'You can have a room in this house and your keep. The wages will be minimal at first but, if you trust me as I'm going to trust you, I think we'll work well together.' Vee smiled at Peg, who was now tracing Ada's cheek with her tiny fingers.

Vee knew she'd won Ada over when she said, 'I can show you awards I've won, but Jack knows I'm the enemy.'

'Let me worry about that,' Vee said. 'Is it a deal?'

Ada started crying with happiness and Peg copied her.

After they'd had their tea Vee took Ada upstairs and showed her a room at the back of the house.

'I'll prepare the bed and clean up – I don't think Madelaine liked housework. Then I'm going to make a stew. I expect Jack, when he eventually comes in, will be starving. I think he'd rather eat here than in the café where people will stare at him. If you want a bath, there's plenty of hot water but don't forget five inches is the limit. There's a spare toothbrush in the bathroom cabinet.'

She thought that later she would ask Ada to help her take the baby's cot upstairs.

Before she began searching for fresh bedding, Vee went into her own room and looked out some more of her clothes, not that she'd got many. She found a skirt and a jumper. Luckily they had the same shoe size so she was able to put aside a pretty pair that she knew she'd never wear again. On the ferries she wore clothes for comfort.

Vee was humming along to the wireless. The dance music was making her feel so much better. Peg was fast asleep in her pram outside the front door in the fresh air beneath the shelter of the porch roof where it was dry, and she had also discovered clean sheets and blankets in the airing cupboard downstairs.

Vee put the clothes for Ada on the floor outside the bathroom and called through the door that she'd be making up her bed.

She was surprised when Ada opened the door, a towel around her, and said, 'I've found bleach and peroxide in the cabinet. Could I use some on my hair?'

'I believe they belonged to Madelaine,' Vee said. 'You might as well.'

Ada spotted the clothes on the floor.

'I'm never going to be able to thank you enough, am I?'

Vee saw the fresh tears in her eyes. 'I've a strong feeling that you'd do exactly the same for me,' she said. It was then she saw the bruises on Ada's lower neck.

Ada tried to cover them as soon as she saw Vee's eyes go towards the dark blue marks. There were bruise bracelets around her wrists too.

'It's not easy living on the streets,' Ada confessed. 'Some blokes came down to the ferry, thought I was fair game . . . They held me down.' For a moment there was silence, a long awkward silence that spoke volumes.

Vee said eventually, 'You're safe here with me.' And so that Ada wouldn't see her cry she went quickly downstairs to start making a meal. She knew that without her forged papers, rape could easily have happened to her too.

Chapter Twenty-seven

Clean nappies were drying over the fireguard and a stew was bubbling on the stove when Ada came down to the kitchen to dry her hair in front of the fire. She was wearing Vee's clothes, and when she took the towel off her head, Vee gasped.

'You look . . . lovely,' she whispered.

Ada knelt on the rag rug and began brushing out her hair. The more it dried, the brighter it became.

'Thank you,' Ada said. 'I'm never going to forget what you've done for me.'

Vee wondered momentarily if she'd taken too much on her shoulders in the relatively short time that Jack had left her in charge. After all, Ada had no papers and Jack was well aware of it. What would he say to Vee giving her the job of looking after his daughter? As for herself, she rued the day she'd asked Sammy Chesterton for help and hated herself for becoming not only a thief but a liar. Oh, well, she thought. She'd worry about that later. There was no turning back now.

'I've been doing as you suggested, giving Peg something cool to chew on,' Vee said.

'Did it work?'

Vee waved towards the hallway. When the rain had come down hard, she'd brought in the pram. Ada jumped up and went to look. Vee heard her saying baby things to the little girl, who was awake, happy and making noises at the toys strung across the front of the pram.

'She's still chewing on it,' Ada called.

Peeved because the happy film music had been interrupted for the news, Vee heard the announcer say, 'There will be four ounces of sugar and two ounces of tea extra for everyone at Christmas,' but they were to go easy on milk because there were more shortages. Vee was grateful when the stirring songs took up where they'd left off.

'That raid last night was bad,' said Ada. Her newly touched-up blonde hair was hanging in a curtain round her face. Vee thought she must have been scared on the boat as the bombs rained down and more so when the men had invaded it.

She wondered whether she should ask Ada if she intended

to pursue the matter with the police, then decided against it. Ada wouldn't want the police involved: she was an alien. She didn't mention that. Instead she said, thinking of Madelaine's body in the air-raid shelter, 'I can't use the Anderson ever again. But I believe Jack's got a Morrison here somewhere. There's certainly one in the café.'

Just then there was the sound of a key in the door and footsteps in the hall. She heard Jack's voice as he spoke nonsense to Peg in a cheerful voice. As he stepped into the kitchen her heart missed a beat.

His eyes met hers. 'Hello,' he said. 'I bet you thought I wasn't ever coming home again.' She shook her head, went over and kissed his cheek. Jack didn't push her away. Instead he smiled.

'That's a nice welcome,' he said, his eyes holding hers.

'Hello,' said John Cousins, as he entered the room behind Jack. 'And who's this?' Both men took off their wet coats and Jack draped them over the end of the fireguard that was free of babywear.

John was staring at Ada.

'I'm Peg's nanny, Ada,' she said.

Vee was surprised that she showed no sign of unease as she put out her hand for John to shake.

Introductions over, Jack said, 'Do you have papers?' Vee

wasn't sure whether he was asking Ada if she had a ration book and medical card or whether she had qualifications, but Ada went to the sideboard, took out her brown bag, pulled from it a large envelope and showed him several certificates.

'I'll put the kettle on,' Vee said, and turned her back on the two men and Ada. This was a ridiculous state of affairs, she thought, as she lit the gas beneath the kettle. Having a bath and bleaching her hair hadn't disguised Ada that much! Whatever was Jack playing at?

Then it dawned on Vee that John had no idea who Ada was. Jack was doing all the talking before his friend started wondering about 'the new nanny'.

'How's Emily's mother?' she asked John.

John grinned at her, the new nanny forgotten. 'Emily's fed up because her mother's a very demanding woman and Emily can't do anything right.'

Jack chipped in, laughing, 'I only met her once, but that was enough!'

John grinned at him. 'The old girl must keep off her feet for a while so I'm eating in the canteen.' He pulled a face. Vee took it to mean the food in the police canteen wasn't too tasty.

'I've got just the thing to warm you on a horrible day like

this. A dish of stew? Not much meat, but there's freshly baked crusty bread to go with it, and I put potatoes to cook in the bottom of the oven.'

Jack was gazing at her. She wasn't sure what she could see in his eyes – gratitude? Then he winked at her and she knew it was going to be all right. Not only was Ada welcome in his home, but he'd told no out-and-out lie to his best friend, John. Plus she and Jack now shared a secret. A feeling of contentment spread through her.

It didn't take long to put out cutlery and dishes and set chairs around the table.

As they ate they talked, the good hearty smell of the food and the warmth in the kitchen promoting conversation between them.

'I was hoping to come and visit you,' Vee said.

'Thank God I wasn't at the police station any longer,' Jack said. He turned to John. 'Will you be needing me any more?'

'Not now her fancy man's confessed . . .'

Vee's eyes shot across the table to Jack's face. 'Apparently he reckons they had a row and she fell. It was his fault, he says,' continued John.

Vee could tell there was something he wasn't saying. 'Don't you believe him?'

'There's a few discrepancies.'

'You think he's covering for someone else?' Ada chipped in.

'Look, I shouldn't be talking about an ongoing case.' John turned towards Jack. 'She was your wife, mate.'

'I shouldn't speak ill of the dead, but she'd not really been a wife to me for a while . . .'

'But I'd stake my job on it that you didn't kill her.' John was adamant.

'I hope you go on feeling that way,' Jack said.

John poured the remainder of his tea down his throat. 'Look, I've got to get back.' His chair scraped against the floor as he pushed back from the table and rose. 'That was a good, filling meal, Vee, thanks.' His plate was scraped clean. It was always gratifying to see a man appreciate his food, she thought.

Jack got up and handed his friend his now dry coat.

'Don't come to the door, I can see myself out,' John said.

'Say hello to Emily for me,' said Vee.

Ada began removing the dirty dishes and started on the washing-up. She had her hands in the sink when Jack returned from the front door.

Vee's heart was pounding as he came into the kitchen. What was he going to say to her? Would he be very angry that she'd made him an accomplice to her crime of giving an alien work?

She was still sitting at the table. His face was inscrutable, but he looked shattered. She guessed they hadn't allowed him to sleep while he was being questioned. While it was true that he and John were friends, he would have been treated like any other person they had taken in for questioning about a murder. But, wait, wasn't she jumping the gun? Was it really murder? And when had Hugh confessed? What was the story behind that?

As he entered the room, Jack stopped and stared at her. 'So, now I have two possible detainees under my roof!'

Chapter Twenty-eight

'You can handle everything here for a couple of days, can't you, Donald?'

'Wouldn't be the first time you've left the Black Cat in my hands, would it?' The old man was sorting out the change in the till. 'Got a bit of fluff you want to take away?'

'If I was anything like the bad boss I'm supposed to be, I should punch your nose for that remark, you crusty old bugger.' Sammy Chesterton put down the glass from which he'd just swallowed the last of his single malt whisky and smiled.

'You do that and I won't be in any fit state to look after nuffink!' Donald slid the till drawer shut, listened for the ping, then finished his own drink.

Sammy Chesterton nodded amiably and, his coat slung

over his shoulders, walked out of the club into the fresh Southampton air.

It wasn't often he regretted anything, but he felt bad that May didn't know where her daughter was. The stupid debt had been paid in full and May and Jem had shown him nothing but kindness. Every time he stepped inside Honeysuckle Holdings he was made to feel like one of her family, fed like royalty, and now that bloody man of hers had him doing chores about the place, like he was some hired hand.

Last week when he'd arrived with a nice bit of gammon, expecting to play a few hands of whist after the meal, Jem had told him, 'We've got a little job to do first. The back bedroom of this place has a rotten window. I've made one up and done most of the preparation but I need someone with a bit of savvy to hold on to the thing while I fit it. Half an hour and it'll be finished.'

What could he do? He'd stood on a ladder out in the freezing cold while Jem had knocked out the rotten window frame in one piece. Of course Jem'd been inside the house, fannying about, while he'd stood on the ladder in his cashmere coat, then pushed the window in so Matey could put in the glass and putty it. Naturally all the crap fell outwards, over him and his nice warm coat.

Still, the grateful look on May's face had made up for his discomfort.

'I've been scared to open that window for ages,' she'd said.

No wonder he'd fallen asleep in the armchair after dinner. Never did get to play whist!

He'd reached his car now, inserted the key and climbed inside. He smiled, remembering he hadn't woken until much later, and when he had he'd found May had covered him with a blanket. Not only that but her damn cat had been sleeping on his cashmere coat and made a nest in it. Hairs all over it!

He put the *Southampton Echo* on the seat next to him and started the engine of his Armstrong Siddeley.

It wouldn't take long to get down to Gosport and, thanks to the skipper who'd jumped into the Solent and rescued the boy, he knew where he could find Vee. And wouldn't May be happy to see her daughter again! It really was the least he could do for her.

There was a great deal of bomb damage in Southampton, with gaps in the rows of houses, like missing teeth in an old man's mouth. Bit like Donald's, he thought.

There was a lot of farmland between Southampton and Fareham but it wasn't long before he was on the main road from Fareham going down towards Gosport ferry.

Bloody Hitler had had a right go at the place. Parts of the main road were like an obstacle course where buildings had caved in. Whole walls had been taken out, leaving the spectacle of half an upstairs room complete with an iron bed ready to fall to the rubble below. There had been a raid last night and he wondered how many unsuspecting people had copped it. Mind you, it wasn't only the bombs that were knocking people off. One day that young bloke was being praised on the news for saving a kiddie, the next his wife was found dead in a shelter! Don't seem fair, really, Sammy thought.

He'd done a bit of phoning around and discovered Vee lived with several other ferry girls in the house owned by Jack Edwards. For her to have saved up to pay him for her ration book and papers she must have worked all hours without spending anything on herself, poor kid. Still, he'd make it right now.

When he reached the ferry, he'd park up, then watch a while. He was looking forward to surprising her.

'You said two?'

Vee stared at Jack and awaited his reply, not that she didn't guess what had happened. But she couldn't help herself: 'Did Regine tell you?'

'No, but she left some papers of yours around where I'd find them.'

Suddenly she wanted to tell him about the ticket fraud. But she kept her mouth tightly closed. She had no proof to show him and it would look as if she was trying to get her own back on the girl.

Ada folded the tea-towel over the fireguard. 'That's the quickest I've ever been sacked from a job,' she said. Her face showed her misery.

'Wait a minute,' Jack said. 'If I didn't want you here I'd have given you away to my mate, the copper. You'd probably have been on your way to a camp by now, wouldn't you?'

'So you're all right with me looking after Peg?' Ada frowned, unsure of herself and his expected answer.

'Of course I'm not, but I'm willing to take a chance if you are.' Vee watched as Ada drew a huge sigh of relief.

'I know how hard you've been trying to make money legally, Ada. I need someone to look after my daughter and you're qualified. The last thing she needs is more upsets, and there'll be plenty of those in this house in the next few months.'

'You won't regret it,' Ada said.

'I hope not.' He turned to Vee. 'She cleans up well. I take it you had a hand in that?'

Before she could answer a small cry came from the pram in the hall. Ada grabbed the cardigan Vee had given her earlier. 'I'll take Peg for a walk.'

Vee listened as the front door opened and she heard the pram's wheels bump down the step and onto the pavement. Jack didn't say anything until the door clicked shut.

'If Regine let you know I was working on forged papers, why didn't you say something to me?'

'What difference would it make whether I sacked you a couple of days after you arrived or much later?'

'It's me who should be asking you that.'

'Ask yourself why I took you on.'

'You needed help, the notice on the boat said.'

'And you didn't ask yourself why it was you I took on?' Jack needed a shave and he looked so tired she wondered how he could cope with everything.

Vee shook her head. 'Why?'

'Something happened when I saw you asleep in the cabin.' He looked sheepish. 'But what could I do? Say, "I really fancy you and I'm married and sleeping with my wife so come and live in my house"?'

It was a long while before either of them spoke. A piece of coal sparked from the fire in the range and landed on the brick surround, then fizzled out.

Quietly Vee said, 'So I've been learning to do jobs on the ferries that I might never need to do?'

'No, that part is real enough. If I lose my regular staff because they want to join the forces, I need reliable people I can depend on to take over their jobs.'

That answer didn't satisfy Vee.

'Never once have you ever admitted you even liked me.'

'Would you have liked a married man making a pass at you?'

Vee hung her head. 'Probably not. But why didn't you sack me when you found out I'm not legal?'

'You're no more a spy than I'm Winston Churchill. I'd like to think I'm a decent enough judge of a person's character.' He was staring at her intently. 'If I could take all the shit my wife was dishing out to me, I could wait until you were ready to tell me the truth. In fact, now is the ideal time for you to explain yourself.'

Vee looked at his beautiful mouth with the corners curved in a smile. 'Shall I make another cuppa? It's quite a story.'

'You have tea if you want. I'm having a proper drink.' He went over to the sideboard, opened the door and took out a bottle of beer. Then he sat on the sofa and patted the seat for her to sit next to him.

'Before you speak, let me ask one question. I have to

work tonight. I've already had too much time off. Will you come with me? We can talk more up in the wheelhouse. But for now I promise I won't kiss you until you've told me everything about your past and then I'll only kiss you if you want me to.'

When she'd finished telling him her story, he set down the empty beer bottle and picked up her hand. His eyes seemed to bore into her soul. He didn't speak, just leant forward and kissed her.

Those lips were everything Vee had thought they'd be, when they came down firmly on hers, sending shivers of delight along her spine. As he broke away he said, 'All this time I've been too scared and ashamed of what you'd think of me to do any more than talk to you. Even that taxed my mental strength at times. Do you know what it means to a man to have a woman beside him who not only cares about him but is willing to risk her life working alongside him?'

'Oh, Jack,' she said. 'I wish you'd been brave enough to do this before.'

'It wasn't right. The timing was all wrong – and I'm not even sure I'm doing the proper thing now. I don't want to take advantage . . .'

She heard the key in the door that heralded Ada's return. Vee sprang away from him, but as she stood up she said,

'You're breaking the law by not informing the authorities you have two aliens in your house.'

'Hellooo!' called Ada. 'We're back. A little girl is hungry.'

Jack rose and gripped her wrist. 'Let me worry about that. I know two wrongs don't make a right, but because the government has lost its head, many people have been forced to do things they never expected to have to do to survive. I have to speak out, Vee. You are the girl of my dreams and I won't let you go without a struggle. I'm not in the right situation yet to prove it to you,' he put his face close to hers, 'but I will, love.' His lips brushed her cheek.

Ada pushed open the kitchen door. She had Peg in her arms and moved towards Vee. 'Take her for a moment, Vee. I need to get my coat off.'

Vee saw she'd worn her old coat over the clean clothes she'd given her. It smelt musty. Ada had no doubt slept rough in it. She determined to get her another as soon as she could. The less Ada reminded people of her origins, the safer she would be.

But before Vee could take Peg, Jack stepped forward. Vee was surprised to see the little girl, small as she was, give him an open-mouthed smile. He was talking to her about her 'toofy pegs', and Vee smiled.

Jack took Peg upstairs with him. He was going to have

a bath and shave, he confided, to get rid of the smell of South Street's police station. Peg could have a swim with her daddy at the same time. He went upstairs carrying her and her yellow toy duck.

Vee was on cloud nine as she lit the gas beneath the kettle. Now her secret was out in the open with Jack, the relief was tremendous. Jack had made it easy for her to answer his questions about her past and had contributed information about his life with Madelaine. Never had she felt so comfortable talking to anyone as she had with him. She felt as if she had known him all her life.

The caress of Jack's mouth was still on her lips and cheek as she stirred the large pan with the remainder of the stew she'd made earlier. Neither she, Ada nor Jack had eaten in the café today, but there was plenty of food here should they want a snack later.

The other three girls came home, but Regine went out again quickly. She was going to the pictures with Paul, but before she left she asked what had transpired between the police and Jack. She seemed surprised that Hugh had voluntarily walked into the police station and given himself up.

'He's not the violent kind,' was all she said.

'Everyone has secrets,' said Vee sharply. She didn't divulge that Jack had told her he knew she was an alien. Regine didn't waste breath on talking to Ada. She accepted her as Peg's new nanny. It was quite obvious that she neither knew nor recognized the other girl. Connie did, though.

As Vee put a shovelful of coal on the fire, Connie said, 'Everyone deserves a second chance. Don't let that bitch Regine spoil anything. She's like a viper in our midst.'

Then she told Vee how successful the takeaway sandwiches had been.

'Does he know?'

Vee realized she was asking if Jack had agreed to their new venture.

She was ready for that. 'He said if you lose him money he'll skin you both alive!'

Connie looked petrified.

Vee laughed. 'It's all right. Jack couldn't very well put me in charge then moan about any changes I made, could he?'

The older woman sighed. 'Every time I tried to talk to Madelaine about anything to do with the café she bit my head off. I hope you stay around for a long time. Jack's much easier to be with now you're here.' Suddenly Connie put her arms around Vee. 'You saw what a gent he was in rescuing me from the church in that air raid. If it hadn't been for Jack I might not be around to tell the tale. He saved me, despite that rogue Hugh shouting about his affair with

Madelaine. Jack's a good bloke.' She let her arms drop. 'I'm not stupid. I've known for a while that he cares for you. Please stay around and make him happy.' Connie paused. 'This business with Madelaine's not over yet, not by a long chalk. Poor Jack's likely to go through a lot of trouble before it's cleared up. Me and Rosie'll be there for him. I hope you will be too. Tell you what . . .' Connie rescued a hairpin that had come adrift '. . . why don't you come with me and Rosie this evening? There's a gangster film on at the Criterion.'

Vee said, 'I've already promised Jack I'll work with him tonight. We've come to a bit of an understanding.' She didn't want to tell Connie everything that had gone on between them, but she knew she could confide in her. 'You don't need to worry. I'll stand by him as well, Connie.'

Connie gave her a heartfelt smile. 'That's good to hear, Vee. But you take care tonight. It's clear, and I wouldn't be a bit surprised if there was another raid. Them Germans are buggers!' She looked at Ada. 'If you'll pardon my French!'

Chapter Twenty-nine

'It's been a while now since I've heard from Vee. I do hope everything's all right.'

'Knowing what you women are like, I guess you want her to help with the wedding.' Jem took off his work boots, went over to May, who was peeling potatoes at the sink, put his arms around her waist and snuggled his face into the back of her neck. 'That's only natural, my love.' He breathed in deeply. 'You smell delicious,' he said. 'Vee hasn't stopped phoning, has she? It's just been a while since you last heard her voice.'

'I suppose so,' she said, turning in his arms and kissing him full on the mouth. 'I think it's a good idea getting a special licence. At least when I do hear from her, we can be married as soon as she gets home.'

'She'll be thrilled to know she doesn't have to stay away

now everything's all right with Bertie Lang – whoops, Sammy Chesterton. I still think, though, that you should have told her he's been visiting us.'

'And if I had, she'd have thought he was out to cause trouble . . .'

Jem sighed. 'Who'd have thought a leopard can change its spots? That man's not half as bad as I thought he was.'

'We all make mistakes,' May said. 'My biggest mistake was taking you for granted all these years.'

'It's water under the bridge,' he said. 'I love you, May.'

Sammy left the car on a piece of waste ground in North Street and walked to the Central Café, which seemed the wrong name, he thought, especially as the place was on a corner. Who knew why people named things the way they did?

It was dingy inside but the tea was good and strong, thick enough for the spoon to stand up in, and it went down well. A Frank Sinatra song was blaring from the wireless. He struck up a conversation with the owner, Bert, and found out the ferry changed its crew of workers at six. The smell of bacon frying made him feel hungry, so he ate a bacon sandwich while sitting at the greasy counter and asked a few questions.

It didn't take him long to discover that Bert was no blab-bermouth and would only talk of inconsequential matters.

'Don't see many women skippering a boat,' Sammy mut-tered, loud enough for Bert to hear. He'd already spread out the *Echo* so it looked as if he was reading the piece about the schoolboy being saved.

'P'raps we're a bit more adventurous here,' Bert said, 'than where you come from.'

Sammy knew it wasn't his accent that had told the man he was new in town – Southampton was only just up the road. His expensive clothes set him apart from the café's usual customers.

'Anyway, the women are doing all sorts now there's a war on.'

Sammy pushed his mug forward for more tea and looked around at the noisy layabouts lounging at the tables. He guessed they'd soon get their call-up papers, and be replaced by another set of youngsters pretending to be big shots.

Sammy wanted to ask if Bert knew where the girl lived. But Bert wasn't forthcoming. The one bit of information he provided was the time at which the crew changed.

Well, he'd have to go down and hang about the ferry to find out if Vee was on duty. He'd rather have been civilized and knocked at the house where she lodged, which could have resulted in a one-to-one confrontation. But it wasn't to be, so he'd have to catch her as she left the boat, if she was working. It was after nine and Bert said the ferry shut down around ten thirty. He'd have a wander around Gosport until then, he decided.

The siren started wailing as he walked past Lloyds Bank.

The main road was empty so he couldn't follow anyone to a shelter and he had no idea where the public ones were. He had two choices: carry on walking towards the ferry or go into a pub.

He wondered if the ferries stopped running during an air raid. If so, and Vee was on duty, she might go home early and then when he got to the boats he wouldn't see her. Bugger it, he'd carry on down to the water – he hadn't come this far to miss her. And if she wasn't working, maybe one of the boatmen might know where she lived.

The noise of the planes grew louder and Sammy stood in a shop doorway to watch the spectacle. Searchlights filled the sky, darting hither and thither in an effort to catch the enemy in their beams. Ack-ack fire started up from the ground forces and then the sky was lit like a huge firework display as bombs dropped from the planes to fall on Portsmouth. The night sky changed colour from black to orange as a hit was scored in what Sammy knew was the city's dockyard.

Carefully he ran down the high street, dodging from shop doorway to shop doorway. Rubble left from the previous bombing raid was piled on what remained of the pavements. He guessed the road needed to be cleared frequently for ambulances and buses. Life had to go on.

The noise was tremendous. The smell of cordite and burning filled the air, and dust stung his eyes. He paused near an alley to lean against the wall.

Suddenly he felt the wall move, heard a rumble and jumped straight out into the street again. Behind him the chimney crashed into the space he'd just vacated. The dust cloud enveloped him and he dropped to his knees. With his arms about his head he waited for something to fall on him, but after a short while he realized his luck was holding and stood up. There was noise all around him but the pounding of his heart was the loudest.

Just ahead he could see the ferry ticket office so he picked his way through the rubble to stand next to the locked door. Sammy wiped a hand across his face. Somehow he'd lost his trilby.

'We gonna make this the last trip, Skip?'

Mac had shouted up to Jack and was waiting below on the deck for his answer. Four passengers had got on to the ferry at Portsmouth. Jack glanced at his watch and shouted back, 'Yes, let's get off.'

Vee, wearing her waterproofs to keep out the cold, huddled against the wheel and stared at the huge fire burning in the dockyard.

'I wish you'd go down into the cabin,' Jack said. 'I've only just found you and I don't want you hurt.' He started the boat's engine. The passengers had gone into the cabin.

'I wouldn't like to think of you up here on your own,' Vee said. 'Anyway, it won't be long and we'll be back on the Gosport side.'

On an impulse Jack removed his peaked cap and jammed it on Vee's head.

'Aye, aye, Captain,' he said, and saluted her smartly.

The siren had started wailing as the boat docked.

Almost immediately, the sky was filled with bombers unleashing their loads. The noise of their engines and the thuds as those shells found targets was terrifying. Vee wasn't just scared, she was petrified. Never before had she been outside during a raid and at that moment she would have given anything to be inside a shelter.

The boat left the jetty, swinging out past moored craft on its journey back to Gosport. The water looked as if golden raindrops flew above the waves . . . It was shrapnel burning as it fell from the skies, hissing as it hit the water.

Below her, Mac had coiled the ropes and was standing with his back against the funnel, using it to protect him, as best as it could, from the falling fire.

She snuggled against Jack. On the way over they'd barely stopped talking. She was glad that he felt able to offload his worries on to her shoulders. He'd praised her for finding a good nanny for his daughter, and when she'd handed him back his keys, he said, 'It's not just the business I'd trust you with, but my daughter and my life, Vee.'

'I love you.' It was the first time she'd ever said those words to any man. 'And I'd like it better if we were out of the line of fire. The bombs won't stop coming.'

'Old Hitler's really giving it to us tonight.' He looked down at her, making her feel safe as, facing the sea, she leant into him.

Vee didn't see the burning shrapnel that fell against his head, face and neck until he'd given a strangled cry and slid to the floor of the wheelhouse.

It had scorched his skin, searing into his flesh, leaving it like melted candle wax before sliding down to burn on the wooden planks. The stench of singed clothing alerted her, along with his cries, and she knew she had to get rid of the burning metal before it started a fire. Had she not been wearing Jack's stout cap, scraps of the molten metal would have fallen into her hair or on to her skin.

No one was at the wheel. She glanced ahead and was relieved the boat was in open water. The shrapnel was too large for Vee to kick over the side and into the sea and she stopped herself trying – its fiery heat could hurt her.

Jack had let the wheel spin and now Vee grabbed at it. Holding it steady with one hand, she felt for the flask in the cubby-hole to use as a lever to poke the hot metal inch by inch until it fell over the side and into the water where it could do no more harm.

'Oh, Jack . . .' Her voice was hoarse, the dust in the air choking her as she threw the flask aside and tried to keep the boat steady. She managed to give a reverse signal to the engine so the boat slowed sufficiently for her to kneel and gauge Jack's injuries. The side of his head was a mess and he was unconscious, lying still and quiet. She was briefly glad he was out of it. She grabbed the wheel once more and set off for the Gosport shore.

There was no time to think, just to act. She wanted to kneel at Jack's side to watch over him – he was badly hurt and bleeding – but she daren't let go of the wheel. Obstacles in the shape of other boats in the channel appeared without warning in front of her, looming straight up in the unreal light.

'Mac!' Vee screamed. By some twist of fate he heard her voice and came running. To her it seemed that they were the only three people on the craft.

When Mac's head appeared as he climbed the ladder Vee could have kissed him.

'Jack's hurt. Take the wheel.'

Now Vee dropped to her knees. Jack was out cold. His face was charred and his neck was bleeding. Some of his hair had frizzled away. She breathed a sigh of relief that the blood didn't seem to be gushing from an artery but was dribbling from a huge wound near his ear. She blessed the bright lights searching for the overhead planes that were still droning above them. She wanted to clasp Jack to her, cradle him in her arms, but she knew she had to leave him lying on the deck while she and Mac docked the ferry.

It needed both of them to berth it. There seemed no end to the noise of fighting aircraft above her. An enemy plane was hit by ground machine-gun fire and Vee watched as it spiralled, whining, into the sea on the Portsmouth side.

'No one'll get out of that alive,' said Mac. Then he asked, 'How is he?'

'Bad,' said Vee. 'He needs the hospital. Oh, Mac,' she said, gazing up into his freckled face, 'I'm so glad you're here.' She took off her waterproof jacket and laid it over the man she loved.

The all-clear rang out as Mac was tying up the boat. Paul had disappeared when the passengers alighted on the pontoon. Vee couldn't blame him – he probably hadn't known what had occurred if he was in the cabin with them. But she was angry that he hadn't been around during the raid or shouted goodnight.

Vee was loath to move Jack, but he couldn't stay where he was. 'We need an ambulance!'

Mac waved his arm towards the jetty where people were moving again, now the bombers had passed over the town. 'It'll take ages. Probably some bad town hits to attend.'

Vee saw a man walking swiftly down the wooden pontoon. He stepped through the open exit gate and aboard the boat.

'Who on earth is that?'

But the moment the words left her mouth she recognized him.

'This is private property, mate, and there's no more trips across the harbour tonight,' Mac shouted, obviously thinking the man was a passenger.

Vee got to her feet and climbed down the ladder. She ran to Sammy Chesterton.

'I've paid in full! You got nothing on me!'

He was smiling! She couldn't believe the look on his face – he was pleased to see her!

'It's all right, Vee. I'm here for May, your mother.'

For a moment she didn't understand what he was saying. What had he to do with May?

'Why? What's wrong with her?'

'Nothing. She's marrying Jem and needs you home.' Her gasp was loud. Her cry, louder.

'Whatever's the matter?'

She had fallen against him, and the jumbled words coming from her mouth barely made sense even to her. 'Jack needs taking to hospital, now!' she finally said clearly. 'Fast.'

'Where is he?' Sammy pushed her away from him and stared into her face. His frown and silence told her he understood.

'On the boat. He's badly hurt.'

Sammy got no further than the bottom of the ladder.

'Go for transport, mate, it's fuckin' serious!' Mac shouted down to him.

Chapter Thirty

Sammy Chesterton sat beside Vee and Mac in the waiting room at the War Memorial Hospital. His warmth was comforting in the room's sterile whiteness.

There had been pandemonium in the place when Sammy had drawn up in his car and run into the foyer. Apparently Gosport had taken another severe beating from the evening raid. But within moments Jack was on a trolley being whisked away, leaving the three of them stunned, until they were offered tea and shown where to wait.

'I took Jack's keys,' said Mac. 'You've got a front-door key. I know how worried you are, so if it's all right with you, I'll arrange for the relief crew to be on hand tomorrow. Then you can stay here as long as you need to.'

'Bless you,' said Vee, now sipping her tea. She looked at Sammy. 'He'll be all right, won't he?'

'Well, he's in the best place,' Mac answered for him. 'Tell you what, I never realized what a bloody big bugger he was until we had to carry him from the boat to your motor, mate.'

Vee looked down at Sammy's cashmere coat. He'd been wearing it when he helped to carry Jack. The dark brown stains on the camel looked ugly, even more so as she knew it was Jack's blood. Sammy had eventually put it around her shoulders when he saw she was shivering with cold.

As if on cue, he said, 'I don't know what it is with your family. That's the second expensive coat you lot have ruined in less than a few weeks. I messed up the other one helping to put in a window at your mum's place. I reckon I'm going to have to order these coats by the dozen!'

Vee couldn't help a smile touching her lips. While they'd been waiting, Sammy had told her of all the happenings at home that her mother had barely had time to talk about when Vee telephoned her. From her initial fear at first setting eyes on Sammy on the pontoon, Vee now knew he wanted only to help her. She broke her silence to tell him and Mac more than she'd ever let on to her mother about her life in Gosport.

'So, you see, I'm terrified there'll be repercussions on Jack for allowing an alien to work for him.'

'We're a close-knit community on the boats, Vee,' Mac said. 'Do you think anyone would ever believe or suspect you might be a bleedin' spy?' He laughed. 'You've risked your life for Jack,' he added.

Vee didn't mention that Ada had no papers.

'I've put a lot of money into our government trying to sort out the discrepancies in the citizenship laws,' said Sammy. 'Canada is pushing ahead with naturalization reforms. It's my opinion there'll be a breakthrough before long.'

'But until then people live in fear of a knock on the door or a flaming torch being thrown through their windows!' Vee was passionate. She put down her cup with a loud bang on the small table.

'You can't blame the English for hating everything German,' Sammy said. 'Two wars are proving they've every right.'

'But it's not Germany as such, surely. It's that Hitler.' Mac was angry, his ruddy face even redder than usual. 'The sooner we beat him the better.'

'We can all agree with that,' said Sammy.

A family came to sit in the waiting room and Vee saw in Sammy's eyes that their conversation must end. The parents and two small boys looked very glum and their faces were marked by tears.

'Mac, if you want to get off home, I know you've got a lot to do sorting out the ferry. I can take Vee back to wherever she's living, then come round, telephone or whatever to let you know what's happening to Jack.' He'd barely got those words out when a nurse rustled alongside them.

'Mr Edwards is stable now. I can allow one of you to see him for a few moments.' She walked away, and Vee jumped up to follow her down the winding corridors.

'Is he going to be all right?'

The nurse, in blue and white, said, 'I can't tell you anything at the moment. Someone will talk to you before you leave. I take it you're a relative?' Vee nodded. She'd have said she was Mary Christmas if they allowed her just a peep at Jack.

Vee drew in a sharp breath. She wasn't prepared for the machine dripping blood into his body or the tiny part of his face that could be seen between the bandages covering his head and neck.

There was a chair beside the bed in the tiny room. She sat down, then searched for his hand and held it. It was cold, clammy even. She willed some of the heat from her own body to enter his, all the while knowing it was futile. 'Can you feel me loving you?' Vee murmured.

The door behind her closed and a doctor stood with notes

pinned to a clipboard that he scrutinized carefully. 'You are Mrs Edwards?'

'We live together.' It was easier than more lies, and she let the doctor make of that what he would. Besides, it was true.

Vee was surprised when he sat on the edge of the bed. 'Mr Edwards is lucky to be with us. He's had transfusions. We've got that under control, but there's not a lot we can do here at the War Memorial for the burns to his face and neck. He's pumped full of stuff to help him sleep and tomorrow we're sending him to a special burns unit that can deal with this better than we can.'

'Where?'

He consulted the notes, then looked at her kindly. 'The Queen Victoria Hospital at East Grinstead. There's a plastic surgery and burns unit there that has been pioneering the way for intensive burns and disfigurements.'

Vee was silent while she took this in. 'Is it very far? Will I be able to visit?'

'It's some thirty miles from London so, yes, I see no reason why you can't visit him.'

'Can I go with him?'

He adjusted his spectacles. 'That won't be possible, but I can give you a number to ring tomorrow. I suggest you go home now and try to rest. He's full of painkillers and it's highly unlikely he'll wake before tomorrow.'

Vee rose from the chair as a scribbled note was handed to her. She folded it carefully and put it into the pocket of Sammy's coat, which she was still wearing. Tears rose to her eyes as she looked down at Jack lying so still. Unsure where to kiss him because of the bandages, she reached again for his hand and squeezed it. But she felt no answering pressure.

Mac had decided to wait to see Vee for news of Jack so Sammy dropped him at his home before taking Vee back to the house. The roads were strewn with bricks and detritus from bombed buildings and Vee saw ARP men and helpers digging in the rubble to find loved ones and possessions. The Women's Institute were helping people recover from shock with hot tea and blankets. It was amazing, Vee thought, how everyone rallied round in emergencies.

Her head was full of Jack's suffering when Sammy pulled up outside the house.

'What's *that*?' He was looking at the car ferry moored for the night.

Vee explained, then asked if he'd like to stay at the house, which was in darkness. She knew he shouldn't drive back to Southampton – he was exhausted.

Once in the warm kitchen, she found that someone had thoughtfully banked up the fire, so she made tea. Vee was glad Sammy had stayed as she wanted advice and had decided he was the best person to offer it.

The house was silent. Vee suddenly realized that no one except herself knew about Jack. Regine, Rosie and Connie would have gone to bed after the raid, as on any normal night, and Ada was no doubt fast asleep with Peg in her cot beside her.

As she lit the gas she said, 'I need to talk to you about what's been going on here. So far, you've gathered I'm in love with Jack, but it's difficult . . .'

He listened as it all poured from her: Madelaine's death, Jack's time at the police station, his friendship with John, who was the detective now handling the case, and Regine and Paul's fraud with the ferry tickets.

'I'm sorry I stole from you. It was an isolated incident and one I've regretted. I've been terrified to tell my mother exactly where I was because I thought you'd come looking for me.'

'I might have done, had I not had such a warm welcome from your mother.' He told her that he and May had known each other at school. 'May deserves happiness with Jem

– he's a good bloke.' He grinned at her and stretched his legs out straight in front of him. 'He seems to think with her taking his name in marriage everything else goes away, but I'm not so sure. Will you and Jack tie the knot?'

Vee sighed. 'It's too soon after Madelaine's death. The murderer has to be brought to justice. There's a question mark hanging over the confession the police have had, and I'd like Mum to meet Jack and accept him, but that won't be until he's out of hospital.'

'What's not to accept? From what you've said, Jack's a decent bloke.'

'Yes, he is.' She took the tray with teapot and cups over to the fire and set them on the small table.

She told him about Peg and how she'd love to have a hand in bringing up the little girl. 'Could you imagine her on the smallholding cramming strawberries into her mouth on a hot sunny day in June?' They smiled at the thought. Vee knew her mother would adore the little girl.

'You do understand that it'll be a long haul before Jack is able to leave hospital? When he does, have you thought how you'll cope with . . . with . . .'

'He's not going to be the same. I do realize that.' Vee pushed a full cup towards Sammy.

'I've heard that the hospital at East Grinstead makes sure

its patients can integrate with society again, especially when heavy scarring might remain.'

'I don't love him for his looks. I love him for the person he is.' She was adamant.

'Jack's going to need all the love he can get,' Sammy said. 'But it will be how he feels about himself that matters most. Some people get very depressed.'

Vee looked into Sammy's eyes. She wondered why she had never given him the chance to listen to her before. Maybe if she'd told him straight out she didn't intend to sleep with him, or indeed anyone, until she had a ring on her finger, there was every possibility they could have come to some other arrangement over payment for the forged documents. On an impulse she asked, 'Do you provide many forged papers?' She drank some tea, relishing the renewed strength it gave her.

He gave her a knowing smile and tapped the side of his nose. 'You have no idea how many upper-class people have a German skeleton rattling in their closet and don't want anyone to find out . . .'

'Really?'

'Yes, really. And a few revered cabinet ministers need a change in the law before their true identities are forth-coming. These men love England . . .'

'Really?' said Vee again.

'That's all I'm saying on the matter,' said Sammy, 'but I've got an idea what to do about the missing ticket money.'

'What? Please tell me! It would be wonderful if I could sort that out for Jack.'

'Let me sleep on it.'

Vee left Sammy drinking his tea and went into Jack's room where she was delighted to discover someone had changed the bed linen. It looked tidy, different. She noticed a suitcase on the floor in the corner and guessed someone had packed up Madelaine's clothing. On opening the wardrobe door, she saw only Jack's clothes hanging there.

She dragged Sammy into the bedroom. 'No sofa for you. This is Jack's room. Sleep tight.' She turned to go, then looked round shyly at him. 'I'm really happy for Mum and Jem,' she said, 'and so glad you came to find me.'

Chapter Thirty-one

'Does that mean you're in charge again, Vee?' Connie was wiping her eyes after being told about Jack being sent to the burns unit. She was eager to know who to go to with any problems now she'd been assured Jack wasn't going to die.

The kitchen smelt of toast and was warm and cosy. Peg was sitting in her high chair with a cushion at her back to stop her sliding. She had a bowl of mush in front of her and was using the spoon to bang on the table top. A lump of wet rusk was stuck in her hair.

Vee had already decided that one person had to make sure everything carried on in an orderly fashion, both in the house and at work. 'I will be, if that's all right with you lot.'

Nods of assent came from Ada, Rosie and Connie, but Regine said, 'You take too much on yourself. You've only been working here five minutes.'

'Until we hear differently from Jack I'll carry on as I did when he'd been taken in for questioning by the police. Tonight we'll discuss this further, all right?'

Sammy had gone out; he'd said he needed some fresh air and wouldn't be too long.

She thought if she got them all together later they could put forward any queries. In the meantime she'd follow up on Jack's progress, make arrangements to visit him and, with help from Mac and the other crew, sort out a new strategy for work.

'I don't have a skipper's certificate of competence to steer the ferry legally,' she said to Ada, when the girls had all gone to work and she was left with Ada and Peg. 'If Jack's likely to be in hospital some time I'll need to make an arrangement with the bank to pay the wages . . .'

Mac had popped in first thing and told her the other crew were ready to work whatever hours were needed to keep the ferries running. Vee was happy about this and, through him, had arranged a meeting with Si. If everything went according to plan, Sammy's plan, they were going to be not only minus Jack but Regine and Paul as well.

'Thank God Jack made me do a stint working at all aspects of the job,' Vee said. 'If Regine goes, I'll step into the breach selling tickets, and maybe Si can come up with a replacement for Paul.'

She had just begun cleaning up Peg so Ada could eat some breakfast in peace when Sammy knocked on the street door. Ada let him in. It hadn't escaped Vee's notice that Ada was tongue-tied whenever she tried to speak to Sammy.

'Whew, it's cold out there,' said Sammy, putting his hands to the fire's warmth. He took off his coat and threw it over the back of a chair.

'Well?' began Vee. 'Tell us what happened.'

'I finally got to see John Cousins and he's agreed to come round tonight.'

Vee frowned. 'I know Regine's going to implicate me . . .'

'That's a foregone conclusion. But if that detective is any good, and if he believes Jack to be as straight a man as he thinks he is, all you do is look surprised and say she's lying.'

'But what if he wants to check my papers?'

'Let him. I've been selling forgeries for long enough to know that my mate supplies the real deal. Why, there's a few in Westminster knows that . . .'

Vee felt better. She looked at Ada, busy making tea for Sammy. Already Peg's eyes were drooping. She lifted her from the high chair, kissed the soft spot on her head and handed her to Ada. She loved the baby's milky, talcum-powder smell. In such a short time Peg had made her way deep into Vee's heart.

'I'll take her out for a walk. She'll sleep better in the fresh air,' said Ada. 'Save me a cuppa. Oh, I wish we had some bourbon biscuits to go with the tea. They're my favourites and I haven't seen one for ages.'

'You're not the only one,' said Vee. 'I'll phone and find out how Jack is.'

'And as you won't be needing me until tonight I'll drive back to Netley and put your mother in the picture,' Sammy said. 'I'm sure she's been worrying long enough.'

Vee spent part of the day going through Jack's books and bringing his paperwork up to date. She was astonished by how much work she could get through when someone else was looking after Peg. In the afternoon, though, she told Ada to take some time off because she missed being with the little girl.

'Sammy is coming back tonight, isn't he?' Ada asked.

'I think you've got a twinkle in your eye for him,' Vee said jokingly. But no one was more surprised than her when Ada coloured.

'You have!' Vee giggled. She laid Peg on her lap and began to change her wet nappy. Halfway through she sat back and watched Peg kicking. 'Who's a clever little Peg, then?'

'Just because I asked about him doesn't mean anything,' Ada said.

'Then why has your face gone even more cherry-coloured?'

'He doesn't act like he's an older man, and he certainly doesn't look old.'

'That's because he's well off.'

Vee was surprised to see tears in Ada's eyes.

'Then he definitely won't want to have anything to do with me. I've got bugger-all.' Ada turned to Peg. 'Sorry for swearing, my love.'

'If he didn't have any money, would you still fancy him?'

'Yes. I like older men. Young ones are only interested in getting drunk and showing off.'

Vee thought about Jack. He wasn't old, but he wasn't like that. Then again, she'd hardly been around him long enough to find out what his bad points were, had she? She thought for a bit. 'I think if you really love someone you take the good with the bad, don't you? But I do agree that older men are generally more settled.'

'I look at him and he makes me want to cuddle him. I don't believe he's settled at all. Why hasn't he married?'

'From what I gathered at the Black Cat, he's travelled, done a lot of stuff on his own, but that doesn't mean he hasn't had a lot of women. When I worked at that club he only had to snap his fingers and the girls came running.'

'I think he's lonely.'

'Don't talk daft! There was this girl in the club who used to go out with him. Greta, her name was. She was quite fond of him. He used to buy her things . . .' Vee stood Peg up on her feet.

'See what I mean?' Ada said. 'He bought Greta's affection. Blokes who do that can't believe women could love them for themselves.' Ada took the wet nappy, went to the tap, rinsed it and dropped it into the bucket beneath the sink. 'And don't think I fancy him because I'm hoping he can get me forged papers. I've got this far on my own during the war and I'll get on with the rest of it!'

'All right,' said Vee. 'I believe you. But you can't rush love, can you?' She looked at the clock above the mantelpiece. 'I don't know about you but I'm hungry again. Worrying about Jack doesn't make me feel any better. Shall we go round to the café and get something hot to eat? We can see how their sandwich venture's going, can't we?'

When Vee and Ada walked in with Peg, it was as if the customers had never seen a baby before. Wide-eyed, little Peg was taking it all in as fingers and faces came from all directions. 'Isn't she a little beauty?' A Glenn Miller song was playing on the wireless and people were crowding around Vee, asking about Jack. It hadn't taken long for the jungle drums to beat in Gosport and Jack was well liked.

Connie dished up Vee's favourite egg and chips with thick doorsteps of crusty bread. Vee was becoming tired of people congratulating her on bringing in the boat. She hated being in the limelight, so when Peg gave a wail as yet another bus conductress filled the pram with her face, Vee said, 'I've had enough, I'm off.'

'You only popped in to see if our sandwich idea was going well.' Connie grinned at her. The poor woman's face was sweaty and her hair had tumbled down from its curly topknot.

Vee had already noted the paper bags on the counter with the contents scrawled on them and she'd seen them fast disappearing. She made a mental note to see if she could buy some bags from the wholesaler with see-through sides to show the tasty fillings to their best advantage. Paper was difficult to get hold of, but she thought she might be lucky.

'Wait till we bring home the takings. I think you'll be very surprised,' Connie said. 'And very pleased.' Then she asked, 'When are you going to see Jack?'

'Do you want more tea before you go?' Rosie interrupted.

Vee shook her head.

'Tomorrow. He's awake and he's expecting me.' The tingle started in her toes and worked its way through her at the expectation of seeing Jack. A phone call earlier to the War

Memorial had confirmed he was stable and could have visitors once he'd settled in at the Queen Victoria.

'I expect you miss him,' said Rosie. 'Well, we all do.' She was trying to pacify Peg, who had got fed up and was bawling.

As Ada wiped her plate with a piece of bread, mopping up the egg, she said, 'Peg'll be having nightmares about all these people poking her. We should take her home.'

'Thank God someone's on the same wavelength as me,' said Vee, looking at the wall clock. It wouldn't be long before Sammy came back to Gosport with news from her mother.

When Vee and Ada reached the house, Regine was in the bath.

Vee knocked softly on the bathroom door. 'Don't forget we're having a chat about the future tonight.'

'I hadn't forgotten,' came the clipped reply. 'There's one or two things I'm not happy about.'

Me too, thought Vee.

Later, John arrived with a constable in uniform. Vee wasn't expecting that. He caught up with her in the hallway.

'I have to go to East Grinstead tomorrow, so if you're planning to visit him, I can give you a lift. It'll save you bothering with trains and buses.'

'Does he know you're going?'

'Yes, it's police business. I've been assured by the surgeon he'll be up and about, getting used to the place. After all, there's nothing wrong with his legs, they said. They plan on operating over the weekend. Then the fun begins.' He made a sympathetic face at her.

'I'd love to come with you,' Vee said. She liked John. He was a kind, understanding man. It was easy to see why he and Jack had been friends for so long.

Shortly afterwards Sammy knocked at the door and came in, carrying a large bag in which there was a huge cake. He handed it to Vee.

She stared at his smart camel coat. 'Is that new?'

He nodded. 'I wonder how long this one will last . . . Your mother made the cake this morning for the next meeting of her Women's Institute. When I said I was coming back to you she made me bring it. Said she expected you were getting skinny without her cooking.'

'Wish I had a mother like that,' said Ada.

'I wish I had someone to make me cakes,' said Sammy. Vee saw him look at Ada as though he hadn't noticed her before but liked what he was seeing now.

Ada put Peg to bed and it wasn't long before Regine appeared, all pink from her bath. Vee could smell the fragrance of her bath salts. She'd put her hair in pin curls and had tied a chiffon scarf around her head. As soon as she came into the kitchen and saw the constable she blushed. Vee knew she hated to be caught without her make-up.

'Why didn't you tell me we had visitors?' She put her handbag down at her feet. She stared at John. 'Any movement on Madelaine's death?'

'Actually, there is,' he said. 'The post mortem shows she hit her head when she fell. That was what killed her. But there was skin beneath her fingernails and bruising to her body so it looks as if she had a fight with someone shortly beforehand.'

The room went silent. It was as if each of the people in that kitchen was in a world of their own, thought Vee. To break the silence she got up and went to the stove to make tea. While she was doing that, she listened to the conversations going on around her. John and Sammy seemed to have a lot to say to each other but their voices were indistinct. Regine had stood a small hand mirror in front of the sugar bowl and was attempting to put on mascara with the little blue brush she kept in her handbag. Vee thought her mother would have had a heart attack if she'd done that. May said putting on make-up should be private, never done in public.

She made the tea in the big earthenware teapot, then put it

in the centre of the table along with milk in a jug. After she'd produced a large knife and laid it on top of the cake, she set down a tray of crockery. Looking at the cake, she sighed. In her mind's eye, she could see May getting everything ready in their kitchen for baking. She imagined the smell while the cake was in the oven, filling the room. She missed her mother so much and gulped back a tear.

Then she sat at the table between Sammy and Ada, facing Regine.

'Have you got Hugh in the cells?' Vee asked, rising quickly again, like a jack-in-the-box. She pulled out a tall stool and beckoned the uniformed policeman to sit, but he refused. She shrugged. John caught her eye and frowned. Vee realized the constable was there on duty, ready to be a witness to anything that might occur, not as a guest.

John said, 'We've let him go.'

There were several intakes of breath.

'I thought he confessed?' Vee said.

'So he did, but he did it to protect his wife.' John drummed his fingers on the table. He was wearing cufflinks that glittered. His shirt was very white against his well-cut dark suit.

'Are you allowed to tell us this?' Sammy queried.

Vee was mulling over his words.

'The press were in attendance. It'll be on the evening news tomorrow,' said John, 'so why not?'

'Come on, then.' Regine seemed very interested. She spat on her brush and ran it along the cake of black mascara. 'Tell us everything.'

'Apparently the scene in the church at the christening was relayed to Hugh's wife, Eleanor. The poor woman was at the end of her tether. If you remember, when the church caught that bomb we all ran for the pub. Madelaine and Hugh disappeared, and Mrs Carter, Madelaine's mother, went telling tales. Eleanor had stood by that bounder knowing he was seeing Madelaine and hoping the affair would fizzle out because they have two little girls. She knew nothing of Peg.'

'Jack always said Madelaine's mother was a cow,' Rosie said.

'Well, Jack was right,' Connie said. She started pouring tea for everyone, then sliced the cake and set pieces on small plates. Its rich smell filled the room.

John added, 'Finding out that Peg was her husband's child sent his wife over the edge. She came into Gosport looking for Madelaine, who had come back alone to this house feeling sorry for herself. When she answered the door, no doubt expecting to see Hugh, and instead found Eleanor screaming at her, she went out the back and down to the air-raid shelter. She didn't want anyone else returning to the house and witnessing the row. The upshot of it all was that they argued, fought, and Madelaine was knocked down, hitting her head.'

'And her body was just left there?' Vee could hardly believe it. She took a bite of her mother's cake. It was every bit as delicious as she'd known it would be. She caught Sammy's eye and his wink told her he found it delicious too.

'Apparently so,' John said. 'You have to remember Hugh's wife was in a right state. She went home and tried to act normal, believe it or not.'

Vee could hardly believe it. 'And we stumbled on Madelaine's body when the next raid began.'

'What I don't understand is why Hugh confessed.' Connie was trying to pin up her wayward hair, without much success.

'Hugh probably did the only honourable thing he's ever done in his life. After he found out Madelaine was dead, he came down to the station and told us he'd hit her and killed her. He made up a story about her flying at him because he'd called out in church that Peg belonged to him. Apparently Madelaine had been on at him to admit to being Peg's father and she wanted him to take her away from Gosport, away from Jack. Of course, without his wife's money the bloke was stony broke.' John paused to drink some of his tea. 'But that's love for you.'

Again there was silence. Vee knew each person was contemplating what had happened.

'So how come his wife's in custody? Your mum makes scrummy cakes,' said Rosie.

'The post mortem showed Hugh was lying. He couldn't have hit Madelaine and killed her. It had to have been a fall on a sharp item, like the top of that garden heater in the shelter.' John motioned to Vee that he'd like more tea. She nodded as he added, 'Hugh's wife broke down and confessed. She still loves him, you see, despite everything. She was grateful he cared enough for her to try to take the rap. She's a mess, poor woman.' He sighed.

'How will the judge deal with her?' Connie asked.

Vee could see she was distraught that Eleanor had been forced to take things into her own hands to stop her husband's affair.

'The judge and jury will take everything into consideration. There are also Hugh's two girls to consider.' He peered at his watch, then at the faces around the table. 'I think we'd better get on with what's next on the agenda.' He picked up his cup and drank the tea. Then he got up and walked round to Regine, who stared at him in amazement as he took the eye make-up brush from her fingers.

'I presume you were going to bed, so why doll yourself up?'

Regine obviously thought the detective was flirting with her, for she said coquettishly, 'Well, I never know who I might meet in my dreams.'

Rosie laughed and Connie smiled, but John said, very seriously, 'You'll not be meeting many men where you're going. I'm arresting you for stealing from the Gosport Ferry Company.'

Regine's face was a picture.

The uniformed policeman was now standing at Regine's side too. He removed handcuffs from his pocket, but John said, 'I think she'll come quietly, without any need for those bracelets.'

He'd hardly got the words out when Regine stood up and yelled, 'You can't prove a thing! If you want a real villain, try taking her down the station! She's a German!' She pointed at Vee, who closed her eyes at the invective now being hurled at her.

After a while she composed herself and stood up.

'I am not a spy,' she said calmly. 'You're trying to deflect the blame.'

'On second thoughts, cuff her,' said John. 'Can you come with me now, Vee?'

Vee's heart was racing. Surely he didn't believe Regine's words. She breathed a sigh of relief when John added quickly, 'We'll need a statement, Vee. We'll also pick up her accomplice.'

'I'm coming with you,' said Sammy. Rosie and Connie were speechless.

'You don't have to,' Vee said, hoping against hope that Sammy would take no notice of her. She needed him by her side.

'I think I do,' Sammy said, rising. 'The rest of you will be all right, yes?'

Connie found her voice. 'Well I never!'

Ada said kindly, 'You ought to let Regine get dressed – she can't go out in her nightwear.'

It was gone midnight when a police car dropped Sammy and Vee outside the house. Inside, no one had gone to bed because they were worried about Vee and wanted to know what was going on.

'Regine's been charged,' said Vee, practically collapsing on to a chair at the table after taking off her coat.

'Rosie, kettle,' commanded Connie, and fresh tea was made.

'We'll be out of leaves at this rate and gasping by the time the government gives us the extra for Christmas,' said Vee.

'Oh, I forgot,' said Sammy, and took from his new cashmere coat's deep pockets three packets of Brooke Bond Green Dividend tea with the orange stamps on the packets. 'Meant to hand that to you when I arrived earlier but I didn't want that detective bloke thinking I was breaking the law,' he said. He hung his coat on the back of the door.

Connie pounced on the tea.

He delved into his other pocket and brought out a large blue sugar bag, 'Look in there, Ada.'

She needed no second bidding and gave a little scream when she saw what was inside. Then she came to Sammy and threw her arms around his neck.

'You are bloody lovely.' She kissed his cheek, and Sammy actually blushed.

Ada bit into a bourbon biscuit and gave a sigh of ecstasy. 'You remembered,' she said, through crumbs.

'You told me they're your favourites,' Sammy reminded her.

Vee caught Ada's eye and winked.

Then she told them what had gone on at the police station: she'd signed a statement saying she'd seen Regine taking clean used tickets from her bag and putting the money for them in a jar in the ticket office.

'Regine told them straight out that she was in partnership with Paul, who saved the tickets he'd previously not clipped. She didn't want to be charged without them knowing all about him,' she said. 'She really is a horrible person.'

'Did they just take your word for it that when you'd been working with her she'd reused the tickets?' Rosie asked.

'Ah!' said Sammy. 'All along she was denying everything, saying there was no proof and that Vee was lying. But the silly girl slipped up. A policewoman came in and took her into another room where she was searched. When her handbag was opened, there was a load of unused tickets inside it!'

Chapter Thirty-two

Jack sat in the rose garden, trying to read Nathanael West's *The Day of the Locust*. It had been on his reading list for a while, but now he had it in his hands he couldn't concentrate on the words. They kept running into one another. He put it down on the seat beside him. Anyway, he wanted to move the bandage away from one of his eyes so the damned white material wasn't obscuring his vision. He had been told by a young nurse that he must not on any account touch his face or neck.

He'd had no idea where he was when he woke in a single room. And then he'd kept falling asleep again until a pretty young nurse popped her head around the door and told him he'd been brought there from Gosport's War Memorial Hospital. She'd given him an injection and he'd slept some more.

He felt no pain. He'd been drinking tea through a straw when a well-built tall doctor had practically filled all the space in his room and explained that they were going to operate as soon as they'd assessed him.

God knew what they were pumping into him, but every time he thought about the ferry and began to wonder what was going on, his thoughts faded into nothingness and he slept.

'Do you remember what happened?' the doctor had asked, catching him awake one morning. Jack had looked at the tall man in a white coat with a stethoscope around his neck. 'I had my hands on the wheel and then nothing.'

Vee's face wouldn't go away. He remembered the worry in her eyes. Instead he thought about Peg and her tiny new teeth, which brought a smile to his heart. Ada seemed the perfect person to look after Peg, but he honestly didn't know how such a little thing had stolen his heart as she had. How could she not be his daughter? He was the one who got up in the night and held her rigid little body when she screamed so that gradually the tears stopped and her little arms and legs relaxed again. Jack was crying. He wanted to hold his daughter now, *his* daughter.

It was all such a bloody mess. Vee's face floated before him again. He'd tried not to fall for her, he really had. She was bright and funny and she got on with things. She never knew he'd watched her with Peg, her arms around the little girl and his Peg leaning into her, safe and relaxed. Babies know a lot. Peg knew she was safe with Vee. Oh, she'd known she wasn't safe with her mother. That was why she'd cried all the time, and you couldn't blame her for it. In a way he was glad Madelaine was gone. He shouldn't wish harm on anyone – but why had his wife taken out her unhappiness on a baby? Madelaine had deceived him and he had been a bloody fool. And look at him now. He had nothing to give Vee. He'd never be able to bring himself to touch her, however much he desired her. He was going to be grotesque. 'You might need another operation,' he'd been told. He was a mess, his life was a mess. There was only one thing he could do and he was going to do it.

And now his head fell to his chest and he slept again.

'You've got visitors.' His shoulder was being shaken gently, and Jack opened his eyes to see Vee sitting on the bench by his side. The nurse made to move away, adding, 'Better your other friend comes in later. Too much too soon and all that.'

So John was here. Good. He had a great deal he wanted to discuss with him, but meanwhile it was better to get it all out in the open.

'These gardens are lovely.'

God, he loved the sound of her voice.

He nodded as best he could. There were so many dressings that he thought when they were taken away his head might fall off. Good. There was still no pain. The sleep had reinforced his decision. It was for her own good.

He looked down at the blue and white candlewick dressing-gown beneath which were white pyjamas, washed and bleached so many times he wondered what their original colour had been. Then his eyes found hers. She wasn't smiling. It was almost as if she knew what he was going to say. This lovely girl needed so much more than he could ever give her.

Vee leant in towards him and found his hand. Her touch was like a million fireflies lighting his body, his heart, his brain. He didn't want to, but for her sake he had to do this.

'I've been a fool.' His voice didn't sound as if it belonged to him. A frown had appeared on Vee's beautiful forehead. He swallowed. 'I've got to let you go.'

She hadn't moved! She hadn't spoken! Perhaps Vee hadn't heard him. 'It's got to stop, now, before I hurt you any more.'

Dear God this was killing him. His guts were twisted into knots. He pulled his hand away from hers, roughly, so that her hand remained palm upwards, her fingers splayed open.

And then he watched as those fingers curled inwards and her hand moved from him to the seat of the wooden bench. Using her arm as a lever, she pushed herself upright and, without even a second glance at him, walked across the grass towards the hospital building. He saw her shoulders move. He thought she might be crying.

But he had done it. He had given her back her life.

'That was quick.' John put down the magazine he'd been thumbing through. He longed for the magazines of before the war when there had been oodles to read and pictures galore. The paper shortage had put paid to decent reading matter.

Vee's high heels stopped clacking on the tiles as she slumped down next to him. He hadn't been a copper all these years not to know immediately when something was wrong, very wrong. Mind, you, the girl hadn't been chatty on the way up in the car. He wondered if it was because she expected him to come out with the words 'forged papers'? Didn't have to be a genius for him to see she was scared of something, so he'd made it his business to look into Sammy Chesterton and all his legal and illegal dealings. A few phone calls, a few words here and there, and he'd discovered her heritage was sound as a bell. Vee was just another person caught up in the country's red tape, which was slowly strangling honest, decent people. And Sammy Chesterton? As long as the bloke kept his nose clean around this area, what he got up to in Southampton was nothing to do with John. Besides, he admired the chap. Sammy Chesterton had built an empire from nothing.

'You'd better go in now.' Vee's voice was hardly more than a whisper. Her face was swollen from crying.

'He's upset you. How?'

She shook her head. 'Please leave me. I don't want you to see me . . .'

But she did cry again.

It was an automatic gesture to pull her to his side for comfort and to put his arm around her shoulders. He let her sob into his jacket. After a while the sobbing turned to sniffs, a few hiccups.

'He's given you your marching orders, hasn't he?'

She looked through a curtain of hair. 'Did you know?'

'Of course not! You're the best thing that's happened to him . . .' He felt in his pocket, pulled out a crumpled handkerchief and gave it to her. It wasn't clean. What could he expect with his missus living at Lee-on-the Solent looking after her mother when she should be in Gosport looking after him? Vee didn't seem to mind though, and wiped her eyes, leaving trails of black mascara on the white cotton. He got up, leaving her sitting and sniffing, and walked along the corridor to where a nurse stood marking a clipboard.

'Excuse me, my friend, the lady around the corner,' he waved an arm expansively, 'badly needs a cup of tea. Could you sort her out?'

Expecting a put-down he was surprised and pleased when she said, 'Show me?'

Together they walked back to where Vee was sitting in exactly the same position as before. The young nurse quickly assessed the situation. 'Stay there, I'll get tea.'

John said to Vee, 'You really do love him, don't you?' He didn't wait for an answer but strode back down the corridor, through the front door, down the steps and out into the gardens.

When John reached his friend, his first thought was that he looked like a snowman with his head and neck swaddled in white bandages. He could see one eye and that eye was shedding the tears that had made his dressings damp.

'Do you realize what you've done?' There was no need to explain what he was on about as they both knew John had come from Vee.

'I did it for her.'

'You did fuck-all for her! That woman saved your life,

saved your home-life, and if it wasn't for her, I wouldn't have two thieves in the cells who've been bleeding you dry!'

John could see the amazement on his friend's face. Before Jack had a chance to ask any questions he waded in again: 'You didn't give her time to tell you anything, just discarded her like an empty fag packet. Try talking! Try finding out she brought that bloody ferry in through fallin' shrapnel and got you to hospital. Try talking about how she's been running around like a blue-arsed fly doing your job for you.' He poked Jack with his fingers. 'Try asking yourself what you've got that makes a woman like that do what she's done for you. She's worth a thousand bloody Madelaines. What's wrong with you?'

Jack was breathing quickly. 'I didn't know . . .'

'Of course you didn't because all you're thinking about is yourself!' Before Jack had a chance to say anything, John added, 'So, you'll be scarred. So bloody what? There's young pilots coming home much worse off than you – legless, armless, blind. This war's taken men's lives and all you can do is sit here and whine, "I did it for her sake"?' He barely stopped for breath before he added, 'Ask yourself why that girl's already taken so much shit from you and the answer is *she loves you.*'

He began to walk away, then glanced back. 'I came to tell you most of what you've just heard. I've had enough, mate. We'll talk again later, all right?' He continued to stalk across the grass.

'Tell Vee I'm sorry . . .'

John stopped. He turned. 'You tell her.'

When he reached Vee she was still sitting alone, but he could see a young lad pushing a squeaking tea trolley towards them down the corridor. It was moving unevenly and it was then he noticed the lad had only one arm. He caught up with him.

'Got one for me? I could do with a cuppa,' he said.

The boy halted.

On the trolley there was a mixture of used and unused mugs, a big sugar bowl and a metal jug that John supposed contained milk. In the sugar bowl there was a spoon, covered with tea and brown sugar.

'Like that, is it?' The lad picked up the large brown pot and poured tea carefully into a clean mug. He was slow but methodical. 'I can feel the anger coming off you in waves,' he said. 'Help yourself to milk – sorry all the biscuits are gone. Gotta be quick at them. Load of gannets, this lot is.'

John said, 'Why can't some people see the woods? Is it because the trees are in the way?'

The boy grinned. 'Tell me about it. Some people are simply blind to everything. This place opened my eyes. You want sugar with that?'

'If you go without sugar for long enough, you don't want it any more.'

'That could be said of a lot of things.' The lad shrugged his shoulder and the empty sleeve flapped. 'I'm getting a prosthesis next week. Wish me luck.'

John said, 'Ever thought you're already one of the lucky ones?'

'A hundred times a day, mate, a hundred times a day.' And the trolley trundled off down the corridor, squeaking as it went.

John sipped his tea and thought about what he'd done.

He'd let rip at his friend when none of it was his business. But it was obvious Jack knew nothing of how he'd come to be at the hospital. Probably since then he'd been too doped up to think straight. But he was one selfish bastard if he thought by letting Vee go he was doing the right thing for her. He'd known Jack for a long time and the best thing that ever happened to him was that girl breezing into his life.

He'd never have expected in a thousand years that the silly bugger would send her packing. Never.

John had driven up today to let Jack know the result of

the inquest on his wife. Now the body could be released for burial. It was up to Jack what he wanted to do about a funeral. That bounder Hugh seemed to have gone to ground. John had sent a uniform round to tell him to come and collect his missus as she'd be released on bail pending doctors' reports, but a neighbour reckoned he was in Cornwall with his kiddies. John hoped he'd take more notice of them than he had of little Peg.

He'd been in touch with the other ferry crew, only to be told by Simon Chandler that 'Young Vee has it all in hand.' And that grumpy old bugger didn't take to many people but seemed full of praise for her. He drank the rest of his tea and left the mug on a marble sconce that held a display of twigs and berries. Someone would discover it next to the ashtray full of butts.

Should he go back out into the gardens and talk to Jack? As soon as that thought entered his head, the anger returned. No, he'd take the poor girl home. Let her decide what she wanted to do. There was a house full of women to look after her back in Gosport. It was at times like this, too, that he needed his Emily at home. Still, only another couple of weeks and her mother would be on her feet again.

John began walking down the long empty corridor to find Vee, his leather shoes tapping loudly on the black and white tiles. It was already dark outside now the days were short and it was so near Christmas. It was cold too – he could see condensation rising on the windows. He wouldn't mind betting the staff had this place looking really homely at Christmas. He'd made enquiries about the Queen Victoria Hospital and Jack couldn't have been in a better place.

John rounded the corner. He stopped in amazement. A warm feeling began moving from his heart throughout his body. What had he said to Jack? Tell Vee yourself? Well, he was doing more than talking to her now.

He'd never seen a woman put one foot out in the air behind her when some bloke was kissing her. Vee was snuggled against Jack and there wasn't room to put a bleedin' pin between them.

Chapter Thirty-three

1946

'Taste, Nanny, taste.' May allowed five-year-old Peg to jam another ruby red strawberry against her mouth, which was already running with juice.

'Yum-yum,' she said, then put her arms around the little girl and turned her in a neat somersault so that she shrieked with pure joy.

'You'll make her sick, Mum, after all those strawberries she's eaten.' Vee, sitting in the shade, fanned her face with the local newspaper. It was hot, one of the hottest days ever, surely.

'Didn't do you any harm, did it?' said May. The little girl, tired now, lay across May's knees and she was rubbing her back in a circular motion.

'She'll be asleep soon,' said Vee, gazing around the field at the rows of strawberry plants at the end of their season. The sky was a deep blue above the green of the plants and the trees surrounding the field, and the air smelt of strawberries and earth, a wonderful combination. In the shade beneath a deckchair, Cat lay asleep, her head on her paws.

'Are you going to wake him?'

May nodded towards Vee's husband, sprawled in a deck-chair fast asleep.

Vee looked at Jack, at his puckered neck and cheek, which were tanned like the rest of him. She rose with difficulty from her own deckchair, picked up the large handkerchief from the table and placed it over the side of his face where the scar was to keep the sun off it.

Even now, after all this time, his skin was too thin to take much sun. On the boat he wore roll-neck sweaters and his hat shaded his face. Every time she remembered the fateful night when she had almost lost him she shuddered with fear, and now was no exception. Jack didn't wake: he snorted, then continued sleeping. Vee smiled at the man she loved.

'No, I'll let him sleep. Not often he gets the chance to relax.' She yawned. 'The sun's so strong today.'

'Isn't it lovely?' May said. Then she sniffed. 'It's about time my husband came back with that teapot. Why do men take longer to do things than we do?'

'I heard a car earlier. I wouldn't mind betting you have a visitor and you know what it's like when Jem and Sammy get yacking. Anyway, it's nice sitting out here with you. Jack needed a break for a few days and where better to come than the country?' From the house they could hear faint music from the wireless, the Merry Macs singing 'Sentimental Journey'.

'I wish you'd take things easier, my girl. The pair of you work so hard.' Vee noted her mother had gone into parent mode, but she didn't mind: it showed how much she cared about her, about all of them.

'What better than to have a husband who loves his work? And you have to admit working alongside him I get to see more of the man I love than most wives.'

May sniffed. 'Are you still in the ticket office most days?'

'Yes,' Vee said. 'I like it. Anyway, it won't be for much longer.' She liked passing the time of day with the customers while she handed them their ferry tickets.

'I hope not.'

Vee smiled at her mother. She felt healthier now than she'd ever done. She picked at a mark on her arm, realized it was a freckle, then said, 'Sammy's coming round to let us know whether he's managed to persuade the Hamble

Boatyard that Connie's sandwiches are better than the food they've been buying in from Southampton.'

'I hope you mean "persuade" and not "threaten"!'

'Oh, Mum, you know Connie's made a big success of selling sandwiches to factories. Since the war ended, life's been on the up for us all.'

'I know, love, and no one's happier for you all than I am. Connie's visit to Australia to see her new granddaughter did her the world of good, and I never thought Rosie would turn out to be quite the businesswoman and driving a van.' She began to laugh. 'Remember those driving lessons Jem started giving her? She frightened the life out of him. He said he'd rather pay for her to have professional ones than ever get in a car with her again!'

'I remember how white he was climbing out of that vehicle. He couldn't walk straight and he was sick on the grass verge!'

A voice behind them shook them both from their laughter.

'Tea's up.'

The two newcomers, both in shirtsleeves, stood each with a tray. Jem had a folded card table beneath his arm and was trying hard to let neither the tray nor the table slip. Sammy's tray was bursting with sandwiches and cakes, and Jem's held the big brown teapot, milk, sugar, cups and saucers.

'Ooh,' said Vee. 'Is that your chocolate cake?'

May said, 'Don't go filling up Peg with it. It's too rich and it'll make her sick. Just give her a little bit.'

All the noise had woken Jack, who opened one eye, took in the situation and winked at Vee. She winked back and he gave her a beautiful smile, then said, 'C'mon, Sammy, pour out the tea. I like being waited on!'

'You lazy git!' Sammy took aim at his outstretched leg with the toe of his polished shoe.

'Stop that!' May's voice rang out and Peg woke with a snuffle.

'Oh, darling, did nasty Nanny shout and wake you up?' Vee was laughing as she leant forward as far as she could and slid the little girl from May's lap to her own.

Peg snuggled down again but after a second or two she struggled up and said sleepily, 'There's chocolate cake.'

'Take this, May.' Jem managed to pass his tray to his wife. 'I'm not putting it down on the ground. There's ants the size of cows waiting to pounce on the food.'

May said, 'Don't exaggerate, dear. You'll scare Peg.'

As soon as the tray had left his hands, Jem shook out the card table and secured its feet. Promptly, Sammy put down the tray of food and May rose, set down Jem's tray and began to pour tea.

'How did it go with the sandwiches?' Jack leaned forward and brushed his hand through his dark curls. The handkerchief slid to the ground and he picked it up, smiling at Vee, knowing she'd covered his scar from the sun.

'Sweet as a nut, mate. The only problem is they want them by seven thirty in the mornings . . .'

Jack frowned. 'I don't think that's possible. Those two girls are run off their feet at that time.'

'Hold your horses,' Sammy broke in. 'I was talking to Mac and he said his younger brother's home from the war.'

'Poor bugger's disabled.'

'He lost an arm, Jack, not his head!' Sammy's voice rose. 'He can drive. That's what he was doing in France in the Tank Regiment. Give the poor bloke a chance.'

'That's you told off,' Vee said. 'I'm willing to bet he could make himself useful in other ways.'

'Fair enough. I'll have a word,' said Jack.

'I want cake!' The little voice cut through the sounds of chatter, birdsong and rustling leaves.

'I want cake *please*,' said May, handing Peg a small piece on a plate. Peg reached for the cake and left May holding the plate. She tutted and Vee laughed.

'Say thank you to Nanny,' she admonished the child, and through a mouthful of cake, Peg said, 'Fank you, Nanny.'

She swallowed quickly, then mumbled, 'I like you better than my other nanny.'

Sammy said, 'So Madelaine's parents do visit?'

'Not often, but it's fair that Peg knows she has other family members.' Jack bit into his cake. 'This is scrumptious,' he said to May, then turned back to Sammy. 'What have you done with Ada?'

'She's spending my money.' Sammy licked his lips. 'Don't suppose I could have another bit of that cake?'

'No, you can't. Leave some for Ada, Greedy Guts. Have a sandwich instead,' said May.

Sammy made a face and raised his eyes heavenwards.

'What's Ada buying?' Vee wanted to know what her friend was up to. Sammy was very fond of her, but Vee hoped he wasn't going to steal Ada away until Peg went to school and she could find someone else to take over in the ticket office. She was going to be a stay-at-home mother.

'I sent her to buy some champagne that's better than the stuff I sell in my clubs,' he told her.

'What are we celebrating?' May asked.

'Hand over that newspaper,' said Sammy. Jack picked it up and threw it at him. He caught it neatly. 'I bet not one of you noticed this piece.'

'Haven't had chance to read it yet' and 'I've been too busy

for papers' came thick and fast. Sammy waved them all to be quiet and began to read from the middle pages. As he held it up, Vee saw that the front page was all about the milkmen's strike for higher wages.

"'Canada is introducing her own citizenship laws dealing with British subjects.

"'A conference decided each country should decide for itself, in its own way, what classes of persons were its own citizens. Each country would accept the citizens of every other Commonwealth country."

'Canada has led the way forward,' he said, looking up from the article in the newspaper. 'When we won the war and kicked Hitler into touch it opened all kinds of possibilities in changing laws that can only be better for everyone.'

'Does "classes of persons" mean each woman as well as men?' May was apprehensive.

'Let me read on and you'll get a better picture,' said Sammy.

"'Change in the law. 1946. No female British subject loses her nationality on marrying. Similarly, an alien marrying a British husband will not be deemed a British subject by marriage alone, but her naturalization will be made easier.'" There was silence while each of them digested the information.

'So, no one will be able to point a finger at a woman who

marries a German and call her a German because she'll keep her British status?' asked May.

'Exactly,' said Sammy.

May began to cry, but between the sobs, she said 'Why, oh, why couldn't this have happened sooner? All the heartache, all the tears, the subterfuge, the burning of homes, the hatred . . .'

She turned from the card table and, oblivious of the newspaper crackling between their bodies, threw her arms around Sammy. 'You helped with this, you gave money to politicians to help . . .'

'May, May.' Sammy was stroking her hair. 'We all in our own way helped bring this about. Each of us has a story to tell of the inhumanity of man to man. But we didn't give up. Our boys fought and died in a war to prevent Hitler taking over Britain. We'll never be trodden down. But if it takes the powers that be a little longer to implement laws to keep our country strong, so be it. We're all only fallible human beings.'

May was still sniffing. Vee knew she was remembering Gus. At that moment Jem moved forward and took his wife in his arms.

Across the field a cloud of dust heralded the arrival of Sammy's car.

May glanced up. 'Can't that girl walk anywhere? Why

does she have to drive so fast?' She dabbed at her eyes. Vee knew her sharp words tried to mask the exhilaration she was feeling at the wonderful news. Good news that they all felt and were about to celebrate with champagne.

Vee reached for Jack's hand.

'I hope she'll go into the house and pick up some glasses,' said May. 'If not she can blooming well go back and get them.' She glared at Vee.

Vee felt Jack's hand stroke her distended abdomen. He whispered close to her ear, so close she felt the warmth of his breath, 'Say "Yes, Mum."'

'Yes, Mum,' she said.

She smiled fondly at her husband, the father of her forthcoming child.

Acknowledgements

To write this book I relied on journals borrowed from the wonderful staff at Gosport Museum and the Discovery Centre at Gosport. I took the liberty of modifying details, facts and events to suit my story. I am a writer of fiction, not fact. The characters – except for the main character, the ferry – bear no resemblance to any living persons.

I have travelled on the ferry boats all my life. Long may they continue to run.